Hardly Strangers

by Rob Massing

Table of Contents

PART ONE

CHAPTER ONE

As the elevator ascended, Chase's body fought to stay erect against the force of gravity sinking his head into his shoulders, his shoulders into his chest, his chest into his lower back. Oh God, his lower back. He was too young to feel so old. Never again. This was the last time. Yes, he said that every time. It was always the last time. But this time he meant it, and no one could talk him out of it, not Billy, not anyone. It was for guys who couldn't feel good about themselves without it, and he wasn't one of those guys, far from it. He was on top of the world, for real.

Sure, it was nice. It was pleasant. That moment, about half an hour after you washed the capsule down, when the warmth spread from your heart, filled your veins and your lungs. It made you smile–but on the inside, because you couldn't let it show. You couldn't look like some kind of novice, some outsider. You didn't want to lose your leverage. The Party Boys would all look away, pity in their hearts.

The ones who couldn't help but smile, that big, open smile, they were the marks, easy prey. Tell them how handsome they were, how hot they were, how much you were into them (they were, and you were, but they didn't hear it as much as they deserved), and they were yours. It was a kindness, really, that he bestowed on them. And they were always the best fucks. Jesus God, they would do anything. Like those two Aussie boys, gymnasts, twenty-two and nineteen (fake i.d.), so eager it almost made Chase change his mind, but oh no, once he got a taste of them, on the densest part of the dance floor, sweaty and smooth-skinned and compact, he was hooked, there was no turning back. The beat started up again, the lights flashed, it was happening, he was there, it was packed, he was surrounded. He gripped twenty-two around the chest while nineteen groped him from behind and kissed his neck, and he flipped and they changed formation and he grinded his hips, pounding to the pounding beat, practically right up the rock-solid ass of nineteen. He was hard as fuck and a little wet and he didn't care, it was so on, they were headed to his place, gonna have to roll on without me, Billy my man, I'll text you when–

The elevator doors opened.

"Fuck. Here we go."

Chase adjusted his slacks, opened his eyes, safe from the morning glare of the gleaming all-white lobby behind a pair of blue-tinted designer sunglasses, and stepped out. He peeked over the rims to give fair and lovely Marissa at Reception her favorite co-conspirator look, her slight, wide-eyed nod a warning of trouble ahead. She tapped a finger to her headset and spoke with deep concentration into the mouthpiece. She flipped her long auburn hair and turned her shoulders toward her computer monitor. Chase completed their transaction with a wink and pushed the sunglasses back up the bridge of his nose.

He plodded past Marissa's desk and down the hallway, passing one empty secretarial bay after another, one empty attorney office after another. However wrecked (temporarily) his impeccable gym body might be on a post-Ecstasy Monday, however heavy (temporarily) his heart, he was always the first to arrive. It was a point of pride. More than that, it was an obligation. Chase Evans was the youngest partner in the storied hundred-year history of the esteemed law firm of Winthrop & Greenfield LLP, the top biller three years running, Chair of the Executive Committee, their national rising star, the hot, young, public face of the firm. They depended on his presence, to set the standard, to encourage and inspire. It was pressure, but it was pressure born of success.

He opened the door to his corner office and yelped out a "Fuck!" as the lights blinked on. He reached for the switch to turn them off, tossed his sunglasses to the desk, closed the door behind him, and hopped into his waiting leather chair. It rocked back with his weight, and on the rebound he planted his feet and rocked it again. He swiveled around to face the city view, let out a sigh, closed his eyes, and rocked some more. Twenty-two and nineteen went nuts for the view, from his penthouse, like a couple of junior real estate agents, but soon enough they returned their attention to the task at hand (and in hand), and after an impressive warmup on the couch (but before they could leave anything behind that wouldn't come out with a good steam-cleaning), they were off to the master bedroom for the main event, the pommel horse and the vault and the balance beam and the floor exercise, mounts and dismounts and sticking the landing and the occasional fall. Nineteen was the first to give it up, catching Chase on his back and pinning him; the boy faced him and straddled him and forced himself down on it, his pretty face twisted in delirious agony. Oh that pretty face. A thousand ships. Chase looked down. His hand worked his fly. His hand slipped under his briefs. He looked up at the view and it was not his penthouse and he gasped at his own recklessness and sat up in his chair.

"Jesus God!"

He looked over his shoulder. Those damned glass walls. Just great. *We believe in transparency* was the Executive Committee's talking point, when they rolled out the blueprints and the renderings. That was a little on-the-nose, but they had taken a vote, the ayes had it, and once a decision was made, they always spoke with one voice. The remodel was only a month old, so Chase could forgive himself this momentary lapse. But it couldn't happen again (not that it happened often).

He zipped up and swiveled back around and rolled across his office to get a better angle. No signs of activity yet, but no time to waste either. He rolled back to his desk, switched on the hard drive, and stared at the monitor. He drummed his fingers on the desk. What was it twenty-two had said? Something bitchy. The precise words were lost to him, but the feeling–humiliation? dismissal?–lingered. A put-down, personal, out of line. Whatever. It was too dumb, they were too dumb (and too young!) to bother him. Those hookups never went anywhere anyway. That was kind of the point.

He held his breath as the emails loaded . . . fifty-one unopened . . . ninety-four . . . a hundred and fifty-three. He exhaled. It could have been worse. It could have been better, too, had he bothered to check his phone or his laptop more than once or twice over the weekend. But a man deserves a break now and again–he shouldn't be the only one holding the firm up–and it was harder (in a good way) than he expected to get rid of nineteen and twenty-two.

He sat back and groaned. Where to start?

"Coffee?" he wondered aloud.

He stared up at the ceiling and swiveled clockwise and counter-clockwise. Yes, he was definitely through with Ecstasy. He should call Billy and break it to him, right now, before he lost his nerve. Or maybe send a text?

A hearty knock on the door–*shave-and-a-haircut!*–jolted him to attention. He steadied himself, sat up, and called out. "Morning, Barnie!"

"And what a l-o-o-o-o-vely mornin'!" Barnie swung open the door and greeted him, arms outstretched, one hand hanging onto the doorknob. She looked up. "Uh, hello, where are my lights? Shit, Lestat, must you always spoil my entrance?"

Chase had to laugh.

Barnie Singer, petite and svelte, wore her bright red hair in a fresh, tight curl with an oversized white bow, and showed off another new thrift store treasure: a form-fitting, black and white herringbone wool jacket with thick shoulder pads, and heels in red leather to match her hair. She reached behind the door and found the switch. Chase winced as the lights came on.

Barnie clasped her hands together. "Did somebody say coffee?"

"Oh, Barnie, you know I wouldn't ask–"

"You're damn right, you wouldn't. What is this, nineteen-sixty-five? It just so happens that I was going downstairs anyway, so . . . usual? Grande two percent latte, double shot?"

"Make that a triple."

"Chase, dear, make that a triple *what*?"

Chase batted his eyes. "Uh . . . make that a triple *now*?"

"Oh, har-tee-har-har. Honestly, you! Anyhoodle, so I guess I'll be going then."

"Okay, so great. Thanks a ton, boss."

"Welcome." Barnie folded her arms and stood in place, tapping a foot. "Ahem."

Chase gave her a blank stare and shook his head.

She rubbed her thumb and two fingers together. "Hello?"

"Oh!"

Chase stuck a hand in his front pocket and felt around. He pulled out the pocket: empty but for a spec or two of lint. He looked up at her, an apology on his face.

"Jesus, never mind," said Barnie. "I'll just put it on your tab. Again." She heaved a dramatic sigh. "It would be so much easier to be mad at you if you weren't so damn good-looking." She whirled in place and headed out the door.

"Why, thanks ever so, Miss B. You're awfully–"

"Oh, bee-tee-dubs?" Barnie called back, as she sashayed away, "your all-hands meeting with Ike Aronson is in the main conference room on 49 in twenty minutes."

Chase laughed. "Yeah, ha ha. Wait, my *what*?!" He jumped up and ran out the door and chased her down the hall. "Barnie, wait!" He caught up to her at the elevators. She pressed the button twice.

"My *what*?!"

"Do you even read your emails, hon'? Something about a change of strategy."

"A change of wha'?" Chase checked his watch. "What the fuck? Is anyone else here? Rachel? Carlos?"

"Beats me, Mr. Evans."

"Did you at least—"

"In a three-ring binder, with numbered tabs, on your credenza."

"And did you tell Ike that I—"

"Please, kid, I've been doing this twenty-nine years."

The elevator door opened. Barnie stepped on, gave a forced smile and a little five-finger wave. "Okay, bye-eee."

Chase turned and hurried past Marissa, running a hand through his hair. "Fuckity-fuck-fuck!"

"Uh-oh!" said Marissa.

He passed a tall, gray-haired secretary–no, Legal Administrative Assistant–Chad, who stood at his standing desk, sipping his steaming black coffee. Chad smiled at Chase and nodded.

"Morning, chief."

Chase smiled back. "Morning, Chad."

He slowed his pace. A young associate attorney–Sophia– checked her phone as she settled in behind her monitor. She waved to him through the glass. He waved back. He relaxed his shoulders. He was Chase Evans, right? He could handle anything. Always prepared, even when he wasn't.

He sat in his chair and rolled up to his desk, back straight, eyes level with the monitor, and took a fresh look at his emails. "Re: URGENT: breach of contract claim." "Re: URGENT: meeting." Distribution: his biggest client, Ike Aronson (originations last fiscal year: 2.3 million, realization: 100%); Aronsoncorp's General Counsel, Brooks Marshall (useless gasbag); Chase's service partners on the Aronson team (and on most of his other teams), Rachel Andolini and Carlos Bautista (brilliant but not cheap); and Frank Sutcliffe, the team's senior associate.

"Wait. Frank fucking Sutcliffe?"

Frank reported to Carlos, rarely to Chase, never to Ike. Smart, but with zero social skills, best kept out of sight. What the hell was he doing on this email chain? Who invited him to the meeting? Chase scrolled down to the invitation, opened it, and accepted.

Eighteen minutes.

He whirled around and grabbed the binder from the credenza. He rose, snatched his navy blue blazer off the hook on the back of the office door, and headed three doors down to Rachel Andolini's office.

He stopped and stood in her doorway.

"Rachel. Thank God."

Rachel sat at her desk, behind a dozen stacks of papers, her face buried in her own copy of the binder, neurotically sweeping back her long black hair. She looked up. She wore no makeup, other than freshly applied ruby red lipstick.

"Chase! You're here!"

"Of course I'm here."

"Oh my God, Chase! What the heck?! Why don't you answer your emails?!"

"I just—"

"Ay-ay-ay, Ike is so pissed off! Like, *so* pissed off! I tried to call you—"

"What the fuck is going on?"

"It's bizarre. Freaking bizarre. Frank Sutcliffe? All of a sudden Ike cares what Frank Sutcliffe says?"

"Yeah, I saw that. Should I be worried?"

"Yes! I mean, I don't know, Chase, okay? I've been going through this freaking binder, trying to figure this out. It would've helped if you–"

"Well, we have eighteen minutes."

"Fifteen."

Chase pulled up one of the two gray upholstered guest chairs on the other side of Rachel's desk.

"Rachel, can you . . . can you move some of this crap over, so I can put my binder down somewhere?"

Rachel stood up, picked up a stack of papers at random, shrugged, and dropped it on the floor. Chase stared down at the mess, grimaced, and looked up at Rachel. They broke out laughing.

Carlos Bautista appeared in the doorway, smartly dressed in a dark gray suit, with a fading tan, his slightly thinning hair neatly combed.

"What's so fucking funny?"

"Oh, shit, Carlos," said Chase, "have you looked at the Aronson binder?"

"Yeah, yeah, it's bullshit. Let me . . . Jesus, Rachel, can you move some of this crap over?"

Rachel swept another stack off the table and onto the floor.

Carlos looked down. "Uh, okay. So that happened."

"Wait, wait," said Chase. "Close the door."

Carlos closed the door. He pulled up the other guest chair.

"So, the nickel summary is, Sutcliffe has this bonkers idea that Ike should bring a cross-complaint against Syndicated for breach of contract."

"Since when does Frank Sutcliffe have ideas?" said Rachel.

"I know, right?" said Chase.

"Well," said Carlos, "that's the thing. His ideas are shit. He's saying Syndicated breached the contract by, get this, suing us for breach of contract. It's total nonsense."

8

"That's idiotic," said Chase. "Everyone has the right to–"

"Correct," said Carlos. "It's *fucking* idiotic. He's got something here about damaging our relationship with the subcontractors, yadda yadda." Carlos flipped through some pages. "Here. 'In point of fact,'–Jesus, who says 'in point of fact'?"

"Yeah, yeah," said Chase, "he's a douche. Anyway, go on."

Carlos took on a haughty British accent: "'In point of fact, one might well argue that by accusing Aronsoncorp of a breach, Syndicated effectively repudiated the license, thereby putting all subcontractors on notice–'"

"Oh, that's bullcrap," said Rachel.

"Fucking bullcrap," said Chase. "I couldn't sign my name to a cross-complaint like that. I'd look like a fucking idiot."

"The problem is," said Rachel, "we have to convince Ike that it's bullcrap."

Rachel and Carlos both looked at Chase.

"What?" said Chase.

"You're the young hot-shot," said Carlos. "He's your client."

"Well . . ." Chase leaned back and stared out the window. He squinted. "I mean . . . it's Ike."

"Uh huh . . . ?" said Rachel.

Chase leaned forward and looked at them both.

"We can't just straddle him and sit on it."

"Right," said Rachel. "Wait, what?!"

"Yeah, excuse me, what?" said Carlos.

"I mean, um, uh, you can't come at him directly, right? He's bull-headed. He'll just dig in."

"I'm sorry," said Carlos, "I'm gonna need you to go back to, uh, to . . ."

"So," said Rachel, laughing, "nice weekend, Chase?"

"Guys, guys, not now, seriously. We have . . . eleven minutes."

"You brought it up, dude," said Carlos.

"Brought what up? No, I didn't."

"Dude," said Carlos.

"Ay-ay-ay," said Rachel, smiling and shaking her head.

\#

Chase, Carlos, and Rachel ascended the staircase and swept into the big conference room on 49, binders under their arms. As the door closed behind them, Chase stopped short. There he was: Frank Sutcliffe, at the other end of the room, seated at the head of the long, white marble table–the head of the table!–folding and unfolding and re-folding a yellow pocket square, smiling. And humming? Was he actually humming? He wore a tight-fitting, dark blue pinstripe suit, with a yellow bowtie to match the pocket square (and yellow socks, probably). His hair was combed straight back, slick with product.

On Frank's right sat Brooks Marshall, flipping through the binder; on his left, another, younger Aronsoncorp in-house lawyer, swiping through his phone. Ike Aronson stood behind them at the window, pacing, hands clasped behind his back, one hand clicking a ball-point pen. He was tall and balding, dressed in a dark suit expertly tailored to make the most of his prosperous bulk.

Frank replaced the pocket square in his breast pocket and turned to his binder.

"Nice of you to join us, Chase," he said, mustering some impressive good humor. "You're late."

"Well, no, Frank my man," said Chase, seeing Frank's tone and raising it, "we're right on time."

Frank wagged a finger. "Everyone knows that 'right on time' is five minutes late."

Ike let out a laugh and stopped his pacing. He opened his arms and smiled at Chase as if gazing upon the son he never had. Chase smiled back and turned to wink triumphantly at Rachel. It wasn't the first time she had misread anger into Ike's innocuous emails.

"Really quite sorry to spring this on you," said Frank, his smile turning brittle, "though I suppose if you had read your emails . . ."

Ike laid a hand on Frank's shoulder.

"That will do, Mr. Sutcliffe. We're all friends here, no? Chase, my *wunderkind*, so good to see you. Carlos, Rachel, you're well?"

The three approached.

"Very well!" said Carlos. "Emily and I are about halfway through that case of exquisite Bordeaux."

"Halfway? What, you don't like it?"

"Ike . . ."

"Rachel, dear, how is our gorgeous little Ella?"

Rachel beamed. "The love of my life, Ike. Thanks for asking. And Sharon?"

"Sharon is . . . eh, Sharon. But I kid. Still the beautiful girl I married thirty-seven years ago."

Ike embraced them each in ascending order of hourly rate. He grabbed Chase by the temples and gave him a kiss on the forehead.

"Still single, my most eligible friend?"

Chase blushed. "Working on it, Ike, working on it."

Ike shook his head. "It's a pity Shar and I don't know more of the gays. She could find someone for you in a minute!"

Ike pulled out the chair next to Brooks Marshall. Chase pulled out the chair next to Ike; Rachel and Carlos took the next two.

"I know we are all very busy," said Ike. "Brooks?"

"Thank you, Ike. Well, needless to say our in-house team has been very, *very* impressed by Mr. Sutcliffe's research. Haven't we, Duncan?"

"Hm?" The young in-house lawyer looked up from his phone. "Oh, yes, absolutely, Brooks, very impressed." He returned to his phone.

"Yes, thank you," said Chase. "His skills are extremely advanced, works very hard, one of our best senior associates. I rely on him constantly."

Frank sat up straight and blessed the assembled.

"Yes, anyway," Brooks continued, "I suggested to Ike that perhaps Frank should step up on this case, and we couldn't be more thrilled with the result."

Brooks patted Frank on the hand.

Chase sneaked a look at Rachel. Rachel raised an eyebrow.

"Please, Frank," said Brooks, "why don't you walk us through your thought process on this?"

Carlos leaned back and coughed. Chase leaned back and looked over at him. Carlos winked.

"I'm sorry," said Chase. "Can I just jump in, just for a moment?"

Brooks cleared his throat. "Please, Chase, uh, I'd really like to–"

"Of course, Chase," said Ike, "Of course. I always want to hear from you, son."

"Thank you. Thank you, Ike. Look, Brooks, uh, look, Frank's idea for this contract claim is . . . it's very novel, very out-of-the-box. I'm quite impressed, too. We all are, right?"

"Absolutely," said Carlos.

"Uh huh," said Rachel.

Frank gave a gracious nod.

"And thanks to you, too, Brooks, for your faith in him, for giving our boy a chance to shine. It's just the kind of thing we try to encourage here at Winthrop. So I'm, we're all grateful to you, truly."

Brooks smiled. "Well, I must say, Chase, that is–"

"But I have to say . . . I've gone through the emails, and through this binder, backwards and forwards, several times . . ."

Carlos and Rachel lowered their eyes to the table.

"And I notice there is nothing in here about a budget for this terrific–but novel, and, well, if I'm being totally honest, problematic–idea. Nothing. You do understand, don't you, Frank, that when we take a new direction like this, we need to look at the cost? I realize as an associate you haven't really been trained to think in those terms, and frankly it's something from a management perspective that we really need to improve on going forward. Just as an example, do you have any idea how many attorney hours are involved in drafting a cross-complaint, especially such an unusual one? Have you thought about what might come next, from the other side? A motion to dismiss? Discovery? Summary judgment? The cost to appear at the hearings on all the new motions?"

"Well," said Frank, fussing with his pocket square, "I–I– I intended to include such details in a later–"

"Yes," said Brooks, glancing toward Ike, "in a later–"

"Look, Ike," said Chase, "all due respect, Frank is an invaluable member of the team, no question, and I appreciate what Brooks is trying to do here, but this is just a little above Frank's pay grade, I'm afraid. He still needs a bit of guidance–"

Ike pounded his fist on the conference table. Chase nearly jumped out of his chair. Frank stopped fussing and smiled.

"Goddammit, Chase!" said Ike. "How long are you knowing me and you speak about me like this? Am I some cheap bastard? Some tightwad? Is this what you think of me, Chase? Huh?"

"Ike! Of course not!"

"Don't I pay my bills, Chase, every goddamn month, on time, no questions asked? Do I ever even ask for a discount, or a write-off, which I am certainly entitled to, with all the business I give you?"

"No, Ike, you don't, but you also don't see–"

"I'm not finished! I don't give a flying fuck how much it costs me, is what I'm telling you. I refuse to let that lowlife crook Marty Perelman intimidate me. He thinks he's such a hot shit, with his big fancy company Syndicated. Which, by the way, he borrowed from every bank in the country to buy that company. Well, let me tell you something. Am I gonna show him! I built *my* company from the ground up! From the ground up! I don't owe nobody nothing! And I did *not* get where I am today by bending over, excuse the expression, for such a fraud as Marty Perelman. I'm going to bleed that motherfucker dry! Do you hear me? We'll see how much of that company he has left when I'm through with him."

Ike sat back in his chair, red in the face. He waved an arm around in the direction of the carafe of ice water on the long counter by the window. "Brooks, someone, can you . . .?"

Rachel rolled her chair back and stood. "I got it, Ike. I got it."

"Thank you, Rachel dear."

"Ike." Chase placed a hand on Ike's shoulder. "Ike."

"What?"

"You ask what I think of you. But now, I gotta tell you, you've got me wondering, what must you think of *me*?"

"Of you?"

Rachel handed Ike a glass of water, turned to look at Chase, then returned to her chair.

"Ike. I always, *always* look out for your best interest. You must know that, after all this time. Not just because that's my obligation as your lawyer. But because I, I admire you, Ike. I look up to you, almost like a . . . honestly, I do. I know how much you've achieved, how hard you've worked. How you started from nothing. I can't even begin to imagine what that must have been like. And when I hear you say these things, that I think you're just–it's, it–well, it hurts me." Chase tapped his chest. "It makes me feel like you don't know me. Do you understand?"

Ike took a long sip from his glass.

"Eh."

"The fact is, I know you, Ike, quite well, I think. I know you're stubborn, you don't back away from a fight."

Ike sat up. "Damn right!"

"But sometimes . . . as your lawyer, I'm telling you, sometimes, you have to . . . you have to choose your battles. Look. We've been down this road before. With the wrongful termination class action, the trade secret cases. But Syndicated is a whole–"

"They didn't get a penny out of me, Chase!"

"That's right, Ike, that's right. But you spent a fortune fighting them. Against our advice, against the advice of your Board of Directors–"

"Oy!" Ike smiled and shook his head. "The so-called Board of Directors. What a bunch of pussies!"

Chase laughed. "I know, I know. But you don't really want to get into a war with Syndicated, now, do you?"

"Too late!"

"No, Ike, it's not."

"It's not," said Rachel. "It's really not."

"It's all been very cordial and civil up until now," said Chase. He closed his binder. "Look, Ike. They're a huge company. They've got more money than God, they've got Dan Rivetti, they've got–"

"What, you're afraid of Dan Rivetti now? Is this what you are telling me?"

Chase backed away. "Now hold on."

"Ike, Ike, Ike," said Rachel, "there's something else. You need to know you're asking us to take a very big risk with this new claim." Rachel looked around the table. "If Syndicated can show that we're just trying to 'bleed them dry,' as you say, that we don't really believe the law is with us, that's some pretty serious bad faith. It's the kind of thing that can ruin a career."

"That's right," said Carlos. "We could be seriously fucked. And I don't know about you, but–"

Ike rose.

"That's not my problem!"

Chase rose and looked him in the eye.

"But it is, Ike, it–"

"You figure it out." Ike poked Chase's shoulder. "You're supposed to be my brilliant legal team. You figure it out!"

There was a tap at the conference room door. Barnie opened it a crack and stuck her head in.

"Sorry to interrupt, Mr. Aronson, just dropping off some coffee for–"

"Not now, Barnie!" Chase, Carlos, and Rachel shouted in unison.

CHAPTER TWO

Chase sat on the hard wood bench in the dimly lit gym sauna, alone, a fresh white bath towel loosely wrapped around his waist. It was too late, almost closing time, but that was the kind of week it had been. Long days and late nights, new pleadings to draft, new research to assign, a new case plan to write, a new budget to estimate, all for what promised to be an extremely costly mistake. He was weak, a coward, stupid. He shouldn't have inflamed Ike with all that talk of money. He should have argued the substance, the merits of Frank's bonkers idea, like he was arguing before a judge. Lead with your strengths. It's basic stuff.

The heater hissed and thunked behind him in its cage.

Three days without a workout was a minor crisis. In the middle of the night Chase awoke in a panic to the thought of his body fat percentage rising, his muscle mass shrinking. Put your career ahead of your fitness, and who would look at you anymore? The next thing you know you're old and fat, desperate for an expensive young "companion" to take care of you in your twilight years. And those guys, well, they would steal from you to buy drugs and they'd host orgies while you were out of town and they'd become meth addicts and they'd end up falling asleep on your silk sheets and never waking up. Or something like that.

Tonight he had doubled his time and increased his speed on the treadmill, added a set for biceps, lower back, upper back, chest, triceps, quads, and deadlifts. Every time he took a break between sets, the image of Frank Sutcliffe, that smug, sniveling jerkoff, smiling through oversized teeth, came back to him. Fuck that guy. This was all his doing. He was just a leech. A loser. Never brought in any business, and now he thought he could go around Chase's back, directly to the client, and get away with it? He wouldn't, not for long.

The sauna door swung open.

"Whatever, dude," said a large silhouette. "You can . . ."

The steam jets switched on, and the loud hissing and pumping drowned out the man's deep voice. The steam rose and obscured his naked body. Chase looked down, then looked up. He closed his eyes, then opened them and squinted. His heart pounded. It was Big Trainer Bro. Just him and Big Trainer Bro. Just him and naked Big Trainer Bro. In the sauna. Sweating together in the sauna.

Chase straightened up, then eased back against the back of the bench, arms resting on his thighs, feet flexing in and out. The chillest dude on the planet.

The door closed. Big Trainer Bro bent over the bench opposite Chase, laid his white towel down, turned around and sat down. He saw Chase through the fog and gave a nod. Chase gave back a nod of his own. Just to be polite.

The bench creaked as Big Trainer Bro shifted his weight.

The steam jets trailed off.

"'Sup," said Big Trainer Bro.

"'Fine, how are you?"

"Huh?"

"Huh? Oh, um, hey. 'Sup."

"'Sup."

"'Sup."

"I've seen you out on the floor. You're a lawyer, right?"

"That's right. How'd you know?"

"I can tell, dude. You guys have a look."

"Um, thanks?"

"Nah, it's all good, bro. It's a good look. Like, on you."

Chase cleared his throat. He re-secured the towel around his waist, for no particular reason.

As the fog lifted, Big Trainer Bro stood and stretched and paced the room, his dick swinging free. He was tall, taller than Chase, naturally dark, with thick, jet-black hair, dark brown-black eyes, full lips, and smooth skin. Perfectly built, not a single muscle group neglected, from his broad, square shoulders down to his thick, hard quadriceps and calves. As if he felt Chase sizing him up (not that Chase was sizing him up), he turned and showed his perfect, round, sweaty ass.

There was no point looking away. No amount of re-securing or adjusting or shifting could disguise Chase's growing enthusiasm. Nothing to be ashamed of, of course.

When he was out on the floor, Big Trainer Bro knew what he was doing, and not just with dumbbells and medicine balls. He looked back, even stared back, just often enough and long enough to give you hope. But no, the man was hopelessly straight. Right? But hadn't he checked Chase out, tonight, doing deadlifts? Caught his eye in the mirror? Or stared at his thighs or whatever? No, Chase had his form all wrong, and Big Trainer Bro couldn't decide whether to correct it. But what about last week, when Big Trainer Bro was training the skinny, old guy, looking bored and distracted; that was when he looked at Chase and smiled and winked. No, he must have had something in his eye.

Maybe he was straight, but maybe not hopeless?

"Uh," said Chase, "so, you're a trainer?"

"Yeah, how'd you know?"

"I'm smart like that."

Big Trainer Bro laughed, a little too hard.

Chase leaned forward, elbows on knees.

"I don't know why anyone would hire a trainer who didn't look like a trainer."

"Right? Hey, I'm Derek."

"Chase."

Derek stepped across and shook Chase's hand, standing right over him. Chase fidgeted, kept his eyes above Derek's waist, went up too high and caught Derek's eye for longer than a split second. There was half a chance this was actually happening.

Derek returned to his pacing and stretching, and added some groaning–so tight, so sore. He didn't look at Chase, but he didn't quite look away. The right guys never cruised Chase, or if they did, they didn't commit. They waited for Chase to commit first. (Because he was hot? Because he wasn't hot?) And Big Trainer Bro–Derek–he had the right guy act down cold. Was he into it or wasn't he? Chase could only sit there on the hot bench, paralyzed, holding his towel down, watching Derek and not watching him, those thick, powerful thighs, that ass, that major cock, which, possibly, was looking a little hard.

No, it wasn't. It was just big. Very, very big. Chase was just tired. He was imagining things. He was full of himself. *That* was what the gymnast had called him. Full of himself. Fine. Whatever. Was he though? Ah, the gymnasts. What were they doing in his head? They were sending him a message. You have too much sex. You don't have enough sex? It's only been a few days. It's already been a few days. You're counting the days, just like an alcoholic counts the days since his last drink. Hi, I'm Chase, and I'm a sex addict. Hi Chase! It's been five days since I last had a dick in my– there is no such thing as a sex addict. Everyone needs sex, some more than others. Right.

"Right?" said Derek.

"Huh?" said Chase.

"Huh?" said Derek.

"Did I . . .?"

"This steam is perfect," said Derek, groaning. "My favorite part of the day, bro." He placed his hands against the wall and walked his legs back and stretched his calves.

"Oh, totally, bro," said Chase,

Derek looked over his shoulder at Chase. "Sweating out all those toxins."

"Oh," said Chase, sitting up, "but you must have a very clean diet."

"Very clean." Derek winked. "Way clean."

Chase closed his eyes. The man fucking winked. Big Trainer Bro fucking winked at him. In the sauna.

Chase stood up. "So look, bro. I don't mean to–oh shit!" Chase's towel came undone and fell to the ground. He bent down, reached out a hand, and stopped. He stood up straight. He placed his hands on his hips.

Derek turned around. He placed his hands on his hips. He looked down in the vicinity of Chase's erection, looked up at Chase's face. He smiled, almost laughed.

"'Sup?" said Derek.

Chase smiled. He looked down in the vicinity of Derek's erection and/or very big penis, looked up at Derek's face. He stretched out his arms and groaned.

"Yeah, so, Derek, my man, I'm thinking I've pretty much sweated out every last toxin in my bod, right? Gonna hit the showers?"

"Yeah?" said Derek.

"Yeah?" said Chase.

"Cool," said Derek.

"Cool," said Chase.

"Just gonna chill here a while," said Derek.

"Oh. Yeah. Nice. Okay, yeah."

"Uh huh."

The jets came back on. The steam rose and filled the space between them, a small kindness sparing Chase further humiliation. Nothing left to lose, he stood his ground and held Derek's dark eyes until they disappeared in the mist. He picked up his towel, held it as he opened the sauna door, tossed it into the hamper and grabbed a fresh one off the shelf as the door closed behind him.

Big Trainer Bro. What a c— no, he didn't use that word.

He hung his fresh towel on the last hook and opened the door to the last stall. He got in, closed the door, turned on the water, gripped his temples, and opened his mouth in a silent roar. You had him, right there, man to man, hard-on to hard-on, and you left the room?!?! What did you think would happen? He stared down at his erection. He turned the water to the coldest setting, but his cock refused to settle down. Big Trainer Bro. Fuck! Not gonna happen.

There was only one choice left to him. No one around except Big Trainer Bro, his big dick swinging around in the sauna, probably stroking away, probably thinking of him. Right. He warmed up the water and pumped out some lotion from the dispenser. Big Trainer Bro, Derek, *nice*. Nice cock, nice ass. Give it to me, Big Trainer Bro. He closed his eyes, stood under the shower head, and stroked. It was good. It was for the best, really. Simple. No mess. No weirdness out on the gym floor.

The shower door swung open.

"Jesus God! What the . . . ?"

Chase opened his eyes. There was Derek, in all his fuckable glory, body glistening with sweat, cock as hard as a rock. So most likely this was now happening.

"Oh, dude," said Derek, "my bad, I thought . . ."

"You thought?"

Derek looked back toward the sauna, then at Chase, on his face a question.

Chase smiled, hand still gripping his cock.

"Did you want to come in, Big Trainer Bro?"

Derek stared but didn't move. He looked again toward the sauna and back at Chase.

"I mean, fuck it. Yeah. Yeah, Sexy Lawyer Dude."

Derek stepped inside the shower and shut the door behind him. "I–I wanna suck that big lawyer cock."

"I bet you do."

Chase wrapped his arms around Derek and pulled him close. Derek put up no resistance, easing his hips into Chase's. Chase ran his hands across Derek's broad shoulders and back, covered in hot sweat; he held him tighter. Derek took a hold of Chase's ass and worked his way up with both hands; he held Chase tighter. Chase took Derek by the waist and guided the two of them under the shower head, let the water engulf them. He was high again, rolling, only this man was real, a fantasy realized, the unobtainable obtained. He kissed Derek's neck; Derek moaned. He worked up to Derek's ear and rolled his tongue around; Derek groaned.

"You feel so good, man," said Derek.

"Yeah?"

"I've had my eye on you . . ."

"I had a feeling."

"I wanna kiss you so bad–I don't usually kiss, it's not–"

"I get it, my man." Chase winked. "There's plenty of other things we can do."

Derek smiled, droplets of water glistening on his face. Man, he was beautiful. He took Chase by his flanks and kissed his nipple, sucked on it gently, rolled his tongue around on it. He pulled back and looked.

"Wow, dude, you could be a fucking Abercrombie model."

"Seriously?"

"I've never seen you with a trainer?"

"Thank you, internet."

"Don't tell my clients."

"Any other secrets?"

Derek's soft, thick tongue slid slowly down Chase's chest, down and across his abs. Chase moaned. Derek's mouth headed toward his cock, slowly, making him wait like only a real pro could. Exactly how straight was this guy? He crouched down and held Chase below the hips. He slid his tongue up past Chase's cock to his thigh, poking it in deep where the leg met the groin.

Chase let out a groan.

Derek looked up, blinked at the water hitting him, stuck a hand over Chase's mouth.

"Whoa, dude, not so loud."

"Can't help it."

Chase opened his mouth and sucked on Derek's fingers. He placed both hands on Derek's head and guided it downward.

"Suck it, Derek. Suck my cock."

"Oh yeah."

Derek grabbed a hold of Chase's hard cock and slipped his tongue beneath, lapping up his balls, taking one, then the other, then both in his mouth. He rolled them around and gently sucked on them, licked underneath, sucked some more.

"Aaah," said Chase.

"Gimme that big fucking cock, dude."

Derek wrapped his mouth around the tip, licked it, sucked on it, licked it, sucked a little deeper, a little deeper, pulled back and exhaled and stroked it and then a little deeper, exhaled, looked up, stared at Chase, stroked, sucked, stroked and sucked, deeper still, and he had it all, pushing his mouth down to the base of the shaft. He closed his eyes, breathing heavy through his nose, the tip of the cock hitting the back of his throat, stuck there, Derek pushing, pushing down, Chase pushing in, then a lunge and it slid all the way down. Saliva and pre-cum dripped from Derek's mouth; he slurped it back in. He moved his hands around to Chase's ass, up to his chest, back to his ass, stroked it.

He was good, Big Trainer Bro, almost too good, too hungry, keeping the whole thing in there, down there, slurping, sucking like a fucking vacuum, such amazing lungs. Probably from all the cardio.

"Ah, shit," said Chase. "Don't make me come, dude, not yet. It's too fucking good."

He pulled Derek's head away; Derek fought back–those traps, those lats, those deltoids, and of course those bis and tris–and got it down his throat again. He gagged a little, let up just an inch or two, then back in, back out, into a rhythm. Beautiful. Still a little hard to believe.

Derek backed off. "I can taste your pre-cum, bro. So fucking good. Wanna taste?"

Before Chase could answer, Derek was on his mouth, the pre-cum sweet and salty. Chase found Derek's tongue and sucked on it. Derek sucked back, rolled around it, over and over. Their mouths joined around their tongues, such a tight fit Chase almost couldn't breathe.

Chase squinted. "I thought you didn't–"

"You have such pretty lips, man, I can't–you drive me crazy. I'm so fucking into you."

"Uh huh."

Chase studied Derek's face and kissed him again. He took Derek's head in both hands, ran his fingers through his wet hair. He smiled.

"I wonder who tastes better."

He cupped Derek's perfect hard round ass in his hands while he tongued his neck, his chest, his nipples. They were as big as silver dollars and dark and pert, and Derek shuddered and cried as Chase spread his tongue over them and licked them and sucked on them. Derek's chest was solid and almost square, as if sculpted from marble. What a sight–the water bouncing off it and running down to his stomach. And his stomach–Chase lost count of the abdominals, there must have been a hundred–and he licked them all, one at a time. He dove down the final few inches, over Derek's navel and down to his enormous, thick, rock-hard cock, and took it in his mouth. It would be a challenge to have it all, but that's what life is all about.

Chase looked up, blinked and blinked at the water spraying his face. Derek stared down at him, nodded, and threw his head back, emitting a guttural plea. Chase rolled his tongue around the tip. Derek held Chase's face in his hands. Chase smiled and took an inch, then another. He looked down at the thing, stroked the shaft with both hands, opened his mouth and slid further down on it, until there was room for only one hand. He pulled back and licked the shaft, tip to balls and back, his tongue wide and flat. He took a deep breath and plunged back in. Derek shivered and groaned.

"Suck my big cock, mother-fucker, suck that bitch with your pretty mouth."

"Oh fuck yeah," said Chase, his voice muffled.

Chase stroked his own cock. It was soaking wet and slick and warm, a mix of pre-cum and water and Derek's spit. Derek's cock was smooth, wet, and leaking with pre-cum, sweeter than Chase's own. The juice was so plentiful, it made a fine lubricant, and Chase's eyes widened in surprise as he took more and more of the cock, down, down. It was so rock hard, it demanded a lot of force. Chase pushed and pushed. It hit the back of his throat. He had to stop, he couldn't stop; he gave another lunge and the monster slid past the limit and he had it all. His mouth was flush with Derek's flat, hard stomach. He gagged, and gagged some more, but stayed with it. He looked up. Derek's eyes were practically rolling out of their sockets. He looked back down, closed his eyes, got back to business, sucking, holding back the gag reflex, slurping and sucking, sliding up and down, slow, fast, slow, fast.

"No, no, stop, wait," cried Derek. "I don't want to yet, I don't want to."

Derek took Chase's head in both hands and slowly, gently, pulled him away. Chase slurped up a mess of pre-cum and smiled. But Derek looked down at him with a changed expression, a hint of a snarl. His snarl turned to a snarly smile, and he turned around. He spread his cheeks and backed himself onto Chase's open mouth.

Chase let go of his cock and used both hands to spread Derek's checks wider.

"Holy fuck," said Chase.

He poked with his tongue.

"Aw, fuck," said Derek. "Aw, fuck. Eat my ass, dude, eat my fucking ass."

Chase lapped him up. He circled around the sweet hole, spreading his tongue wide and licking that ass, teasing around the edge, poking in and out; he stuck his face in deep, and rammed his tongue right in. Derek groaned. Chase groaned.

"Aw, man," said Derek. "So fucking nice."

Chase rammed in deeper, sucked at it, licked the edges and sucked some more. The shower water soaked his face as Derek's perfect round hard ass enveloped him. He licked his asshole, tongued him, licked him, sucked him; he buried his face in deeper, as deep as he could go, then deeper still, and sucked on that sweet ass.

"Aw fuck, aw fuck, I'm gonna come, I'm gonna come!"

Derek shuddered; he pulled away and turned around and shot his load on Chase's face, thick, streaming ropes of it. He stuck his cock in Chase's mouth, pulled out, came some more, shuddered, and came some more. Chase swallowed what he could, got his mouth back on Derek's cock and took the rest of that sweet, sweet cum, sucked on it some more as Derek cried in ecstasy, still shuddering.

Chase was ready, he was ready to go. He stood up. Derek knelt down and brought Chase's cock to his mouth and right down into his open throat. Chase lost all control and fell back against the shower wall, coming, coming right down Derek's throat, and Derek drank it, drank it all in, until it overflowed his mouth and back onto Chase's cock. Derek pulled back and swallowed hard and licked up what was left and stood up, nearly out of breath.

Chase pushed himself off the wall and into Derek's arms. They kissed again, one last, long, cum-filled kiss, and they stood and held each other, panting, chests heaving together.

Big Trainer Bro. Imagine that.

CHAPTER THREE

Frank Sutcliffe stared at the email.

Frank - so sorry to do this to you on a weekend, but Chase is a little worried that Syndicated may try to argue that New York law applies on the breach of contract claim—could you make sure we've got our bases covered on that?

- Carlos

Yes, so sorry. So very, very sorry. How utterly transparent. Of course they gave him this pointless research on a weekend. They were punishing him. For seeing something they didn't. For knowing Ike Aronson better than they did. Ike went for it, just as Brooks predicted, and it didn't matter to Ike if Frank wasn't running the case, if Frank was just some nobody in the trenches who did all the work but took none of the credit. And if Frank's idea made Ike question his faith in his little *wunderkind*, that vain, shallow fraud, Chase Evans, all the better.

Wunderkind! What, exactly, did he do, had he ever done, to earn that name? True, it took a lot of hard work to be born with good looks and charm. *Ha ha.* So maybe Frank never reeled in the big clients, so what? Nine years under his belt and he might never make partner, but he refused to pretend he was anyone's friend just for the promise of a big payday. Everyone did it now, but that didn't make it right. His father never did it, nor his father before him. They were men of honor. But now, *You eat what you kill.* Such a nasty business.

And a lonely one. Chase may have looked like he was top of the world, but deep down, surely he wasn't. He was past thirty and still single. They said he hooked up with a different man every week. Frank had seen Chase in the morning, before his third cup of coffee, and it wasn't pretty, even on that pretty face. That pretty, chiseled, full-lipped, blue-eyed face. There was a hole in his heart, and all the hookups in the world weren't going to fill it. And all the drugs–God knows, the man partied every weekend. He couldn't keep it up forever. This wasn't going to be the last time he got caught napping.

"Oh, to hell with this."

Frank switched off the computer.

#

Chase stood at the window, following the path of the helicopters circling in the distance, the lights of the city twinkling below. The beams of their searchlights crisscrossed the clear night sky, chasing down a fugitive or a traffic jam, or just making their presence known. A blinding light landed on him. For a brilliant moment it filled the penthouse, turning night into day. He stood frozen in place, blinking, waiting for his vision to return.

Growing up in a middle-class neighborhood in the Valley, condemned to ground-level like everyone else, he never adjusted to their angry appearance without warning in the middle of the night, their harrowing, machine-gun clatter that split the air, rattling the doors and windows. Keeping us safe, his father would say, so deadpan no one ever knew if he was serious.

But they roamed in silence tonight, on the other side of the thick glass that wrapped around the apartment. They were his helicopters now, his metal dragons, patrolling the kingdom. Add an early-decade Tracey Thorn club remix pumping through the sound system, and they were his private light show, his airborne dance, and he directed the choreography. He even danced a little himself.

The only thing he lacked–the only thing–was the full three-sixty view. A middle-aged hedge fund guy, Victor, with a blonde, supermodel-looking wife, Dinah, and her Corgi, Wicker, owned the ocean-facing half of the floor. One day, Chase would make an offer. Everything was for sale. An engineer and an architect and a real estate associate had already worked out the blueprints and the permits. Chase would bring down the walls between the two units and create a showplace, the finest spot in the city, with views from the mountains to the Pacific. Imagine that.

In the meantime, Victor was Chase's dear friend, not just to make the inevitable negotiations frictionless, but because a guy who managed twenty billion dollars of other people's money could always use a better high-end litigator on retainer, if he ever just happened to lose faith in the current one.

Not long after Chase moved in, he hired a chef and a bartender and invited Victor and Dinah and a few carefully curated friends over for cocktails and hors d'oeuvres and dinner. He listened, and listened, to Victor's stories: his first billion-dollar deal, the time he outbid that movie actor for that rare Hockney charcoal, the vineyard in Napa Valley he bought just to stock his wine cellar.

It required an impressively inflated ego to suggest, as Victor did more than once, that everything he had, he deserved, and luck had nothing to do with it. Dinah, fortunately, was gifted with the wit and humor to see through his pomposity and cut him down to size, with the occasional conspiratorial wink at Chase. In Chase she earned a devoted fan. A good couple of decades separated Victor and Dinah, but to judge from the way they looked at each other, the way they laughed at each other's corny humor, their marriage was no mere arrangement.

The phone rang. Chase picked up. "Billy boy!"

"Hey, C-note, waddup?"

"We are totally getting some tonight, Billy the Conqueror."

"Because we are so not thirsty, Chase Manhattan. Let me see your handsome face, *chico*."

Chase tapped FaceTime. "Whoa, you mean let me see *your* handsome face, *chico*. Pull the phone back, let me get a good look."

Billy wore a tight white t-shirt, which showed off his dark skin and muscular upper body and biceps. He had given his hair a modified buzz-cut, emphasizing his even, well-shaped hairline and setting off his thick, dark eyebrows. He had on round, oversized, black-rimmed glasses.

"Thoughts?" said Billy.

"You are looking smoking hot tonight, *jovencito*. I would totally hit that."

"Oh, please, *mijo*, don't even."

"For the reals, my man."

Chase met Billy their very first day of law school. They formed a study group with two women whose brilliant legal minds were a severe mismatch for their poorly tuned gaydar, which led to some awkward, but harmless, misunderstandings. Amped up on the cutthroat pressure, Billy and Chase hooked up on the eve of their first semester exams. They crushed the exams; the sex didn't quite make the grade. Second year, they were elected co-editors of Law Review; they tried again, and their marks improved. It happened a few times, but they fought–Billy was too needy; Chase was afraid of commitment. They were meant to be friends. Best friends.

Like Chase, Billy got multiple offers from the best firms, but he hated the grind of Big Law, the pressure to bill hours and bring in business; so he put up with it long enough to pay off his student loans and then went into the non-profit world, taking an executive position at the LGBT Center. He'd never have a penthouse, but he loved his life, and he was giving back.

"Which Porsche are you picking me up in tonight," Billy asked, "the red one or the blue one?"

"Oh, ha ha," said Chase, "you know I have only one Porsche. I think I'll take the Tesla tonight. I'm feeling virtuous."

"Who knew virtue was so expensive?"

"See you in a minute. Love-you-bye."

"Love-you-bye."

Chase turned up the dimmer switch and checked out his reflection in the window. With Billy dressed in white, he had better change to black, but his jeans nicely featured his world-famous booty, and the hair was perfect.

It was so on.

#

Billy Alarcón put the phone down.

Smoking hot? Boy, please. Dial it back.

Saturday night with Chase was always quite a thing. Out all night dancing and partying and whatever, it was no sweat for Billy, with his schedule designed for a normal human. But Chase, always working, working, working, plus this–his energy was a marvel. He could have left Billy behind, a million times, but it never happened. Chase took care of him, in his way. Chase was his hero, in his way.

There was that time, but it was a lifetime ago, and it was all settled and behind them now. But there were other times, now and then, when something was up, he could feel it, and it still hurt a little. It was almost like he could get to feeling sorry for Chase. Which didn't make a whole lot of sense, but anyway it was only almost. So best to let it pass, and it always did. And then he had his best boy Chase back, and what could be better? Nothing. Nothing could be better, no doubt. No doubt whatsoever.

It was too hot in the apartment. It was such a nice, comfortable night outside. He went downstairs to wait for Chase out in front.

#

Chase and Billy turned into the long driveway and circled around to the valet.

"A restaurant with a private driveway," said Chase. "Only on the west side."

"It's just beyond beyond," said Billy.

They stepped out of the car. The restaurant's big, heavy wood and metal door opened as some early drinkers poured out, snapping selfies and counting likes on Insta. Billy pretended not to eavesdrop; Chase dragged him inside.

"Mm," said Chase, "what smells so good?"

They stood at top of the stairs and looked down, Chase hooding his eyes with one hand. Single Edison bulbs hung from long cables, lighting each of the small, high tables where the noisy bar crowd overflowed. To one side, three sous-chefs in spotless white stood at a big, open window, busily preparing, occasionally glancing up at the staircase. Chase pressed a hand lightly to Billy's back as he scouted the crowd. He spotted Rod and Terry at the bar and shot his hand up and waved; they waved back and beckoned them down.

"Oh no, those two?" said Billy.

"What? I told you. We love Rod and Terry."

"Well, sure, but they're so . . . married. I mean, like, practically straight."

"They're hardly that."

"Aren't they having a kid?"

"Oh, come on. I think it's adorable."

They made their way down the stairs. Chase glanced over at the hostess table; an extremely thin, pretty young woman in a floral print dress smiled apologetically and held up five fingers; Chase winked and gave her a thumbs-up.

"Boys, boys!" Chase cried. He gave Terry and Rod each a big, warm hug and a gentle kiss on the cheek. "Miss you guys! What's up?"

"Well," said Terry, eyeing Chase and Billy up and down, "y'all didn't need to go and get all gussied up just for us, okay?"

"Oh, ha ha," said Chase. "We're going out after, obvy."

"Heavy sigh," said Rod, as his wire-rimmed glasses slipped down his nose. "Remember going out after, baby? Oh, to be young again."

"We're the same age!" said Billy.

Terry laughed. "We never went out after, Rodney." He pushed Rod's glasses back up and pecked his cheek.

"Maybe *you* didn't," said Rod.

"Ooh!" said Chase and Billy.

The bartender spotted Chase, up-nodded and worked his way over, squeezing behind a barback. Chase leaned in and shook his hand.

"Good to see you, Chase."

"Yeah, good to see you . . . wait, wait . . ."

Dark hair, perfect features, part-time model . . .

"Montenegro . . ."

"Yes . . ."

Chase looked up, idly scanning the shelves of liquor bottles.

"You like Djokovic, but not Raonic . . ."

"Yes . . . and you like Nadal."

"Nikola!"

"Got it, man!" Nikola smiled.

"Boom!"

They high-fived.

Nikola set down some napkins and leaned forward and propped his elbows on the bar. Chase ordered a round.

"You're welcome to join us, boys," said Chase, turning around and patting his front pocket. "I have enough for everyone."

Terry rolled his eyes. "Of course she does."

"Ecstasy?" asked Rod, with studied disinterest. Terry shot him a look.

"You a quick one, Hot Rod" said Chase. "Though some of the kids are calling it 'Molly' nowadays."

"Same shit, different decade," said Terry.

"Don't be a hater, now, Terry," said Chase.

Terry wagged a finger. "Girl . . ."

"But Chase," said Billy, "I thought you said never again."

Chase grinned. "I always say never again."

"But you said this time you mean it."

"I always say this time I mean it."

Nikola laid the drinks on the bar, and Chase handed them out. They'd barely taken a sip when the maître d', dressed in business casual black, found Chase.

"Your table is ready, Mr. Evans. Sorry for the delay."

"Delay?" said Terry, turning his head and splashing his cocktail.

The boys took their drinks and followed the maître d' through the high bar tables and out past the glass partition to the patio, where the ceiling was higher and the crowd was louder. At the very full dinner tables, tiny, battery-operated candles provided the only light, other than cell phone flashlights, which the diners aimed at their menus.

They proceeded to a table near the center of the room, warmed by a raging fireplace.

"Righteous!" said Rod. "This is, like, pop star seating."

"Eh," said Chase, "more like TV star."

"Basic cable," said Billy.

"Recognize," said Chase. "It's the Golden Age of Basic Cable. We don't mock."

Billy reached over and mussed Chase's hair. "I would never!"

36

Chase pulled back in horror. "*Ay, chico,* the hair! *Que haces?*"

"*Dios mío! Lo siento, chico.*"

Chase smiled. He reached over and rubbed Billy's buzz-cut.

"Dear Lord above, you two," said Terry, "get a room already."

Chase and Billy looked at each other, then let out a laugh.

"Oh, ha ha," said Chase.

Chase and Billy ate light, picking at the beef tartare and crispy chicken and sipping their negronis with a grapefruit twist. Rod and Terry ate hearty, devouring the short ribs and black cod and yams and maitake mushrooms, with multiple refills on their mezcal-aloe vera cocktails.

Terry patted his stomach. "This boy's eating for two now, okay?"

Rod rubbed Terry's back. "It's true. He's so nervous, you'd think he was the one giving birth."

Terry pulled away and blinked at Rod.

"What?" said Rod, shaking his head.

"Uh, excuse me, no." Terry snapped his fingers. "This is the part where you tell me I'm just being all crazy and shit and I've never looked better. Am I right, boys?"

Chase and Billy nodded eagerly.

Rod removed his glasses and leaned into Terry; Terry backed away until he nearly fell off his chair. Rod took Terry's face in his hands.

"Terry, my baby, my beautiful, smoking hot, beautiful—"

"You already said beautiful."

"Beautiful, beautiful, gorgeous hunk of man, you have never looked better."

"And what was wrong with the way I looked before?"

Rod sat back and tossed his napkin to the table. "Oh boy."

Chase and Billy laughed.

"Okay," said Terry, "I give it a seven on a scale of . . . one hundred."

"Terry!" said Rod.

"Okay, maybe eight." Terry moved toward Rod and gave him a big kiss.

"Aaaaaaaaaw," said Billy and Chase. They gave a golf clap.

"Get a room, you two," said Billy.

"Oh, don't you worry," said Terry. "We'll be having our own private after-hours tonight, okay?"

"Okay?" said Rod.

"Holy shit," said Chase, his attention suddenly drawn across the restaurant.

"What?" asked Billy. "Where?"

"Frank fucking Sutcliffe. As I live and breathe."

"The research-slash-loser dude?" said Billy. "Where? Which one?"

"Top of the stairs—don't look!"

They all looked.

"You guys!"

Chase scooted his chair out, stood, and smoothed his t-shirt. "I should probably go say hey."

"There she goes," said Terry.

Chase meandered around the tables, keeping an eye on Frank. Frank hooded his eyes and looked around. His hair was down, product-free. He wore jeans and a polo shirt. He descended the stairs and pushed through the crowd toward the bar. He nearly reached the counter; he leaned this way and that, standing on tiptoe and tentatively raising and lowering his hand, taking an elbow in the gut from an oblivious patron and reacting with a helpless laugh.

Chase came up behind him and grabbed his shoulders; Frank flinched.

"What are we drinking, Frank ol' boy?"

Frank turned around. The annoyed look on his face briefly turned to a smile.

"Chase! I thought . . ."

Then Frank shook his head, as if trying to erase a bad memory, and his expression landed on neutral.

"My man," said Chase, "look at you! Out on the town! I don't believe I've ever seen you out before."

"Yeah, well . . ."

Chased leaned back, folded his arms, and stroked his chin. "So I'm guessing . . . vodka?"

"Uh . . ."

"Okay, so that's a yes. Don't go anywhere. Tonic? Rocks?"

Chase raised two fingers. Nikola spotted him.

"Wait!" said Frank.

Chase looked over.

"Jameson. Neat. Please."

"My man!" Chase turned to the bartender. "Two Jamesons, neat!"

Nikola nodded.

Chase turned back to Frank. "A man after my own heart."

Frank rolled his eyes. "Yeah, that's it."

"Gotta say, I like your weekend look, Frank. It's actually kinda cute, if I'm being honest."

Frank squinted. "Uh, thank you?"

"Oh, give it a rest, Frank. We're off the clock."

Frank patted him on the shoulder. "This implies you were ever *on* the clock."

"Oh, snap! Hello, paging bitter, party of one?"

Chase scanned Frank's face, searching for the smile he thought he'd seen a moment before, or at least a hint that Frank had even heard him, but Frank looked away, wearing an oddly vacant expression, looking everywhere but at him.

"I get it, Frank. You're pissed off about the last minute research assignment. Yeah, sorry about that, but–"

"No, I'm not–oh, it's nothing. I know how this works."

"Um, okay, that's not at all dark and paranoid. Look, you still got your Saturday night, right? Anything fun on the agenda?"

"Chase?"

Someone tapped Chase on the shoulder and handed him the drinks. Chase handed one to Frank. Frank took a long sip, scanning the crowd.

"Haven't decided yet," said Frank, "though I have a pretty good idea what's on *your* agenda."

"Oh really? Do tell."

"Finish a light meal here with your crew, then go kill time at a bar, then to an after-hours club where you'll do drugs, dance all night, pick someone up, take him home, fuck, and after you're done, lose his number."

Chase nodded. "A little shaky on some of the details, but all-in-all, pretty spot-on. How did you know?"

"Oh, please. You're such a cliché."

"Ouch, dude, for reals. I guess that means you're not joining us?"

Frank let out a big laugh.

"Aha!" said Chase. "I knew I could do it."

"Yes, Chase, you can actually make me laugh." Frank flashed his eyebrows and mimed smoking a joint.

"What's this now?" Chase slow-clapped. "Frank, I had no idea!"

"There's a lot you don't know about me, Chase."

"Evidently!" Chase patted Frank's arm. "Well, maybe we should remedy that. Someday. Anyway, I'm gonna head back to my crew. You have a good night, stoner!"

"Yeah, okay. You—"

Chase grabbed Frank by one shoulder and worked his way around him. He found a woman without a drink, winked, handed his drink to her, and kept going.

"Thanks, Chase!"

Chase stopped and turned around. Tall, thin. Long, straight blonde hair, tennis tan. White camisole.

He wagged his finger. "Scottsdale."

"Uh huh!"

"A-a-a-a-a-a-amy? Amy!"

She smiled. "Bingo!"

"What's up, Amy?"

She smiled, kissed Chase's cheek, and turned to her girlfriends, raising her eyebrows as he passed behind her. They nodded.

"I think he's gay though," one of them said.

Chase turned his head. "Just never met the right girl!"

They laughed and raised their glasses.

Before reaching the glass partition, Chase looked back. Frank was lost to the crowd.

Frank was right; Chase really didn't know that much about him. Chase liked to get to know people; he liked people. But Frank was a really hard person to like. Especially now, now that he had pulled his little stunt. There was a real stench of desperation about it. About him.

"Wow," said Billy, as Chase returned to the table. "I can't believe that was Frank Sutcliffe. He's not at all how I pictured him."

"He's kinda cute?" said Rod. "I mean, in a sad puppy dog kind of a way."

"Right?" said Billy. Billy and Rod and Terry nodded.

"Those deep blue eyes," said Terry. All three nodded again.

"You guys are pathetic," said Chase, as he took his chair and scooted in.

"We're lost without you," said Rod.

The waiter came by with dessert, miso donuts dipped in caramel, which Billy and Chase pushed to Rod and Terry's side of the table. Chase checked his watch and asked for the check. As the waiter walked off, Terry leaned forward and took his wallet from his back pocket.

Chase put a hand to his chest. "Terry, sweetheart, you're breaking my heart. Do you really have such a low opinion of me? Put your money away."

"You hardly ate!" said Terry.

"That's not the point."

"Listen to the man," said Rod. "I mean, how dare you, Terry?"

Billy clucked his tongue. "Honestly!"

The waiter returned with the check. Chase handed him his credit card. The waiter took it and walked away.

"So Terrence," said Chase, leaning back.

"So Chase," said Terry.

"Have you heard anything from Caroline about my pitch?"

"Oh, that. Yeah, she's still thinking."

"Thinking? I don't like the sound of that."

"Well, it's down to you and one other firm."

"Which firm?"

"Girl, you know I can't tell you that."

"Aw, come on. Okay, how about you just use their initials?"

"Oh, high-larious, nerd."

"Well, it was worth a shot. Anyway, I'm pretty sure I know which. They're a bunch of assholes, you know."

"Oh my God . . ." said Billy. He looked toward the staircase.

"Oh my God . . ." said Chase.

"What?" said Terry and Rod as they turned around.

"Mr. Frank Sutcliffe, playa," said Chase.

Frank was at the top of the stairs, heading toward the door. A tall man in a leather jacket held onto him, arm hanging over his shoulder. Frank turned his head and took a last look. He caught Chase's eye, nodded, and turned away. The door closed behind them.

Chase whistled. "My man."

#

A miasma of steam and mist, glowing in the shifting colors of the lasers, greeted Chase and Billy as they made their entrance at After Hours. The smell of sweat, punctuated by the occasional, vague gasoline sting of poppers, wafted towards them. They waded in among the Party Boys densely packed on the dance floor. Chase nodded his head and shifted his shoulders and chest as he drifted, a hand in Billy's, with Billy just ahead, leading the way. They were new arrivals, fresh meat, so Chase let the boys take him in first, holding his gaze just above theirs, glancing down at their bodies, naked above the waist, now and then accidentally on purpose bumping against their chests, or politely grabbing their shoulders to balance himself as he passed them by.

Billy stopped in the dead center of the dance floor and turned to face Chase. His brown eyes were wide open and unblinking; he wore a permanent smile verging on laughter.

Chase grabbed him by the belt. "Drink, *hijo*."

Billy tilted his bottle too high; the water spilled, splashing his face and dripping down. He laughed; Chase laughed. He handed Chase the bottle. He took off his glasses, dried them off with the t-shirt hanging off Chase's belt, and put them back on. He examined his chest and arms, wiped himself down, and slapped his stomach with pride. The boys nearby whistled. Billy looked at Chase, held out his arms in a big shrug.

"What can I say?"

Chase opened his own bottle, held it over his head, and poured. He shook out his hair, wiped himself down, and slapped his stomach with pride. The boys nearby whistled *and* cheered. Chase held out his arms in a big shrug.

"What can I say?"

Billy took Chase by the wrist and raised his arm above his head.

"*El ganador, y todavía campéon!*"

"Wait, wait," said Chase, closing his eyes. "I believe . . . yes, we have achieved liftoff, people."

"*Bravo!*"

Chase threw his head back, feeling the mist and hearing the music for the first time. He breathed in deep, and exhaled, as if relieved of a great burden. He was here with his boy Billy. Everything was in its place. He would fix the whole Ike Aronson mess. He always did. He was Chase fucking Evans.

The music was an indecipherable collage of drum and bass and cymbals, haunting voices like Gregorian chants on meth, rushing water and crashing waves. Chase listened for the pop song hidden in the chaos, but it was so transformed by the DJ's mixing board that it was unknowable. It hypnotized him, aroused him. It rose and fell, rose and fell, in sync with the lasers, each crescendo a little louder and faster and more urgent than the one before, the crowd aching for resolution, until it seemed there was nowhere else for it to go; one last crescendo, the lights so bright they were blinding, and then a moment of darkness. Silence. Stillness. All at once, the lasers flashed back on, the video screens blinded them once more, kicking off a new beat. Everyone roared in Ecstasy and hopped up and down, clinging to each other. The cycle began again.

Chase watched Billy, whose eyes were closed; he danced in small steps, rolling his hips, rotating his arms in small, parallel circles at his sides. Chase tried to sync their steps, stepping forward where Billy stepped back, stepping back where Billy stepped forward, stepping on Billy's toes. Billy opened his eyes and laughed, shook his head.

"Don't step on four, *cabron*."

"What?"

"*Ay*, forget it. Just do your white man disco dance."

Chase shrugged and smiled. He resumed his white man disco dance, feeling the music, bobbing his head and swinging his hips and shoulders, raising his arms in the air and howling like a wolf. Billy mocked him, moving stiffly, off the beat, meowing like a kitten. Chase rolled his eyes. Damn, he loved Billy. He wouldn't say it, not now, not while they were rolling on Ecstasy. It would just make everything weird. He wrapped his arms around Billy's shoulders. Billy held Chase at the waist.

Billy turned Chase's head so that he could speak into his ear. "Hey, Chase?"

"Yeah?"

Billy drew a deep breath. "Oh, nothing."

"Oh no, you can't do that, dude. What?"

"Just . . . thanks."

"For what?"

"I don't know. Everything?"

They held each other. They swayed together for a moment, feeling each other's chests rise and fall.

Chase spoke into Billy's ear. "Hey, Billy?"

"Yeah?"

"I love you."

"*Ay, chico.*"

Billy kissed Chase on the forehead. Chase kissed Billy on the forehead, then on the mouth, then on the forehead again.

"Do you think I'm a cliché, Billy?"

"What?" Billy squinted at him. "Are you serious right now? Totally the opposite. You're one of a kind, *papi.*"

"Frank Sutcliffe told me I'm a cliché."

"Frank Sutcliffe? Fuck that guy. But, I mean, don't actually."

"You seemed pretty into him."

"Um, ew?"

"Thank you! I mean, what was up with you guys drooling over him tonight? I almost took it personally."

"Aha," said Billy, "our plan worked!"

They laughed and broke their embrace. Chase looked around. It wasn't easy to separate the feelings, the high from the love from whatever else, but it couldn't be Billy. Not that it *couldn't* be Billy, but it wasn't . . . it wasn't a good idea. Their friendship was too important to him.

"It's not a good idea, right?"

"Yes," said Billy.

"Yes, it's not a good idea, or yes, it is a good idea?"

"Yes."

"Billy."

"Chase, stop. You know it's harder for me than it is for you."

"Aw, Billy."

"No more 'I love you' tonight, okay?"

"Yeah, it just slipped out. I'm sorry. Maybe I'm feeling a little needy."

"It's okay." He took Chase's hand. *"No te preocupes. I promise not to tell."*

Billy looked away, his meandering eyes a little glazed and sleepy. Chase kept half an eye on him, not enough for Billy to notice but enough for Chase to know Billy was there. Billy's gaze sharpened, his eyes landed. Chase followed their direction, to a spot on the dance floor where the fog had lifted. They both watched a group of men forming a circle, imperfect, changing, breaking, and forming again. Some were younger, some were older; they ranged in physical type and ethnicity; the style of their clothes and haircut and accessories signaled a distinct variation in income. It was hard to say who was with whom, if anyone was with anyone. Yet something unseen united them: closing their eyes and smiling, opening them and laughing, reaching out and holding each other, in groups of two or three or four or five; they all seemed to be in on the same secret, something forbidden to everyone else.

The strobe lights pulsed at just the right rate to imitate time standing still. That was when Chase spotted him. He had never laid eyes on him before, that was certain, yet there was something familiar about him, as if Chase had known him since the beginning of time. Different from the others, better somehow, but still one of them. The man focused all of himself on everyone around him in turn, sharing something intimate, recalling a memory, singing together some great lyric they both loved, taking a selfie five times until they got it right; and from the beatific expressions on their faces it seemed that he left each man better off, happier, each believing in his heart that he was special.

It didn't make sense, all this idolatry, nor Chase's own fascination. There had to be a more earthbound explanation. It was all his imagination, a projection. Or he just really, really wanted to fuck the guy. Maybe they all did. No, probably they all did. Sandy brown hair, wavy but not quite curly, with dark eyebrows and big, almost too big, green eyes and a wide, natural smile, a strong chin and chiseled cheekbones. Fair-skinned, just a hint of chest hair, tall and lanky, with beautifully developed abs and upper body. More like a high school quarterback than a gym rat. Of course Chase wanted to fuck him.

"Hey, Billy." Chase looked over, but Billy's back was turned. "Billy?"

Billy ignored him, or didn't hear him over the music, or the snapping of the paper fans, or the thoughts in his own head. Chase turned once more to watch the man, but the fog had rolled back in. Chase would find him again, but not if he looked for him. Simple.

Billy tapped him on the shoulder. "Whatcha lookin' at?"

Chase turned around. "Huh? Me? Nuthin'."

"Uh huh. Do you want to move?"

"If you want to."

It was easy to lower his gaze and look into the eyes of the men around him, now that the only man who mattered was out of sight and out of mind. He was friendly Chase, easy Chase, uncommitted Chase. And just like that, they stared back at him. They danced with him. The braver ones smiled, or licked their lips, or stroked his arm, or held him, or kissed him softly, on the neck, or kissed him deep, on the mouth, or stuck a hand down his jeans, over his briefs, or inside them. He reciprocated, or didn't, a reward for their bravery, or because he wanted to, or wanted them, or didn't; nothing at stake, nothing to win, nothing to lose.

He let the man with the softest, smoothest skin and the prettiest mouth hold him very close, but not very tight, so they could each rest a hand on the other's chest, while they kissed a little, talked a little, but still moving, still dancing. Their hands crept down to each other's backsides, and the man was just as smooth there, and so it was on, Chase had himself a winner for the night. He kissed the man a little more, closed his eyes, got hard, eased into the man's wandering hands, did some wandering of his own.

"I'm Chase."

"David."

Chase opened his eyes. The man with the big green eyes looked back at him. Chase blinked. This was some powerful Ecstasy. Or it was an omen: the man with the smoothest skin, perfect as he was, just wouldn't do. Chase frowned at David and shook his head. He kissed him on the cheek. He dropped his arms to his sides and backed up a step. David looked at him, confused, perhaps angry, but not entirely surprised. David stood a moment, staring, until a contented smile returned to his face. Chase reached out to run an apologetic hand through his hair, but David escaped his grasp. He turned and disappeared into the crowd.

That was a mistake. The man was perfect, or close enough. Omens do not exist. He could have spent the rest of the night with the man with the smoothest skin, groping and making out on the dance floor, groping and making out and more on the way home, clothes coming off in the elevator, jerking and sucking in the shower, fucking in the great room overlooking the city, fucking on the bed.

He was making himself hard, too hard. He had to stop torturing himself. Never a wrong move. He took a sip of water. He needed some air. He needed a break.

"Billy, I gotta . . ."

But Billy wasn't there. He looked around. Billy was gone, without saying goodbye.

48

Chase smiled. "Well, good for you, my man. Guess I'm gonna have to roll on without you."

Two large, gentle hands gripped his shoulders from behind. He adjusted himself. He turned around. He gazed up into a pair of big, green eyes. Not just a phantom this time, unless . . . no, it really was him. Up close, the man was even more beautiful, if that was possible.

"Did you lose your best boy?" the man asked.

"Billy? Yeah. How did you know?"

"I saw you guys before. You look very sweet together."

"We're not together."

The man smiled. "I'm Mike."

"Chase. What happened to your groupies?"

Mike cocked his head and squinted. "My what?"

"All those guys, the ones you . . ."

"Oh yeah. Don't worry about those guys."

"I'll try not to."

Chase placed his hands on Mike's waist. Mike placed his hands back on Chase's shoulders.

"Is this okay?" Mike asked.

Chase wrapped his arms around Mike's back and rested his head on Mike's shoulder. "This is better."

"Oh," said Mike. "Hello." He pushed himself against Chase's erection.

"Oh, that," said Chase. I guess I got a bit of a head start."

"Where'd he go?"

"I sent him away."

"What? Why?"

"I don't know. Maybe I was hoping for something better."

"Did you find it?"

Chase slid his hands down Mike's jeans. "I'll let you know."

Mike moved his hands from Chase's shoulders down to his back. Chase looked into Mike's eyes, but had to look away. It wasn't just that he was too perfect too be real, though he was that too. Mike had a way of returning Chase's gaze, direct, undefended, with a sense of utter calm that seemed to come from deep, deep inside him. It was too much to bear, too familiar, from someone Chase was sure—pretty sure—he had never met. And yet how else to interpret it, except that Mike knew Chase, or knew something about him, perhaps something Chase didn't know about himself? Or could it be simply that Mike looked at the whole world that way? Maybe it didn't matter. But it did explain the groupies. Who wouldn't worship a man who looked at you like that?

"Mike?"

"Yeah?"

"I don't know you from Adam, but I think you're amazing."

Mike laughed. "Sure that's not just the Ecstasy talking?"

Chase nodded, looked Mike in the eyes, took his head in both hands, and kissed him.

#

The sun was just coming up as Chase and Mike threw each other onto Chase's bed. Chase grabbed at Mike's pants, unbuttoning and unzipping, but Mike took has hands, saying "wait wait wait." He lay on his back and pulled Chase up on top of him, brought Chase's mouth to his and kissed him, hard. They opened their mouths and brought their tongues together, inhaling and devouring each other. Chase came up for air and then began again, tasting Mike's sweet breath, then covering Mike's face with his mouth, kissing, licking, taking him all in.

Mike moaned and said, "oh fuck, oh fuck, oh my God Chase."

"Mike, you're amazing. You're so amazing."

"Shhh, shhh," said Mike, "Just kiss me."

Chase kissed Mike's salty neck, kissed his ears, came back to his mouth and took him again. Their hands traveled down now as they kissed, caressing each other's sweaty skin, holding each other, squeezing each other, rolling over and back, over and back. Chase raised his head and looked down at Mike. Mike nodded.

"Yes. Yes."

Chase took a deep breath. He kissed and licked Mike's chest, his nipples, his stomach, his flank, he grabbed Mike's pants and pulled, took them off and tossed them to the ground. Mike's tight black briefs were wet with perspiration and sticky with pre-cum. Chase nuzzled there, at Mike's last line of defense, tasting everything, grabbed the briefs and pulled them down, inhaling Mike's beautiful strong legs as he threw the briefs on top of the pants.

He took Mike's cock in his hand, admired it, stroked it. Mike let out a groan.

"Oh, Jesus," said Chase.

He stuck a hand down his own pants and kept stroking Mike with the other. He looked up and saw Mike, beautiful Mike, looking down at him, a look of pained euphoria on his face. He closed his eyes and held Mike's cock and took the tip in his mouth, circled it with this tongue; the pre-cum forming a sinew connecting them. Mike stretched his arms out over his head, then brought them down and rested them on Chase's head, stroked his hair.

Chase went down on Mike's cock and kept going until he had all of it.

"Oh fuck," Mike cried.

It was stiffening now, growing in Chase's mouth and throat, finally so fully erect that Chase could hardly breathe. It felt so good, he wanted more. He forced himself down on it even more, as far as he could go, and then just a little farther. He held it there as long as he could, until Mike couldn't take any more and pulled out.

Chase exhaled, panting, and lay on his back. Mike sat up, grabbed Chase's jeans and pulled them off. He went straight for Chase's fully erect cock, spreading his tongue and licking it all the way up and down and up and down, taking the shaft now in both hands as he moved his tongue to Chase's balls.

He spread his tongue again, opened his mouth and managed to get both balls inside, and he sucked on them gently, rolling them around in his mouth. He spread his hands over Chase's chest, stroked it, while his mouth stayed below. He pulled Chase's crotch into his face, grabbed Chase's legs, and spread them. Then he pulled them up, so that they rested over his shoulders, and again pulled Chase's crotch in closer. He took Chase's cock in his mouth, sucked on it, then took it in his hand and stroked it while he ran his tongue down past Chase's balls, and followed the trail that led to Chase's hole. He licked around, teasing, as Chase writhed in anticipation.

"Oh fuck oh fuck," cried Chase.

"Mmmm," said Mike. "Fuck yeah, so sweaty. Oh yeah."

Mike stopped and pulled away, setting Chase's legs down on the bed. He felt along Chase's stomach and chest. Then he lay back, his mouth facing Chase's cock, and maneuvered himself so that his cock was within easy reach of Chase's mouth. Chase took the hint and sucked Mike's cock, easing it up and down, while Mike got back to work on Chase's cock. They lay like this side by side, taking each other's cocks, sucking and licking, teasing each other's balls, moaning, groaning, taking turns deep-throating, then deep-throating together, gasping for air, Chase so overwhelmed he could barely go on, but he wanted to go on and on and on. He never wanted to stop.

Mike lay on his back and lifted Chase over and on top him, and they sucked each other's cocks this way, with the weight of Chase's body bearing down on Mike's mouth and forcing his cock in deep, so deep that Mike had to pull Chase up by the hips to get some air, while Chase eased down on Mike's cock from above. Then they flipped over, now Chase feeling the weight of Mike's body and his cock forced down his throat. He relaxed, let his arms falls to his side and let Mike's cock in, opened his throat and took it, and Mike let Chase's cock go, sat up and looked down at Chase sucking his cock. He slid it in and out, slapping Chase's face with it, and gradually eased off, pulling his cock up and letting his balls fall into Chase's mouth. Chase opened wide, sucked them and licked them, slobbered on them, jerking himself off. Mike pulled his balls away and moved again, giving Chase his ass.

"Oh my God," said Chase. "Oh fuck."

He took Mike's ass cheeks in his hands and stroked them, spread them, tilted his head back. His opened his mouth and spread his tongue and took Mike's hole–Mike shuddered and gasped–and Chase tongued him there, tasting his sweet, sweaty hole, and he spread Mike's cheeks some more and dove in, stuck his tongue up and licked, going deeper and licking and sucking and licking, going deeper, Mike moaning and groaning in ecstasy, Chase keeping his hands there stroking that beautiful ass, stroking all over Mike's body, putting his hands anywhere but on his own cock, so sure he would bust if he did.

Mike stroked his own cock, moving his ass up and down over Chase's face; he got up and turned around and sat back down, facing Chase, so Chase could watch him while he felt himself up, his chest and his stomach, running his hand through his wet hair and pulling his head back. Looking up at this, it was almost too much for Chase. He thought he might come without touching himself. He grabbed Mike by his hips and pulled him up, off his face, and he looked up, face glistening with sweat and saliva, and smiled. Mike looked down at him, utterly soaked in sweat. Chase had never seen anyone so beautiful. Mike stroked Chase's hair, stared into his eyes, smiled.

Mike got down and lay on his back, brought his head to the edge so it was hanging off the bed.

"Gimme your cock, Chase."

Chase got up off the bed, came around and stood at the edge. He held Mike by the shoulders and gave him his cock. With Mike's head back like this, he could take it all, and Chase held him and fucked his mouth, moving fast, really fucking him, down his throat, Mike's moans muffled by the volume of flesh filling him, Chase's entire body flexing with each thrust. He went faster, faster, saying "take that cock, let me fuck your face, take that cock," Mike nodding and taking it, his eyes tearing up. Chase pulled out and gave Mike his pre-cum to lick and swallow, then pushed back in and fucked his mouth some more.

"God, I wanna fuck you, Mike, I wanna fuck you so bad," he said as he thrust in and out of Mike's mouth.

He pulled out and stepped back and stroked himself. Mike sat up. He turned around and half-stood, took Chase's face in his hands and kissed him, licked the sweat off his face and kissed his mouth, and they opened their mouths and shared the sweat and pre-cum, and filled each other with their tongues, mouths sucking tight, breathing hard and fast.

Mike pulled away, turned over, climbed onto the bed on all fours.

"Fuck my ass, Chase. Fuck me."

Chase had to take a minute. Holy fuck, that beautiful, round ass, the way Mike's slim waist tapered up to those beautiful, broad shoulders, his back solid muscle. Chase fell on top of him, wrapped his arms around his chest, spoke into his ear.

"No, not this way. I want to see your face when I fuck you."

He turned Mike's face toward him and kissed him. He backed off and helped Mike turn himself over.

He stood at the edge of the bed. He reached across to the nightstand and pulled out the lube. Mike spread his legs and stroked himself. Chase opened the lube bottle and held it up, let it drip onto his hand, then onto Mike's tight ass. He took a finger and gently grazed Mike's asshole, as Mike squirmed; he stuck a finger in gently, slowly, reaching in an inch, then two, and stroked inside, as Mike writhed and groaned. He took two fingers, repeating the motion, as Mike groaned more, louder, saying, "Of fuck, fuck me, Chase, fuck my ass." Chase looked down at him in wonder.

You're amazing Mike, he said, this time only in his head.

He dripped some lube on his own cock and stroked himself, then he reached down and stroked Mike's cock. His body began to tremble; he had to take deep breaths to control himself. He looked down at Mike's face–Mike was nodding, yes, yes–and he grabbed his cock and grazed Mike's asshole with it, back and forth, up and down, and now Mike was breathing heavily, saying, "give it to me, Chase, give me that big cock," and Chase positioned himself, stepping forward, and took his cock and gently inserted it in Mike's hole, just an inch or two, to get him ready. He stayed there, fucking him with just the tip of his cock, watching Mike writhe in agony-ecstasy, waiting, until he cried, "give me more, Chase, give me all of it, I want it, I want it." Chase lifted Mike's legs up, held one in each hand and slowly, gradually, but without stopping, gave Mike his cock, all of it, an inch at a time. Mike was so tight, he couldn't go too fast.

Mike grabbed his own cock and stroked it, wincing as he felt Chase's cock pushing, pushing past his resistance–he didn't mean to resist but his body could only take so much. He was breathing through it, short, quick breaths, as the hard shaft went deeper and deeper. He shuddered and cried out, "holy fuck!" and Chase was all the way in, ramming up against him.

Chase kept ramming him there, feet firmly planted on the ground, his hips flexing and his glutes tight, so he could use all his strength to fuck Mike's ass. He couldn't believe how tight, how perfect his asshole was, and he watched as Mike tensed his body, taking his cock, watched all his muscles rippling. Mike felt so good. Chase eased up on him, still fucking him deep, but now more gently, and as Mike's face relaxed and turned into a smile Chase was glad, glad the man he was fucking was enjoying it, enjoying him, and in this way they could make it last, they could fuck and fuck and fuck, and it wouldn't be all force and submission but also something else, something they were doing together, not just using each other.

He scooted Mike back on the bed and fell on top of him, kissed him, held him, and Mike wrapped his arms around Chase's back, and they both smiled and moaned softly to each other, and it was still fucking hot, but also it was nice. Beautiful. He loved looking at Mike's face, staring into his eyes–but not for too long–holding him and fucking him and kissing him, and Mike was all there with him, they were totally together, minds on nothing but each other, and they fucked like this for what seemed like forever.

Until Mike began to shudder, and he picked his head up, and he cried, "Oh, fuck, I'm gonna come, I'm gonna come, keep fucking me I'm gonna come," and Chase stayed inside him and thrust a little harder, and pushed himself up, held himself up so Mike could jerk himself off, and Mike stroked and stroked and stroked and then he came, came so hard the cum shot up nearly to his chin, coming all over, leaving a mess of cum all over his chest and stomach. Chase kept fucking him, just a little longer, and he leaned down and licked up some of Mike's sweet cum, and he kissed Mike's mouth and they shared the cum, and he kept kissing him, until he couldn't take another second and he pulled out, and Mike said, "come in my face, come in my face," and Chase climbed up and sat on Mike's chest so his cock was in Mike's face, and he stroked and stroked and stroked and came on Mike's face, came in big shots all over Mike's face and in his hair, Mike with his eyes closed but his mouth open, and a big drink of Chase's cum went straight into Mike's mouth, and Mike licked his lips and swallowed, and Chase came down and kissed him, licked the cum off his face, kissed him, closed his eyes and kissed him, and they kissed with their tongues all the way in each other's mouths, swirling around, licking the cum, swallowing each other's juice. They couldn't get enough of each other, even after all the sucking and fucking and coming, and they stayed together kissing and panting and holding each other, caressing each other, until at last their breathing slowed down.

Chase climbed down from on top of Mike, lay down next to him, on his side, his back to Mike. Mike turned onto his side, and Chase backed himself into Mike, and Mike wrapped his arms around Chase's chest. Chase closed his eyes.

#

They sat in the hot tub, squinting into the sun. It was a clear, cool afternoon, and Chase could have stayed there all day, with Mike, with Mike's arm around his shoulders. He closed his eyes.

This was not the usual Sunday. Mike was different. Not just the way he looked, not just the look in his eyes, not just the sex. He had an effect on Chase, touched him somehow, in a place no one else had. It had something to do with the strange, recurring sense that he had known Mike forever. It wasn't frightening, not exactly. It wasn't sad, not exactly, or maybe it was a little sad, but a beautiful kind of sad. Was it relief? Relief from what?

A vape pen sat on the deck. Chase looked at it, picked it up, held it out to Mike. Mike shook his head.

"Don't let me stop you though," said Mike.

Chase brought it to his lips. He squinted. "Nah." He put it down.

Was that because Mike refused it, or would Chase have abstained anyway? It wouldn't be so bad, right? Doing something a little different for someone you liked? Just as long as you didn't take it too far. Anyway, he really didn't need it this time. He didn't need it to ward off the post-Ecstasy blues. He was with Mike.

Mike turned to look at him.

"Chase," he said.

"Mike?"

57

"You're amazing."

Chase eased back into Mike's embrace, a new thrill coursing through him.

CHAPTER FOUR

Chase removed his sunglasses as the elevator opened. He stepped out and smiled at fair and lovely Marissa at Reception.

"Good morning, Marissa. New haircut?"

"Why yes, Chase," said Marissa, blushing and patting the soft curls above her shoulders. "How kind of you to notice!"

"Très glamorous!"

"Why, thank you, kind sir!"

"Certainly, m'lady."

"You're awfully chipper for a Monday morning."

"Just the start of another week at Winthrop & Greenfield, printing money!"

"Ha ha yes, of course. Good weekend, I take it?"

Chase shrugged. "Eh, you know, same old same old."

"Yeah, me, too."

"Better than a poke in the eye!"

"I suppose."

Chase strutted through the reception area, stopped, and turned.

"Oh, say, Marissa, have you had your coffee yet?"

Marissa held up a mug. "'fraid so, Chase, but I do appreciate the offer."

"Well, next time."

She nodded. "Totally."

Chase walked down the hall to his office. He opened the door and gestured to the air like an orchestra conductor, and the automatic lights turned on. He bounced into his chair, sat back, whirled around, and looked out the window.

"Lovely," he said.

Another beautiful, clear day, the distant mountains set in dark relief against the pale blue, early morning sky.

He turned to his desk, sat up, rubbed his hands together, held them above the keyboard, and froze. A manila envelope jutted out from under the keyboard. That was a rather odd place for Barnie to deposit his mail, even the confidential Executive Committee stuff. He peeked over the top of his monitor out to the hall. He got up, closed the door, and sat back down. He slid the envelope out and opened it. Inside, a copy of an old article from the *Philadelphia Journal*:

Accused Law Firm Embezzler Found Dead of Apparent Suicide

May 18, 2000, Philadelphia. Francis Powell, Jr., 51, former managing partner of the law firm of Powell & Powell in downtown Philadelphia, was found dead in his Villanova home late yesterday from a gunshot wound to the head, an apparent suicide. Powell had been accused of embezzling $15 million from his partners and had been arraigned and released on $1 million bail.

The embezzlement charge, brought May 13, came as a shock to the Philadelphia legal community, given the prestige Powell & Powell had earned over nearly half a century in the city. Sources with knowledge of the firm's management have told the Journal that unbeknownst to most members of the partnership, the firm's financial condition had worsened considerably in the past 2-3 years.

Powell is survived by his wife, Martha Sutcliffe Powell, and two sons, Francis "Frank" Powell III, 15, and Lawrence Powell, 11.

According to Philadelphia police . . .

"Frank . . . holy shit."

Chase slipped the photocopy back into the envelope, jumped up, threw open the door, and jogged down the hall to Rachel's office. She looked up from a new pile of documents. Old piles of documents had spread from her desk to her two guest chairs. More piles were growing on the floor against the wall.

"Holy shit, Rachel."

"What?"

Chase closed the door behind him. He held up the envelope. "How the fuck did you find this?"

"Find what?"

"Oh, ha ha." He handed it to her.

She opened it and scanned the article. She slumped back in her chair. "This is wild, Chase. Freaking wild."

"I know, right?"

"I don't remember this guy, Francis Powell. I mean, this was in Philadelphia, I was barely out of high school. But it's freaking wild that no one ever put it together, that this was Frank's father."

"Oh, come on, you're such a bad liar."

"I swear, it wasn't me. When the heck would I have time?! I'm so swamped with this new freaking cross-complaint, Ike's calling me three times a day, the memo on the motion to dismiss, the–"

"Okay, okay, I believe you. You're a very sincere whiner. So Carlos then?"

"Chase! He's buried in this crap, too, *and* he's co-chair on a three-day arbitration with Harvey!"

There was a knock on the door. Barnie opened it a crack and stuck her head in.

"Did somebody say coffee?"

"Not now, Barnie!" Chase and Rachel cried in unison.

"Oh-em-gee! Sorry!"

Barnie closed the door.

"I saw him out the other night," said Chase.

"Who?"

"Frank!"

"Frank goes out?"

"Right? So trip on this. He says to me, 'There's a lot you don't know about me.'"

"You think he meant *this*? That's playing a little close to the edge, isn't it?"

"Who knows? He's just creepy enough."

"Ya got me there. Thing is, though, I'm not really sure what you're supposed to do with this."

"I'll think of something. But it doesn't leave this room, okay? Well, except Carlos."

"Understood."

"Francis Powell the Third. It suits him. Pompous little douchebag."

"So, nice weekend?"

Chase shrugged. "Eh. Average."

"Uh-oh, I know what that means."

Chase grinned.

"And you're caught up on your emails?"

"Rachel! Don't even!"

Rachel raised her hands above her head, fending him off.

"Jeez! Just asking!"

"Yes, Mommie Dearest, I'm all caught up. Went through them last night, and again this morning before I left the apartment."

"Gonna see him again?"

"Gonna see who again?"

"Ay-ay-ay!"

#

Frank gripped his binder of cases, in alphabetical order and indexed, with numbered tabs, and stood in the doorway, his eyes on Chase. Chase spoke on his headset, eyes on his monitor. Frank never met one-on-one with Chase like this. This was progress. Nothing to get too excited about, of course. A little recognition was nice, but it was long overdue, and it was just Chase. Just another lawyer, a colleague, nothing more than that. He shifted from one foot to the other, glancing around the office, never letting Chase entirely escape his view. He stood up straighter, pushed his chest out. The binder was getting a little heavy. He was this close to tapping on the door jamb.

He looked at his watch. Five minutes early is right on time.

Finally, Chase looked up, acknowledged him, and gestured to a guest chair. Chase held up an index finger and tapped his earpiece and spun his chair around to face the window. Frank sat down across from him, laying his binder on Chase's desk.

"Yeah," said Chase, "just walked in. Yep! Okay, good luck today. My love to Harvey." Chase fell silent a moment, then laughed. "Yeah, bye." He hung up the phone and twirled around to face Frank.

"Frank, my man! How are you?"

"Good, Chase, very good, thank you. How are–"

"That's great, Frank, great, great. I'm not even gonna ask you about your weekend, because, I mean, hello!" He winked. "Well done, my man, well done. Who knew?"

Chase picked up the binder and opened it.

"So what little gift have you brought me today?"

"Those are the cases on New York law as it applies to the new contract claim, per Carlos's request. I've prepared a–"

"Huh? Oh, right, right, right, your research project, ha ha."

"Ha ha?"

Chase flipped through the first few pages and closed it, placed it back on Frank's side of the desk.

"You can put that aside for now, Frank. Carlos will brief me later. I'm sure you did a thorough job. You always do, my man!"

Frank cleared his throat, adjusted his tie, and looked at Chase.

"Well, that's fine, Chase, but if that's the case, I'm not sure what—"

"Frank, can I just say, first of all, congratulations. I can admit when I've been outplayed, right? You saw something I didn't, and you took the initiative, and you went for it. So good on ya, Frank. Can't say I love your methods, going behind my back and all that, ha ha, but hey, you won Ike over. That's huge. When your biggest client insists on spending a bunch more money on you, how can you say no, right?"

"Exactly! I'm so glad you—"

"So here's the problem, Frank, as I see it. Ike runs a big company, right? But Ike also has a Board of Directors, and he reports to them, but of course you knew that. They do *not* like the way he spends money, Frank. And this new claim, and all the fees we'll be charging them? Well, I don't think the Board is thrilled. To them it's not smart, it's not going on offense, blah blah; it's just Ike lighting money on fire. Again. It makes me look bad, it makes the firm look bad. Worst of all, it makes Ike look bad. We can't have our biggest client looking bad. Do you get that?"

"Sure, Chase, I suppose, but—"

"So if you thought, I don't know, that somehow this baller move of yours was gonna put you at the head of the line for partnership or something, well, think again, okay? If your new breach of contract claim gets thrown out, well, I don't know what to tell you, Frank. If it somehow manages to survive, best case scenario, you get to keep your job. But partnership? Well, I don't think that's *ever* gonna happen. And I have a lot to say about whether it does. A *lot*."

Chase stood up. "So, we good?"

Frank stood up, too fast. His head spun. He steadied himself, gripping Chase's desk. He took a quick look at Chase and turned to go.

"Frank?"

Frank turned around.

"Yes, Chase?"

"Your binder."

Chase stared down at it, his hands on his hips.

"Yes, of course," said Frank.

Frank picked it up and turned again to go.

"Oh, and one more thing," said Chase.

Frank turned around again, breathing hard. He stared at the floor.

"Please, Chase, what?"

"Chill out, dude, come on! So . . . Saturday night."

"I thought you weren't going to talk about that."

"I changed my mind. Maybe you were a little . . ." Chase flashed his eyebrows and mimed smoking a joint. ". . . But you told me there was a lot I didn't know about you. Do you remember that?"

"I guess."

"What do you suppose you meant by that?"

"I don't know, Chase. Look, I really need to—"

"I couldn't stop thinking about it. Weird, right? It's just Frank Sutcliffe. Who cares, right? So, I'm just wondering, maybe there's something you need to tell me? Something I should know? About you?"

Chase leaned across his desk and stared at Frank. Frank stared back.

"Chase, I . . ."

"You what, Frank?"

Did he have something to tell Chase? Was Chase trying to tell *him* something? Did Chase know something? The perspiration now flowing under his arms and soaking the back of his neck, could Chase see it through his shirt? Frank's shoulders hunched up, squeezing his neck. How must that look? He took a breath and lowered them.

"Wait," said Chase. "I think I know."

"You know?"

"Do you love me, Frank? Do you want to marry me, Frank, honey? Is that what it is?"

"I . . ."

Frank turned and fled.

He darted down the hall, so fast Barnie stopped talking and look up from her phone; he headed through the reception area, past Melody, or Melanie, or Mary Ann, or whatever it was. He pressed a button for the elevator and paced. The door opened and he got in, turned and propped himself against the wall. He shirt was drenched; he shook with a chill.

He got off the elevator and ran outside. He slowed to a walk. He took out his phone and dialed.

"Brooks Marshall's office?" said a woman's voice.

"Oh, hi," said Frank, through labored breath. "Is Mr. Marshall there?"

"Who may I say is calling?"

"Frank Sutcliffe."

"Hold the line, please, Mr. Sutton."

"Sutcliffe."

The line beeped.

"Frank?" said Brooks.

"Brooks, oh my God, Brooks, I am so screwed! I'm gonna lose my job! You said I was gonna make partner, you *promised*, and now I'm gonna lose my job!"

"Whoa, whoa, whoa. Frank. Calm down."

"He knows about us. What am I gonna do?"

"Who?"

"Chase!"

"Knows what?"

"Brooks! Don't do that!"

"Frank, you're being ridiculous."

"He kept trying to get me to tell him something, but I can tell, I can just feel it, he already knows. He's on to us."

"He doesn't know anything. He's just trying to scare you."

Frank laughed. "Yeah, well, he's pretty good at it."

"He can't hurt you, not as long as I've got your back. Okay?"

"But Brooks—"

"Frank! Please, you have to calm down. The worst thing you can do is let Chase think he's gotten to you. Do you understand that?"

"Yes, yes, of course."

"Okay, okay. So just, just calm down, go back to work, try not to worry so much, okay? Frank?"

"Okay, okay, but—"

"I've got to go, Frank. We'll talk later."

Brooks hung up.

Frank found a dark green metal bench and hunched over, gripping it to steady himself. He kept his head down and his eyes open, to slow the spinning. He breathed in deep, held it, and exhaled; and again. When the spinning finally stopped, he turned and sat down. He sat back. He loosened his tie. He looked around. The bench was in the shade, his shirt was still wet, and he was shivering. People on nearby benches were smoking, most of them alone, like Frank.

A bearded man in khakis and a white dress shirt sat down next to him on the bench and took out a pack. He stuck a cigarette in his mouth and looked over, held the pack out to Frank.

"Oh, no. No, thank you."

"You sure? You look like you could use it."

Frank smiled. "What, you mean this?" He looked down and unstuck the wet shirt from his chest.

"I'm Zach."

"Frank."

Zach put the pack back in his shirt pocket.

"Actually," said Frank.

Zach smiled. "Sure."

He took the pack out again, shook out a cigarette. Frank pulled it out, stuck it in his mouth, held it, his hand trembling. Zach leaned forward with a lighter, steadied Frank's hand, and lit the cigarette.

Frank inhaled. He looked at Zach. Zach smiled.

Frank wasn't going back to the office today.

#

Chase folded his hands behind his head and leaned back in his chair. He'd never seen another lawyer look so scared. It was a surprisingly satisfying feeling. Had he been too rough? Maybe. Poor Frank. The world had dumped a lot of shit on him. Only fifteen, and his father shoots himself in the head. His family ruined. Frank made a little more sense to him now. Never the same from one day to the next, as if he didn't know what kind of a man he wanted to be. One day high and mighty, the next a scared, sniveling kiss-ass. One day charming and almost attractive; the next slouching and hiding in the library.

But always and forever a world class jerkoff.

He sat up and looked at his monitor. He scanned his emails, opened Rachel's new draft of the Aronsoncorp cross-complaint. It was a very hard case to make, even for Rachel, the best writer in the firm. As he slogged his way through it, he knew right away how Syndicated would respond. The cross-complaint was an attempt to punish Syndicated for exercising its First Amendment rights. Is was frivolous, just an excuse to drive up Syndicated's legal fees. The worst part was, they had a point. Anticipating what the other side would argue was an essential skill, but sometimes it could be depressing, seeing it so clearly. He ran his hand through his hair and gritted his teeth.

His phone vibrated. He leaned over the desk and picked it up.

"Wow, that was fast. Too fast?"

He unlocked the phone and opened the text.

Chase, amazing Chase. Just wanted to let you know I'll be out of town for a while. I'll be in touch. Mike L.

He read the message again. He stared at the phone, squinted at it. He stared and shook his head until the screen went black.

"Oh, ma dude, that is some weak-ass bullshit."

Very, very weak. Why didn't Mike just ghost him, instead of trying to sell him such a pathetic line? It was beneath him. It was so obviously a lie, it almost felt like Mike wanted him to know it. In that case, why not tell the truth?

Chase laughed. Imagine that: actually thinking, even for a minute, even for the time it took him to read the text, that he knew the guy well enough to know what was beneath him, to know if he even gave a shit about the truth.

"I mean seriously. I'm Chase Evans. Chase fucking Evans. Nobody breadcrumbs Chase fucking Evans. Deuces, bro."

He tossed the phone to the guest chair across from his desk and returned to Rachel's draft. He minimized it and checked his emails. There was yet another draft, with comments from Carlos.

"Shit! It's a fucking moving target."

He closed the old draft and opened the new one and started from the beginning. Remember that time, not even twenty-four hours ago, when Mike was different? Guess not. But he *was* different. There *was* something there, something new, something a little scary. Mike was scared. It was new for him too. Mike felt like he'd known Chase forever, too. Yeah, what a pretty story. Mike really did have to go out of town for a while. But why? What was he hiding? Was there someone else? No, Chase wasn't going there. He was done. If anything was going to happen now, it would have to be–

The office phone rang, once, twice, three times . . .

"Barnie?!" Chase yelled.

The ringing stopped.

Barnie yelled back. "It's Billy!"

"Use the intercom, Barnie! Jesus!"

"Sorry!"

The intercom rang.

"Sorry," Barnie whispered. "First line."

Chase pressed a button. "Hey." He leaned back.

"Hey, baby," said Billy. "You okay?"

"Always. You?"

"Monday blues. Saturday night though? Oh my God! Best. Ever."

"Right? Where did you go? I didn't see you after–"

"For real? You gave us a ride home, airhead."

"I did?"

"Yeah! You, and me, and your blonde-haired boy, Mike, and–"

"Light brown. Oh, and your boy James. Yeah, I remember now. He was fucking fine."

"So fine. We fucked for days. I am so sore. I'm not even kidding you right now."

Chase laughed. "I can't believe I forgot about that."

"Not very professional, *hijo*. Maybe you were right about quitting Ecstasy."

"Hmm . . . ."

"What about you and Mike?"

The strange sadness that wasn't quite sadness pressed against Chase's eyes.

"It was amazing, Billy. He was fucking amazing. I'm getting hard just thinking about it."

"Gonna see him again?"

"See who again?"

"Chase! What the fuck is wrong with you, boy?"

"Guys like that, you know . . . "

"Guys like what? I really liked him, Chase. So did um, um . . ."

"James. Yeah, so did I."

"You didn't just like him, Chase. I know you, *mijo*, better than anyone, better than you know yourself even. If you ask me, you were way into him."

"I was, Billy. I *was*."

"You sure you're not just coming down off your Ecstasy?"

"Billy . . ."

"Shit, gotta go. Gotta take a call from the CEO. But this conversation is not over, *hijo*. Talk later?"

"Sure, later."

"Love-you-bye."

"Love-you-bye."

Chase dropped his face into his hands, ran his hands through his hair. He picked his head up and stared at his monitor.

"Fuck."

He stood up.

"Damn you, Billy."

He went over to the guest chair and retrieved his cell phone. He opened Mike's text.

Chase, amazing Chase. Just wanted to let you know I'll be out of town for a while. I'll be in touch. Mike L.

He read it again.

Chase, amazing Chase. Just wanted to let you know I'll be out of town for a while. I'll be in touch. Mike L.

"'Amazing Chase.' Christ, what an asshole. It's like a big, wet kiss while he stabs me in the heart."

Or was it just your garden variety brush-off from a hot guy he fucked once, with a kind word to soften the blow?

Well, either way.

Chase typed. *Cool story bro.*

"No." He backspaced.

Cool.

He hit "send."

#

Mike looked out the window, down at the city far beneath him. Why was the sky always so blue when he left this place? Why did it always feel like leaving home, when he was supposed to be going home? Almost a decade now, he'd been some kind of wanderer, adrift but settled, alone but attached. He saw himself slipping out with Chase, amazing Chase, down to Clifford's house by the beach, rolling around in the sand with him like in an old Hollywood movie, making love on the couch with the curtains billowing in the ocean breeze.

Sooner or later, he had to make a change. He couldn't keep this up much longer. But Chase wasn't the answer. That feeling that they'd known each other forever, it was just a feeling, nothing more. Chase was just a hot guy who fucked him once, rolling on Ecstasy, feeling things he probably had already forgotten.

Mike had a long flight ahead of him. He looked over. Clifford was already out, earplugs in, sleep mask on, snoring softly. Mike patted Clifford's hand. He reclined his seat all the way back and brought the footrest all the way up and closed his eyes.

CHAPTER FIVE

Kevin Lacey sat on the edge of his son's bed.

"Michael, I don't care if you make a single scrimmage. I don't care if you sit on the bench all season. All I want–all Mom and I want–is for you to study hard and get good grades and make something of your life."

Mike looked up from his duffel bag.

"I know, Dad."

"And don't be intimidated by those rich city kids and their fancy prep schools. You're smarter than all of them."

"You don't need to worry about me, Dad."

For Mike, getting good grades at Brown was the easy part. Actually learning something was the bigger challenge, though no one else seemed to notice or care. They were all just killing time until law school, or business school, or a management training program, earning their lady's and gentleman's B's and C's, taking their junior year abroad in Venice or Tokyo or Rio.

In French poetry, why did they just scan the meter, when they should have been asking why Baudelaire was always writing about death or wine? In the Concerto, why did the half-drunk Hungarian professor regale them with the story of that time he auditioned for Leonard Bernstein, when they should have been listening to Mozart and Beethoven and Mendelssohn, searching for motifs and feeling uplifted by transcendent violin solos? In English Literature, why did the balding, bespectacled T.A. seem more interested in cruising Mike than in the exploring the narrative arcs of *Paradise Lost*?

Not one to rock the boat, Mike tuned out in frustration, and turned his attention to the blank pages of his notebook. He sketched in pencil, a habit born of daydreaming, back in high school. By now it was something of a passion, and he noted with pride the improvement of his technique, despite a lack of formal training. After a slow start with landscapes and still lifes, he had moved on to, and become obsessed with, young, barely clothed wrestlers, in semi-erotic poses, seen from multiple perspectives. These caught the eye of Marius, sitting behind him in French poetry, who followed him out after class.

"I wrestled at Choate, you know."

"You wrestled at what?"

Marius invited him back to his dorm room to study, which for some reason involved Marius sitting at his desk wearing nothing but a pair of tight gym shorts. Mike got the message and made himself equally comfortable, and within a few study sessions (and after some wrestling instruction), Mike had his first real boyfriend.

For Thanksgiving break they drove Marius's hand-me-down BMW from Providence down to New York, to stay at Marius's family's penthouse on Central Park South. Marius insisted they weren't as rich as they seemed–it was a rent-controlled apartment that originally belonged to his grandfather. But Marius's father worked on Wall Street, and his mother was a candy bar heiress who played tennis, lunched with the ladies, and raised money for the Metropolitan Museum, or the Metropolitan Opera; Mike never could keep it straight.

At dinner, while Marius's two younger sisters competed for Mike's attention, Mr. Wasserman tried to talk him into a summer job at his firm, and a smitten Mrs. Wasserman begged to take him shopping on Madison Avenue and find him a proper wardrobe. Mike's idea of Wall Street, glamorous and fast paced, didn't match the reality, a horde of spoiled, arrogant frat boys who hadn't changed since college. A shopping spree, on the other hand, appealed to him, not because he was vain, nor because he harbored any illusion that the clothes made the man, but because of Mrs. Wasserman, Elaine. She had an easy affection and warmth for him that his own mother lacked (though she had her own good points). She spoiled him because she enjoyed it, not because she expected anything in return.

For Christmas, they took him skiing at Aspen. A natural athlete, Mike picked it up quickly; within a few days he joined Marius on the black diamond runs, beating him to the bottom of the mountain by their last day. For New Year's Eve, it was back to Manhattan and a masked ball hosted by one of Elaine's society friends. Mike went shirtless, scandalizing the conservative crowd and making Marius beam with pride (Marius was more discreet, in a tight, semi-transparent t-shirt).

Sophomore year, Marius accused Mike of loving his family—and his family's money—more than him. Mike defended himself, but half-heartedly; he did love Marius, but he couldn't be sure that he would have loved him without Central Park South, or Aspen, or all the finer things he had quickly acquired a taste for. Anyway, they were both so young, years from graduation. There would be plenty more love in the future before either of them was ready for a real commitment. They parted as friends.

He rebounded with skinny, curly-haired Todd, a painter, aspiring filmmaker, and occasional actor from the Rhode Island School of Design down the hill. Todd picked Mike up at one of the theater people's off-campus after-parties, notorious for their free-flowing alcohol, weed, and sometimes acid. He encouraged Mike to think of sex not as a means to an end–the first step toward a "relationship"–but as an end in itself. They didn't need to possess one another; their minds should always be open to other guys, other experiences. That was all it was–experience, grist for the mill. Often they prowled the bars and sex clubs for a third or fourth.

Mike showed up at Todd's RISD gallery openings with a bouquet of sunflowers and a bottle of Cabernet. He solicited Todd's critique of his pencil sketches. He came up with something he hoped was original to say about the pieces hanging in Todd's apartment, but when he described one of them as "minimalist," Todd blew up, haranguing him that it was abstract expressionist, which would be obvious to anyone who wasn't just a dumb jock at a preppy corporatist diploma mill. Mike just laughed; he told Todd he certainly was dumb for not realizing what a pretentious poser he had been dating.

"You mean fucking!" Todd shouted, as Mike headed out the door.

Christian from the football team–now there was a genuine, honest-to-goodness, dumb jock. He was as hot as he was dumb, and after a few drinks at a frat party he got frisky, sneaking a hand onto Mike's ass, and, when Mike returned the favor, following him into the bathroom. Mike never pushed, but happily made himself available whenever Christian give himself permission to do it again. Christian was a different creature when he hooked up with Mike–loud, voracious, submissive–but it was hopeless from the start. Christian never allowed them to be seen in public together. There was nothing to talk about except football. Mike was destined to be the youthful experimentation phase before Christian found a blonde sorority sister to wear his letterman jacket and bring home to Mom and Dad.

Senior year Mike applied for a seminar in ancient Portuguese history. His major was American Literature, but he had been hearing students gushing over the Professor Tavares for three years, and not just about his pedagogic skills. In the admission interview, he got tongue-tied regurgitating the tidbits about the Visigoths he had memorized the night before. When the professor thanked him for his time and lowered his eyes in sadness, Mike's rejection was all but certain. But he got in. It made no sense.

The seminar gathered around a great, scarred wooden table in one of the older, Gothic style buildings, in an echoing, high-ceilinged, walnut-paneled classroom, with portraits of ancient deans lining the walls. There was no last row, no place to be inconspicuous. Feliciano Tavares introduced himself with the admonition that they must call him Feli. He strutted around the table with an athlete's cockiness. He filled out his khakis just a little better, his glasses and thick hair were just a little more fashionable, his shoulders just a little broader than you would expect of a middle-aged Portuguese history scholar. He looked straight through Mike. At first. Which was just fine. At first.

When, by the third class, Mike gathered the courage to raise his hand and speak, Feli stood and faced him, feet planted, arms folded over his chest, and listened. Something in the tilt of his head or the openness of his gaze revealed a man of great kindness, and suddenly Mike's words came easily, even flowed, made sense to him, made sense to his classmates, who nodded and smiled. When Mike finished, Feli nodded once, clapped his hands and said "Good," turned his head, and moved on. Mike sank into his hard wooden chair.

Not long after, on a crisp spring morning, Mike's coffee buddy and freshman year hall-mate Nancy took the seat next to him and happened to catch a look at his notebook. She elbowed him and nodded down at it. He barely realized he had been sketching a new portrait, this one begun not out of boredom but something quite different. It resembled in every detail the dark-eyed man standing on the far end of the great wooden table. Mike broke out in a sweat and glanced up; was everyone looking at him? Were everyone's eyes darting from him to Feli and back? And what about Feli? What was he looking at? Had he seen the portrait? Mike looked over at Nancy. She shrugged.

He lingered after class, flipping through his notes, flipping through the syllabus, flipping through the textbook, fooling no one, looking up to watch Feli, who was half-sitting on the table, chatting with the last of the hangers-on (there were always hangers-on), his hands in constant, enthusiastic motion. As the others drifted out, one by one, Mike drew closer, taking deep breaths, straightening his papers. He deposited everything in his backpack and set the backpack on the table. He nodded to Feli. Feli nodded back. Feli got up, went to the door, poked his head outside, came back in, and closed the door behind him.

He folded his arms across his chest and leaned against the wall.

"Michael."

"Feli."

"Something is up?"

Mike smiled. He forced a laugh.

"What is funny?"

"You are, Feliciano."

"This is what my mother calls me."

"It's a beautiful name. Feliciano."

Feli used his foot to push himself away from the wall. He took a step closer.

"What are we doing here, Michael?"

"I don't know. You're hard to read."

Feli laughed. "And you are not?"

Mike moved toward him, his pulse racing, until they were at arm's length.

"Am I still?"

"Maybe not so much."

Feli grabbed Mike by the shoulders and kissed him. He held the kiss until Mike kissed him back, then pushed himself away.

"I shouldn't have done that."

"Why not?"

"The university is very strict. We could be a scandal."

Mike smiled. "I like the sound of that."

"No, no. It's not funny. I would lose my job. But."

"But?"

"You are graduating this year, yes?"

Mike nodded.

"Can you wait for me?"

After graduation, for their first date, Feli took Mike to dinner at a Portuguese restaurant in Fox Point. Without a classroom to perform for, Feli lost his swagger, but Mike liked him better that way, vulnerable and a little insecure, maybe even intimidated. He needed Mike's validation, more than Mike needed his. He needed to be pursued, or at least to be met halfway. For Mike it was a new sensation, and a thrill, to know that someone so attractive and accomplished was just as human as he was.

They spent the summer at Provincetown, in a house that belonged to a group of Feli's friends, who rotated in and out without much warning and threw impromptu, raucous parties with the least excuse. Feli taught Mike to cook, taught him about wine. He tried to teach him Portuguese, but mostly they lapsed into French, suffering the mockery of the friends but bravely soldiering on. They all went out to the bars together; Mike didn't mind the idea that they might be showing him off, though they claimed they just didn't want him missing out on the joys of youth.

When Feli went back to Providence in the fall, Mike stayed on. In the off-season he could have the place virtually to himself. The friends encouraged him to stay as long as he pleased. Living apart from Feli, he had plenty of time to think. He was too young to be tied down, especially with someone whose future was already written. He loved Feli, but he wasn't prepared to spend the rest of his life in a college town, buying the groceries and going to the gym while his husband, Brown's most eligible gay professor, revisited temptation every time an eager, handsome student needed help with a passage in the textbook.

Feli cried, but he said that if their roles had been reversed, he would have done the same. A part of Mike wished Feli had fought a little harder, even though he knew that wasn't who Feli was.

Word of the breakup traveled fast; Mike awaited the call from one of the friends asking him to find someplace else to stay. His parents would happily welcome him home, but it would feel like defeat.

One December day, he got a call from Jordan, or Doctor J, as they called him, of the Boston contingent.

"What are you still doing there, brother?"

"Yeah, I'm really sorry, Jordan, I totally understand if–"

"I mean, the weather is miserable! Everyone is in South Beach now."

"South Beach?"

"Damn straight! Meet me at Logan Airport in two days. I've got your ticket, my assistant Bobby will send you the deets. Hope you're okay with business class?"

"Well, um . . ."

"Oh, *I'm* sorry, did you have something better planned? Yeah, didn't think so. South Beach!! See you in a minute, lover!"

They stayed at the Fontainebleau, where Jordan met up with his own group of friends, all with rooms on the same floor. The friends fawned over Mike, dressed him in tight white jeans, a tight white tank top, and some tasteful bling, and took him out to their all-night dance parties. The friends followed a strict party drug protocol: Doctor J allotted the dosage and controlled the timing, and kept everyone hydrated, but not too hydrated. Alcohol was out of the question.

Mike danced with Jordan and the friends, at first. But he drifted away, alone, just to explore, just because it was all so new and quite possibly wonderful, and then something changed. A strange new feeling struck him. Wherever he looked, he saw men, men who were more like gods than men, looking back at him, an exclusive club of gods, descended from Mount Olympus. Taller, more muscular and leaner, more beautiful, better. With perfect heads of hair, smooth, clear skin, sparkling eyes, and radiant smiles. They smiled at him, and he smiled back at them, and they opened their arms to him. It was just a moment in time; his membership could be revoked without notice; the feeling could leave him as easily as it had come upon him. But for now at least, he was blessed.

He made new friends of his fellow gods. They exchanged numbers and emails. They promised each other to meet again. He went home with one of them. Afterwards, late the next morning, he crawled into bed with Jordan.

"I feel so good," he said.

Jordan rolled over to face him, smiled, tousled his hair.

"Those South Beach boys, right?"

Mike gave him a kiss.

"I love you, Jordan."

"I know you do, dude. But not like that."

"Not like what?"

"You're sweet. Let's get some sleep."

Back in Boston, Jordan gave Mike a set of keys to his brownstone in Back Bay, a credit card, and a car, because it was what friends did for each other. Mike didn't argue. And when he slept with Jordan, just every now and then, that, too, was what friends, some friends, did for each other.

"No regrets," they always said after.

It had nothing to do with the keys, or the credit card, or the car. Jordan even said so, and Mike didn't argue. After all, he was still free, hooking up with other men, dating other men. Out of respect for Jordan, for their friendship, he never brought them home. That would have crossed a line.

In the spring they went to the White Party in Palm Springs, where the West Coast contingent owned remodeled mid-century houses with pitched ceilings and floor-to-ceiling glass, and kidney-shaped swimming pools and custom built hot tubs and artificial lawns. Mike fell in love with the desert: the warm, still, dry air, the palm trees, the clear, pale-blue sky, the convertible sports cars, even the misters that cooled down the patios. He could see himself there.

He spotted Feli on the dance floor. He ran over to him, practically knocking him down, and held him tight for a while before releasing him and taking a good look.

"Feliciano! I didn't realize until just this minute how much I missed you."

Feli shook his head.

"Michael, it is as if you have graduated."

"What are you talking about? I graduated a year ago!"

"No, no. I mean, again."

"Again?"

"You are still you, beautiful, charming, confident. But you are *more* than you. You are . . . "

"I am what?"

Feli held out a hand, flat and level, at chest height, then raised it above his head.

Mike looked up.

"So that's a good thing, right?"

CHAPTER SIX

"Michael, baby, wake up. We're landing."

Mike opened his eyes and blinked at the good, kind man tapping his knee.

"You slept like a rock," said Clifford.

Clifford gently punched Mike on the shoulder.

Mike stretched, yawned, and raised his seat. He looked out the window. It was raining, in sheets.

In the town car on the way to the apartment, Mike's eyes followed the windshield wipers while Clifford prattled on about the dance parties and the new restaurants, the latest couplings and hookups and breakups, and Poor Rob, so handsome, and smart, but hopelessly single! Mike smiled, picturing Poor Rob in his retro Captain America t-shirt, with his receding hairline and his blue-gray bedroom eyes, a good enough guy, if a little reserved, standing near the edge of the dance floor sipping his bottled water and smiling.

"I wouldn't feel too bad for Poor Rob," said Mike.

Clifford looked down at his phone, swiping through his emails.

"And who was that guy you hooked up with? He was extremely attractive."

"Not just attractive," said Mike.

"True. He was super-hot. My God, such pretty lips."

"No, that's not what I meant. He's an impressive–anyway, his name is Chase. I liked him."

Clifford checked his watch, looked out the window.

"Impressive how? HNWI?"

"Sorry?"

"High net worth individual?"

"Jesus, Cliff."

"Oh, come on, Mikey, just kidding around."

That was Clifford. Couldn't help himself. But it gnawed at Mike just a little. It was tacky, but it wasn't altogether unfair. Not that he could have guessed about Chase when they met. Or could he? Had he developed some sort of instinct? He shook it off. Even thinking about it was tacky.

"So I was thinking," said Clifford, "maybe we rent a movie, order Italian, open a bottle of Pinot?"

Mike placed a hand on Clifford's knee and slid closer to him.

"Sounds ideal."

Clifford put his arm around Mike's shoulders.

"And then we need to talk."

Mike sat up. "Oh, Clifford, we've been through this."

"Shh. Shh. After dinner."

"Well, then can we skip dinner and talk in the morning? I'm wrecked."

#

In the morning it was as if Clifford had forgotten he had anything to talk about. They slept late, made breakfast, and went to the gym. Mike pushed Clifford, starting with the core, making him hold the plank, one hand at a time; then switch from hands to elbows and back to hands again; then reach down and backward to meet the knees, keeping his hips level; then bring his knees up and back, flexed feet touching the floor one at a time; until Clifford was red in the face and shaking.

"This is how it's done, Clifford. No backsliding!"

Clifford collapsed onto his stomach and reached for the water. Mike snatched it away.

"You have to earn it, dude."

They moved on to squats.

It was good getting back into their routine. As much as Clifford whined, Mike's program was working. Just look at him: Clifford was as fit as he had been in years, certainly in the time Mike had known him: bulked up, slimmed down, turning heads again, on the dance floor, at the beach, at the gym. The new glasses Mike had chosen for him, the new haircut Mike had talked him into, everything was working.

"What?" said Clifford.

"What?" said Mike.

Clifford rolled his eyes, positioned himself under the barbell, and faced the mirror.

"Never mind."

#

After his shower, Mike put on sweatpants. Still dripping a little, his hair a little wet, he came into the master suite and sat on the edge of the bed. Clifford's bathroom was steamed up; Clifford stood just within Mike's sight-line, draped in a towel, leaning up against the sink, humming and whistling as he shaved.

"Someone is awfully pleased with himself," said Mike.

Clifford turned his head. "Why shouldn't I be?"

"No reason I can think of."

Clifford rinsed off the razor, unstopped the sink, and splashed his face. He took off his towel, dried himself off, and put the towel back on. He walked into the bedroom, still humming. He approached the edge of the bed and stood against it, making room for himself between Mike's legs.

Mike tugged at Clifford's towel.

Clifford wagged his finger.

"Oh, no you don't."

Clifford secured the towel and spun away. He flexed his biceps and looked back at Mike over his shoulder.

"All those boys at the gym would be on me in a minute if they knew . . ."

"If they knew what?"

Clifford spun back to face Mike.

"Don't be an ass."

"I'm not. Come here, Private."

Clifford put his hands on his hips.

"Fuck you, Mike."

"You're already hard, Clifford. I can see it through your towel."

"That's just because I'm huge."

"Prove it."

"No."

"Prove it."

Clifford exhaled. "Goddammit." He unhitched his towel and let it drop to the floor.

Mike raised his eyebrows. "Maybe it's both. Holy fuck."

"Why don't you come here and suck my big cock, you big cocksucker?"

Mike rose. He came and stood in front of Clifford and grabbed Clifford's cock. He smiled. "What do you think the boys at the gym would do with this?"

Clifford took Mike's shoulders and pushed him down; Mike knelt in front of him.

"Suck my big cock, cocksucker."

Mike licked the tip. Clifford pulled it away. He slapped his cock against Mike's face, back and forth across his cheeks, slapped it against his nose and his temples. Mike chased it with his mouth, got his lips on it, got the tip in his mouth and sucked. He ran his hands up Clifford's stomach and chest, then up and down his back and down to his ass. He pulled Clifford's body closer.

Clifford pulled out and turned away.

"No. I just showered."

Clifford bent over to pick up his towel. Mike tackled him to the ground and pinned him down.

"Mike! What the fuck? Let me go! Jesus!"

Mike released him and sat up. "Sorry! I thought we were just wrestling."

Clifford sat up. "That's not what it felt like."

"Okay, sorry!"

Mike got up and sat at the end of the bed. Clifford got up and put on his towel and sat next to him.

"Since you asked," said Clifford, "it felt like you were angry with me."

Mike rubbed Clifford's back. "I would've asked."

"I know."

"I'm not angry. Well, maybe a little. I thought *you* were angry."

"I am. Well, not really."

They both laughed.

"Clifford."

Mike kissed him. Clifford kissed him back, with a hunger Mike had not felt from him in a while.

"Is that how you kissed what's-his-name, Chance?"

"Clifford, don't do that to yourself."

"So thoughtful of you, Mike, to worry about me like that."

"I do worry about you. And it's Chase."

"Chase, Chance, what difference does it make?"

"Fuck, I don't know. No difference, I guess."

"That's right." Clifford rubbed Mike's leg. "You don't know him the way you know me."

"Let's just forget about him, okay?"

"I will if you do."

Mike tried kissing Clifford again. The hunger he felt from Clifford made him hungry in return. They fell back on the bed. Mike leaned over him and stroked his erection under the towel. Clifford stuck his hands down Mike's sweatpants.

"Can we just do this now?" said Mike. "Please?"

"Shut up."

Clifford pushed Mike off him and pulled down on Mike's sweatpants with both hands. Mike lifted his hips and helped Clifford slide them off. Clifford leaned over Mike and stroked his cock.

"You have such a nice cock, Mike."

Clifford threw off his towel. He got on top of Mike and rubbed his own cock against Mike's. He propped himself up, arms extended, shoulders back, and grinded his hips, letting out a quiet groan.

"You look hot," said Mike.

"I am hot."

Clifford pushed himself up by the hips and took ahold of his cock.

"I want to shove this monster cock down your throat, Mike. I want to shoot my fucking load down your throat."

"You wanna make me your bitch."

"You *are* my bitch."

"I *am* your bitch. I'm your fucking cocksucking bitch."

Clifford backed off the bed and stood up.

"Suck this monster cock, you little bitch."

Mike sat up and slid forward and reached for Clifford's cock.

"No," said Clifford. "On your knees, bitch."

Mike fell to his knees.

"Crawl."

Mike got down on all fours and crawled toward Clifford. Clifford stood over him, waving his cock around, slapping Mike in the face with it.

"Beg."

"Please, please, please let me suck your cock."

"My what?"

"Your big fucking cock. Your big mother-fucking monster fucking cock. Please let me suck your monster fucking cock."

Clifford slapped his face with it again.

"Yes, yes, smack my face with your big, hard cock. Make me feel it."

"Oh, shit, I wanna fuck your mouth. I wanna fuck your mouth with my big cock. Open your mouth so I can fuck it."

Mike opened wide.

"Close your eyes."

Mike closed his eyes. He waited, mouth open, tongue out. Clifford stroked himself, working up some pre-cum and letting it drip on Mike's tongue. He grabbed Mike by the temples and pushed his cock into Mike's waiting mouth.

Mike groaned. Clifford groaned. Mike closed his lips around the cock.

"Suck that cock, bitch. Suck that cock, bitch."

Mike nodded and opened his eyes.

"Close your eyes!"

Mike nodded and closed his eyes. He sucked on Clifford's cock, trying to take it, trying to breathe, trying to keep his eyes closed. Tears ran down his face. Saliva and mucus and pre-cum dribbled out of his mouth and onto Clifford's cock and onto the floor. He slurped it up.

Clifford pushed, pushed his cock harder.

Mike squeezed his eyes shut and tried to breathe, fighting not to choke on it, letting out a muffled noise that wasn't a groan, but more like the sound of an exhale with nowhere to go. He pushed again, running out of air, trying to force another exhale.

He backed off, swallowed, wiped his mouth, wiped the tears.

"I can't."

"Yes, you can. You're a good little bitch."

"But Clifford, you're so fucking hard."

"Get the poppers, cocksucker."

Mike got up and hurried to the kitchen. He found the bottle at the very back of the freezer and hurried back.

"Want some?"

Clifford shook his head. "Just suck my cock, Mike."

Mike got back down on his knees in front of Clifford's cock. He opened the bottle, exhaled, held one nostril closed, and brought the bottle to the other nostril. He breathed in, a long, deep, snort, and held it. He closed the bottle and put it on the floor.

He sat back and stared at Mike's enormous, rock-hard cock. His breathing changed, slowed, became heavier, fuller; his body felt warmer; he could feel the blood running through his veins, could hear his heart pounding; his brain wanted to burst out of his skull; he was sailing high above himself.

He grabbed Clifford's cock again and slid his mouth down on it. He breathed in, closed his eyes, and went down. He grew unmoored and giddy; he kept going, feeling it sliding down; it felt so, so good, sliding and sliding. It was so hard, and wet, and he liked the feeling of all that hardness in him, filling him up, liked feeling how much it pleased Clifford.

"Oh, yeah, oh fuck yeah, oh yeah, suck my monster fucking cock, you like that, don't you, bitch?"

Mike nodded.

"What was that, bitch?"

"Mm-hmm, yeah."

"Oh, fuck yeah, that feels so fucking good, what a fucking little bitch cocksucker."

Clifford took ahold of Mike's head again and pushed himself forward; Mike took ahold of Clifford' ass and pushed himself against Clifford's cock, pushed it up against the back of his throat.

Clifford groaned. "Fuck, you're amazing."

Mike reached for his own soaking wet, rock-hard cock, and stroked. He tried to hold Clifford's cock against his throat, held it as long as he could, until he couldn't breathe. He pushed Clifford away and gasped for air and coughed. He searched around for Clifford's towel, found it, wiped his face, got back on his knees and looked up.

Clifford looked down.

"You okay?"

"Yeah."

"I'm really close, Mike. You're fucking amazing."

"It's a monster fucking cock."

Mike picked up the poppers and took another hit. He got warm again, sailed away again, grabbed Clifford's cock with his hands, took a deep breath and opened his mouth and slid the cock in, sliding, sliding, feeling the hardness, feeling Clifford shaking, breathing, feeling Clifford feeling him, wanting him, pushing in and holding it, harder, harder. Mike stroked himself, let go and took his hand and grabbed Clifford's ass with it, took a finger and rammed it up Clifford's hole.

"Oh my God!"

Mike pulled out and took two fingers and rammed them up Clifford's hole, stroking himself with his other hand, sucking that big, throbbing monster cock, feeling it pressing against his throat and sliding farther down. He stayed there, on Clifford's cock, fucking his ass with his fingers, and Clifford shuddered and shuddered and shuddered and came and came and came, and Mike stayed on him, fighting his instincts, forcing his throat open, and he felt the hot geyser of Clifford's cum shooting down his throat, and he stayed there and now Mike was coming, coming, coming, shooting all over the floor and all over himself, and he gagged and choked and Clifford came again, more hot cum and Mike tasted it, drank it, opened his mouth as wide as he could, opened his throat as wide as he could.

Finally, his body made itself do what he would not, it coughed and coughed and choked and forced him off Clifford's cock, let the cock go, let it slide away. Mike turned away and got the towel again and coughed into it, panted into it, wiped his face and his neck and his chest.

He looked up at Clifford, who was standing over him, his head all the way back, looking up the sky, his arms outstretched, his chest heaving. Clifford laughed and ran both hands through his hair, dropped his arms to his sides, and looked down at Mike.

"Wow."

Mike smiled. He stood up. He held Clifford and kissed him.

Clifford looked at the floor. "What a fucking mess."

Mike got the towel and wiped the floor. He picked it up and tossed it at Clifford.

"Ew! Mike!"

"Guess you'll need to find some other bitch to finish the job."

Clifford laughed, then burst into tears.

"Clifford?"

"Oh, shit, shit, don't look at me."

"Hey."

Mike went to embrace him; Clifford turned away. Mike embraced him from behind.

"Shh," said Mike. "Shhhhh."

"I just can't do this anymore, Mike. Maybe it's easy for you, to be half-in, half-out like this, but I can't. I can't do it anymore."

"Clifford."

"Is it really so hard to fathom, that I want you all to myself?"

"I thought we loved each other."

"I think maybe love means something different to you."

Mike let him go.

"Maybe it does, Cliff."

Mike went to sit on the bed. He held his hand out. Clifford moved toward him and took his hand and looked away.

"Clifford? Do you want me to . . . to leave?"

"I'm sorry, Michael. I'm really, really sorry. I can't have you living here anymore. It's just too damn much for me.

PART TWO

CHAPTER SEVEN

Billy showed up at Chase's place early, like any loyal best friend, but also because he missed his *hijo* and they had to hang for a minute. Chase was gone missing from the club scene. It wasn't just that though. Something else was different, and it definitely started right after that weekend, when Chase met the hot boy Mike. Chase met hot boys all the time, because Chase was all that, but usually, no one kept his interest, and he just said seeya and moved on. He told Billy Mike was just another statistic, and besides that he had a shit-ton of work and he didn't have time for anyone else anyway.

Billy wasn't buying it, and he said so. Chase couldn't hold out for long with Billy, that wasn't going to fly, so he admitted it was Mike who said it, seeya, but that was fine with Chase because it was just a question of who said it first, they both were over it, and he was even glad Mike texted him because he didn't have to be the bad guy, not this time. Maybe Chase saw himself as some kind of player, or wanted to, but mostly he was just like everyone else, afraid of getting his heart broken, so when he got the text he put the worst spin on it he could think of, almost out of instinct. Wasn't it at least possible that Mike was telling the truth? Maybe he really did go out of town; maybe he really would be in touch.

Some guys are real, some guys don't play games. Why not at least believe it until you know different? You have to stay optimistic. You have to believe in fate, just a little bit. Nothing good ever happened without a little help from fate.

Billy and Chase nibbled at the stuffed mushrooms as the caterer Shawn set them out, standing at the kitchen island, with an old movie playing on the big screen in the great room. For parties Chase played black and white movies, sound off, music on–just for atmosphere, not for actually *watching*. The "classics" were for the olds. There was this one guy, came on to Chase at a pool party in Boys Town, made him watch "Magnificent Obsession" and "Pillow Talk," lying together on the dude's not quite wide enough couch, but Chase fell asleep halfway through. To be fair, the few dates they could arrange were on Sundays, and Chase was still a mess from Saturday night. Sweet guy though. Cooked dinner for Chase on his grill on the patio, vegan ice cream with raspberries and blueberries for dessert. Really sweet guy. The Sweetest Guy in the World, Billy called him, just to rub it in.

The bartender was supposed to show up when Shawn did, but he hadn't. What if the guests started arriving before he did? No point pestering Shawn about it; he would get there when he got there. But with your biggest client on the way, and when you could use a drink yourself . . .

Chase cleared his throat. "Shawn. The bart–"

"He's just running a little late, Chase, that's all. It's all good, I promise. Can I fix you something in the meantime?"

Chase checked his watch. "Sure, why not? I'll have . . . just whatever. Please."

"One of those for me, too, please," said Billy.

"Coming right up."

"Look at you," said Billy, hovering over the seating chart laid out on the island. "Nothing left to chance. Ike, that's your client, right? At the head of the table?"

"Uh-huh. His wife Sharon to his right. It's 'Shah-ron,' not 'Shay-ron.' His GC, Brooks Marshall, to his left. Then Brooks's wife Katherine–she goes by 'Kat,' whoever the fuck Frank Sutcliffe is bringing, then Frank, then you, on my right."

"Frank Sutcliffe? For real?"

"Billy! We're all one big happy family. Or are you just worried you can't keep your hands off him?"

"Yup, that's it, dude. And on your left?"

"My partner Rachel Andolini, her husband Jake–"

"Oh, Rachel. Love her."

"Yeah, she's awesome. Then my partner Carlos Bautista's girlfriend Emily, then Carlos, then Barnie."

"Barnie? Your secretary?"

"Legal Administrative Assistant. We love Barnie."

"And?"

"No 'and.' I'd be lost without her."

"Uh huh."

The doorbell chimed and Chase crossed the kitchen to the monitor by the door to see who was downstairs. It was Barnie, mugging for the security camera, holding a bottle in one hand and flowers in the other.

"Hi Barnie! Come on up!"

Chase buzzed her in.

"Shawn, you sure your bartender has the right address?"

"Dude, chill," said Billy. "Are these people a bunch of drunks or something?"

Shawn handed them their drinks. Chase went for a sip, but Billy caught him by the forearm.

"*Hijo*, where are your manners?"

Billy raised his glass, and Chase, giving Billy his sincerest hangdog look, raised his glass and clinked Billy's.

"To friends," said Chase.

"To friends."

The elevator door opened and Barnie appeared, in a black blouse and black skirt, and knee-high red boots with heels she could barely balance on. She held her arms out wide.

"Ta-da! Oh-em-gee, this place! Private elevator? Look at these fabulous views!"

Shawn took Barnie's bottle and flowers and set them down on the island.

"Oh, thank you, dear. I can't believe you're still single, Chase–unless, hello, who is this gorgeous Latin lover?"

"This gorgeous Latin lover is Billy," said Chase.

"Billy!" Barnie gave him a big hug. "I should've known you'd be such a hunk from your sexy voice! *Delicisio!*"

Billy blushed. "What's up, Barnie?"

Barnie gasped. "Is that 'My Favorite Wife'?"

"Sorry?" said Chase.

"On the TV. 'My Favorite Wife'? Cary Grant and Irene Dunne?"

"Um, sure. I guess."

"Oh-em-gee it's one of my all-time *favoritos*. Can we turn the sound up?"

Barnie charged between Chase and Billy, nearly knocking Chase over, and practically skipped her way into the great room.

"Where's the remote?"

She chose a long couch and settled in, legs crossed, one arm resting along the top.

"Why don't you dub it for us, Barnie?" said Chase.

"Okay, so now Cary is saying–"

"Barnie!"

"What?"

"Kidding!"

"Oh, you!" Barnie flicked her wrist. "Just hand me a cocktail and I am set!"

Chase shot a look at Shawn. Shawn nodded and began another drink. Even Shawn was looking a little perturbed. Her phone vibrated and she picked it up, started typing. No,

Chase wouldn't ask. What was the point? She would just say something reassuring, whether she meant it or not.

While mixing drinks and texting, Shawn laid out four trays of hors d'oeuvres on the island. Chase picked up a tray and Barnie's drink and brought them over to her. He stood behind the couch, idling as she stared at the screen, engrossed in her silent movie, oblivious to him. He exhaled and tapped her on the shoulder. She reached back, eyes still on the screen, and explored the tray with one hand, landing on a spanakopita triangle.

"Oh! Hot!"

Chase handed her a napkin. She wrapped it around the hors d'oeuvre and set it on one knee. She reached her hand back again, and Chase handed her the cocktail.

"*Gracias!*"

She roared with laughter and slapped a cushion.

The doorbell chimed again. Billy, standing near the monitor, stepped up and pressed the intercom and called out, "Who is it?"

"Aw, Billy!" Chase cried. "You don't just–"

"Hello? It's Frank Sutcliffe."

Billy smiled.

Chase exhaled. "Well? Billy?"

Billy buzzed him up. "Can't wait to get a look at his little friend."

Barnie turned around. "Frank is here?" She stood up, twirled, and headed back to the kitchen. "That little triangle doo-dad was to die for!" She grabbed another off the tray.

Chase came over and stood by Billy, half-turned to face the elevator door. He took a long sip of his drink.

Billy looked at Chase, then at his drink, then back at Chase.

Chase looked at Billy. "What?"

"I'm not saying a word. Not one word."

The door opened. Frank peeked out. His hair was gelled and spiked; he wore red jeans and a black sweater, and a black leather jacket festooned with zippers. He glanced over at his date, smiled, took the man's hand, and stepped into the apartment. His date was a half a foot taller, built like a truck-driver, wearing a black t-shirt, brown leather jacket, faded jeans, and heavy leather boots. He had a three-day beard, short hair combed straight down and dyed blazing white, and thick silver earrings in the shape of the letter *pi* in both ears.

"Chase," said Frank, "this is Atlas."

"*Atlas*? For real? Hi. This is my friend Billy."

Frank stared at Billy. Even Chase's friends looked like movie stars.

"Hi Frank! Hi!" Barnie came up behind Chase, waving.

"Oh, hi," said Frank.

Frank looked around the apartment. Quite a space, so much potential, fallen into the wrong hands. The hands of too much money. Too much new money. Too much Chase Evans. Showy, immodest, practically begging for attention. It had that so-called "modern" look, cold, lots of gray, lots of glossy white, lots of stainless steel and right angles, the kind of thing Chase would have hired a very expensive, very unoriginal decorator to do. Nothing here to envy. Nothing at all.

Atlas squeezed Frank's hand. "Frank?"

"What? Oh! Sorry, I was just admiring the fabulous views. Chase, your place is magnificent. Don't you think, Atlas?"

"Off the hook," said Atlas.

"Please, guys, come on in."

Chase took their jackets.

Frank wandered through the kitchen, glancing down at the trays of hors d'oeuvres, and stopped behind a couch to stare at the television. It was the biggest screen he had ever seen. An old black and white movie, sound turned off. He looked over; Atlas was still beside him, rubbing his back. Atlas came close to his ear, whispered, "could you imagine fucking in this place, on top of the fucking world?"

Frank laughed. We should fuck right here, right now, he thought.

"But we won't," he said.

Atlas stepped back. "Whatever, Frank." He walked away. Oh, there goes Atlas. There were so many places they could do it, and they hadn't even seen the bedrooms yet. There were probably a half dozen, and as many bathrooms. But he was too judgmental. Good for Chase, good for him. All his dreams were coming true. Who could deny someone their dreams? Only someone blinded by envy. Not Frank.

His gaze was drawn to the helicopters and their beams of light dancing in the distance. There was the moon, too, half-full. Did it look bigger from up here? No, it actually was bigger, because up here, on top of the fucking world, they were closer to it, up here in the stratosphere, above the clouds. What was he doing here? It was some kind of trap. He didn't belong here, only the Right Kind of People belonged here. They could stand and look out the window and not get dizzy, not feel like the whole building was swaying, because to them all of this was just nothing, just normal, just their every day, they never gave it a thought. Thinking, thinking, thinking thoughts.

"Say, it's quite a view, ain't it?"

"What. What?" said Frank.

Barnie took Frank's arm. "Everything okay, Frank?"

"Sure. I mean, why?"

She leaned in and whispered. "You've been glued to that spot, staring out the window, for about ten minutes. Don't look now, but–"

Frank turned around. Rachel and Jake, Carlos and Emily, Brooks and Kat, all stood around the kitchen island with Chase, Billy, and Atlas.

"Don't worry, hon'. I don't think anyone noticed you."

Barnie guided him Frank by the elbow and walked him into the kitchen.

"So I've just discovered that Frank here is an even bigger fan of Cary Grant than I am! Isn't that right, Frank?"

"Is that so?" said Brooks. Brooks took his wife's hand. "Kat and I were just saying how much we adore 'The Philadelphia Story.' So romantic!" He smiled at Frank. "Don't you agree, Frank?"

"Philadelphia?" said Frank.

Barnie rubbed Frank's shoulder. "Actually, I rather prefer 'Bringing Up–"

"Oh, yeah," said Atlas. "'The Philadelphia Story.' She gets blitzed on champagne on her wedding night, right? What's-her-name, Audrey Hepburn?"

Carlos and Emily laughed.

"*Katherine* Hepburn," said Kat.

Chase looked at Frank. "'The Philadelphia Story'? I'm guessing it takes place in Philadelphia? Doesn't seem like the most romantic place, Philadelphia. I think–ouch!"

Chase turned and glared at Rachel.

"What the fuck, Rachel?"

Rachel glared back at him.

"I'm from Philadelphia," said Frank.

"You don't say," said Chase. "Did you find it quite romantic, Frank?"

Carlos laughed.

"What's going on?" said Frank. "What's so funny about Philadelphia?"

"Hey!" said Barnie. "Why don't we open that bottle of wine I brought? The guy at the wine place said it was *fabuloso*."

"Great idea!" said Rachel. "Is there . . ."

Shawn handed Rachel a corkscrew.

"Actually, I could use a good, stiff drink," said Carlos.

"Me too!" said Jake.

"Frank?" said Carlos.

"What?"

"Couldn't you use a drink? What about you, Atlas? Chase, I thought you said there was going to be a fucking bartender at this rager."

"Oh, don't you worry, my man," said Chase.

The doorbell rang.

"That should be Mike," said Shawn.

"Who?" said Chase.

"The bartender. He just texted me."

"Thank God," said Carlos.

Billy went to the monitor, pressed the intercom, opened his mouth to speak, then stopped himself. He peered in closer to the monitor, took off his glasses, moved still closer, and hovered.

"Oh. My. God."

He put his glasses back on. He stepped back, turned, and broke into a big smile. With a flourish, he pressed the button.

"It's Mike."

Chase turned to face the elevator door. The entire kitchen turned to face the elevator door. Leave it to Billy to make a whole production out of a late bartender. Chase allowed himself to feel a little sorry for this guy Mike. It was his own fault, but he was going to have his hands full the moment he stepped off the elevator.

The door opened.

"Oh my God," said Barnie, as her jaw dropped.

Something rose in Chase's chest. He shuddered and pushed it back down. There he was, this guy Mike, momentarily frozen, his big eyes wide, as if stunned by the unanimous, gawking welcome. As if. Because obviously, he was so not used to this kind of attention. How sweet. Dressed in black tuxedo slacks, a white dress shirt, and a black bowtie, with a black duffle bag over his shoulder, rocking the bartender look, because of course. Except for a new, neatly trimmed beard, right on point, with just a hint of red in it, nothing had changed.

"Mike, hi! It's Billy. Remember me?" Billy stuck out his hand.

Mike grabbed it. "Of course I do! Nice to see you again, Billy."

"Shit, what am I thinking?" Billy gave Mike a big hug. Mike laughed and hugged him back, raising him up off the ground.

"Dude!" said Billy.

Billy turned and smiled at Chase, his face bright red.

Mike stepped forward and faced Chase. Chase turned and faced Billy.

"Chase," said Mike. "Chase?"

Chase looked at Mike. "Mike."

"Chase," said Rachel, "so he's a little late. Give the guy a break."

"Come on, you two," said Billy.

Billy put a hand on Mike's shoulder. He put the other hand on Chase's shoulder.

Mike held his arms out wide, gave Chase half a smile, cocked his head.

"Wait, what?" said Rachel.

"Fuck it, sure," said Chase. He smiled and took half a step forward and gave Mike a hug.

"I'm really sorry about this, Chase, no joke. When I realized it was your place I tried to find someone to cover for me but–"

"Dude, why? Don't give it another thought." Chase patted Mike on the back. "You look great. I like the beard."

"Oh, yeah." Mike rolled his eyes. "You don't think it's kind of . . . over?"

"You decide when it's over, don't you, Mike?"

Mike squinted. "Um, ouch?"

"What?" Chase looked at Mike, at Billy, and back at Mike. "Oh! Oh, no, that's not what I meant. Ha ha, no, dude. I meant–well, anyway, whatever."

Chase held onto Mike's back and turned to his guests.

"Everyone, this is Mike, the bartender. All your prayers have been answered."

"Uh, hey," said Mike. He gave a shy wave.

"Bourbon on the rocks!" said Carlos.

"Carlos!" said Emily.

Billy whispered in Chase's ear.

"It's fate, Chase."

"No, it isn't, Billy. Uh . . ."

Chase turned and fled to his bedroom. He closed the door. He sat down on the bed. He fell back and put his palm to his forehead.

"Fuck!"

If this was fate, then fate could just fuck right off. Just when he thought he had finally got this motherfucker out of his head. It was fucked up. It was bullshit. How many times had he heard the ding of the text message and glanced at the phone, expecting Mike? How many times had he started a message of his own? But Mike never would have replied. Or his reply wouldn't have been enough. And Chase couldn't risk sitting around waiting for it, driving himself crazy.

How many times had he thought, this is something I should tell Mike? At the gym, in the car, getting ready in the morning, even when he was shopping with Billy. About how his mother used caller I.D.-blocking and then got mad when he didn't pick up; how the express line always took longer than the regular line but he got in the express line anyway; how his little punk nephew would always say, "Uncle Chase, you still don't have abs"; what a gorgeous wide shot it was, the desolate highway, the state trooper's car pulling up from the horizon all the way into closeup, an R&B version of "California Dreamin'" on the soundtrack.

But just because you talk to someone in your head, day and night, doesn't make him anyone special. Just because you're thinking about someone, all the damn time, doesn't mean he's thinking about you. In fact, odds were extremely good he wasn't thinking about you. After all, Mike never did text again. After all, Chase had finally put him out of his mind.

Asshole.

There was a knock at the bedroom door.

"What?!"

Billy came in, climbed onto the bed with Chase, and straddled him.

"*Dios mio*, look at this fucking loser."

Chase laughed and pushed at Billy's chest. "Fuck you, *perrita*."

"What are we gonna do now?" said Billy.

"We?"

"Come on, Chase. You're my boy. You think when you have a problem, it's just your problem?"

"What problem?"

Billy rolled off and collapsed on the bed next to him.

"Exactly! It's like, move along, people, nothing to see here. People are always running off to their room and closing the door like scared little bitches right in the middle of a party for their biggest client when the smoking hot bartender they're still totally crushing on shows up out of nowhere. I mean, when *doesn't* that happen?"

"I just need a second, Billy, that's all. It has nothing to do with . . . what was his name again?"

"Oh, ha ha."

"That's just your little fantasy."

"And you're just a scared little bitch."

"Nice try, *chico*. I see what you're doing, and it ain't gonna work.

Billy got up, took Chase's hand and pulled him up.

"Come on," said Billy.

"Wait–how's the hair?"

"You mean other than the receding hairline?"

"Oh, don't even."

"Just kidding. No I'm not. Yes I am. No I'm not."

"Ugh!" Chase shook Billy by the shoulders. "Dude, I'm seriously gonna kill you!"

It struck just the right note, the two of them laughing over an inside joke as they returned to the party. Well done, Billy boy. Barnie was back on the couch, with her newfound companion, Atlas, catching him up on Cary Grant's antics thus far, with a brief digression on the whole Randolph Scott thing. She held a glass of her *fabuloso* red; he nursed a bottle of dark beer. At a small table near the window, Carlos gave a demonstration, to giggles and laughter from Emily, Rachel, and Nick, of the series of nervous tics Rafael Nadal cycled through before every serve: tugging at his shorts, tugging at the shoulders of his shirt, wiping behind his left ear, wiping his nose, wiping behind his right ear, and again. Carlos drank bourbon on the rocks; Emily drank a margarita; Rachel drank red; Nick drank a whiskey sour. Brooks and Kat sat on another couch, each with a glass of white (Kat's with an ice cube), Kat straightening Brooks's tie and brushing the lint from his shoulder.

In between stocking the bar and taking drink orders, Mike opened the cabinets above the bar to inspect Chase's wine collection. He kept half an eye on Frank, who was grinding his teeth, staring without blinking, mumbling to himself, swaying like a metronome. The guy clearly was having a bad reaction to something, probably Ecstasy, probably from a bad batch. But then none of that stuff was exactly pharmaceutical grade.

Mike looked across the room to the kitchen, where Chase and Billy huddled close together, laughing, but it was Shawn who glanced back, in a flash, with a none too pleased look on her face. He shrugged and looked around and under the counter, found a stack of cocktail napkins to fan. Surely she would understand why he had tried to get out of the job, if she knew. Except that now that he was here, it occurred to him that he hadn't really tried all that hard. He was meant to be here. He was lucky to be here, with a chance he never could have arranged by himself. It was a little unkind of fate to drop it on him, so unready, but fate was a bitch sometimes. Fate didn't care about your plans.

He filled a tumbler halfway with ice water and parked it on the counter.

"Hey, chief," he said to Frank, "drink this. On the house."

Frank turned to him. "Who, me?"

Mike smiled and nodded. "Just sip it."

"Why?"

"It has magic powers."

Frank picked up the glass and examined it. "What is it?"

"Magic? It's like supernatural."

"No, I meant the–"

"Sorry. Dumb joke. I'm Mike, by the way."

"Frank. You're the most beautiful man I've ever seen, Mike."

"You're very sweet, Frank. Thank you."

"You see that guy, over there, Mike? With the white hair? That's Atlas."

"*Atlas*? For real?"

"He's my date. We met on Grindr."

"Nice."

"And you see that guy, over there, the handsome middle-aged gentleman in the suit, holding hands with the nice blonde lady? That's Brooks. He's my boyfriend."

"Your *boyfriend*?"

"Well, maybe boyfriend is the wrong word. Side piece? He's my side piece. Or I'm his side piece."

"You're not kidding, are you?"

Frank smiled.

"Well, Frank, I'm impressed. Does Atlas know about Brooks?"

"Nope!"

"And the pretty blonde lady, does she know about you?"

Frank made a swooshing sound and passed a hand over his head. "Sure would be a shame if somebody spilled the beans though."

"Frank, buddy, why would you do that?"

Frank winked. "I have my reasons."

Mike nodded. "You're a very interesting dude, Frank."

The doorbell rang. In the kitchen, Chase left Billy gabbing with Shawn, and went to check the monitor. He took a good, long look around the apartment. Everything was in place. He buzzed Ike and Sharon up and stood ready to greet them. Across the room, Mike and Frank seemed to be getting along just great, which was just fine because Mike was a naturally friendly guy and being friendly was part of his job. Plus someone needed to keep an eye on Frank, who was barely holding it together. It couldn't have been just because Chase had toyed with him, Rachel's kick to the shin notwithstanding; something was up.

Ike Aronson burst out of the elevator, dressed flawlessly, as always, in a bespoke dark suit with a pale blue tie, and carrying a magnum of champagne. Sharon followed, a wafer-thin woman of medium height, dressed in a sparkling gray evening gown that fell delicately off her shoulders, her gray-brown hair swept up in a luxurious bun. Her facial rejuvenation was of the highest caliber.

"Chase my boy!" said Ike. You remember Sharon."

Sharon smiled. "So lovely to see you, dear."

"Sharon," said Chase, "you look smashing."

They gave each other a kiss on each cheek.

Ike gripped Chase by both arms.

"This place, my boy, such a knockout!"

Ike and Sharon inspected the apartment like prospective buyers, marveling at the view, praising the fabric choices, the kitchen colors and granite grades, assessing the art and photography, guessing the artist, looking for dates and signatures, and embracing each of the guests in turn. Ike acknowledged Frank with a pat on the shoulder and handed Mike the champagne.

"Please, young man, can we open this right away?"

Ike picked up a toothpick from a glass dispenser on the bar, stuck it in his back teeth. He turned and leaned against the counter and folded his arms across his chest.

"So, Chase, my boy, how much does a penthouse like this set one back?"

"Zillow!" said Carlos.

"Shazam!" said Ike. "No, never mind, I retract the question. But tell me this. You only have half the floor? Seems a pity, doesn't it, so high up, so lovely, a bloody fortune I'm sure, but no ocean view?"

"The other half belongs to Victor Donaldson," said Chase.

"Your neighbor is Victor Donaldson? The hedge funder? Victor's a friend–well, oh, perhaps more of an acquaintance. Well, we have business."

"Of course you do," said Chase. "You know the vineyard he bought, Stag Hill? He practically filled my wine cabinet with it."

Ike turned to lean sideways against the counter.

"Ah yes, Stag Hill." Ike shook his head in sorrow. "Unfortunately for our friend Victor, Napa suffered a terrible, terrible drought right after he bought it. Such a shame."

"But fortunately for you," said Mike, as he turned and opened an upper cabinet, "most of the Stag Hill in Chase's cabinet is from before the drought."

Mike took out a bottle of pinot noir and set it down.

Ike slapped the counter.

"Very good, young man! Very, very good! How do you know this?"

Mike shrugged. "I know a little bit about wine."

"A little bit! I'm impressed, son, very impressed. It's good you know these things. You'd be surprised. I try to tell my kids, but, oh no, they can't be bothered, right Shar?" Ike picked up the bottle and inspected the label. "Excellent choice, son. Why don't let's open this one, let it breathe a little while we pour the champagne?"

"Right away, sir," said Mike.

"Please, call me Ike. And I can call you . . .?"

"Mike."

"Ha! Mike and Ike! I love it!"

Ike offered his hand for Mike to shake, then gripped Mike's hand with both of his. "I like this guy!" He pinched Mike's cheek. "And quite a looker, too. Am I right, dear?"

"He's very handsome, yes," said Sharon.

"Single?" said Ike.

Mike blushed.

"Ike . . ." said Sharon.

"Either of my girls should be so lucky. One divorce apiece. And counting!"

"Ike!"

"What? It's true!"

"You're terrible, dear. Just terrible. Ignore him, Mike. He can't help himself. Everybody, ignore that man."

"I'm sorry," said Chase, "my Accounts Receivables department won't allow it."

"Correct," said Carlos, "they sent out an email last week. 'Under no circumstances are you to ignore Ike Aronson.'"

Ike beamed. "In that case . . . ," he put a hand on Mike's shoulder, gripped him at the base of the neck, "can we make a place at the table for this fine gentleman?"

"Oh, no," said Mike, "I–"

"Oh, no," said Chase, "I don't–"

"Sure we can!" said Billy. "Chase, you didn't tell me your client was such a righteous dude!"

"Billy . . ." said Chase.

"Ha ha!" said Ike. "Did you hear that, dear? I am a righteous dude! That's what the young man–it's Billy?"

Billy nodded.

"That's what Billy just said. Very wise, very wise young man, this Billy. Chase, this is your . . ."

"Friend," said Chase, "though sometimes . . ."

"You're a fine judge of character, Chase. This I have known about you from the word 'get-go.'"

Frank giggled. "The word 'get-go'!"

"What? What did I say, Frank?" Ike reddened. "Did I say it wrong? What?"

Frank froze. "Oh, no, uh . . ." He took a gulp of his water and looked out the window.

"It's not 'from the word "get-go,"' love," said Sharon, patting Ike on the arm. "It's 'from the word "go"' or 'from the get-go.'"

"That's what I said!"

From behind the counter came the pop of the champagne cork. Barnie cheered and clapped. Mike laid out a dozen crystal champagne flutes on the counter and poured equal amounts in each. Chase and Billy passed them around.

Ike raised his glass and cleared his throat. He took Sharon's free hand and clasped it in his.

"I just want to—wait, Mike, sweetheart, pick up a glass and join us."

Mike looked at Chase.

Chase nodded. "Please join us, Mike."

Billy patted Chase on the back. Chase glared at Billy. Billy smiled.

"Now," said Ike, "I promised Sharon I would not talk about business tonight. She says it's vulgar. This is what my dearest calls me. Can you imagine this?"

Sharon shook her head "no," emphatically, then nodded "yes," emphatically, eliciting gales of laughter.

"Vulgar?" said Carlos. "What a bunch of horse shit!"

More laughter.

"First of all, let me just thank Chase for opening his lovely home to Sharon and myself. I know you—we—have a big day coming up, so I just want to say, win or lose, thank you, Chase, for everything you've done to make life miserable for that fucker Marty Perelman and his piece of shit company Syndicated! And let me just add, win or lose, you better fucking win!"

Carlos and Chase laughed.

"And I swear, Sharon dear, that is the last vulgar remark you will hear for me all evening!"

"I'll drink to that!" said Sharon.

"Hear, hear!" said Chase.

"Hear, hear!" said everyone else.

"You want to thank Chase?" said Frank.

All eyes turned from Ike to Frank.

"What?" said Ike.

Mike put down his glass and took Frank's arm. "Frank, buddy."

Frank batted him off. "Get your hands off me! I'm not your buddy! You want to thank *Chase*, Ike? What about me?"

"Watch yourself, young man," said Ike.

"No, you watch yourself, Ike."

Barnie gasped.

"For fuck's sake, Frank!" said Carlos.

Mike got a better hold on Frank's arm. He twisted Frank around so that they faced each other. He took Frank's glass and set it down on the counter and gripped both of Frank's arms.

"Look at me, Frank."

Frank turned his head away. Mike held Frank by the chin and turned him back.

"I said, look at me."

Frank closed his eyes.

"Frank, come on, just take a deep breath and look at me."

Frank took a deep breath and opened his eyes. He stared back at Mike.

"Frank, you're my buddy, aren't you?"

Frank nodded.

"Okay? Good, good. You've just had a little bit too much . . . to drink, okay?"

Frank stared.

"Okay? Frank?"

"Yeah, okay."

"Now, listen to me. You and I, we're just gonna take a little break, we're gonna go sit down and chill somewhere, just you and me. Chase, can I–"

"Please," said Chase.

"Okay, Frank?" Mike dropped Frank's arms and took his hand. "Come on, Frank. Just keep your eyes on mine. Can you do that?"

"Oh yes, I can do that."

"Good, Frank. Hold my hand. Eyes on mine."

Mike guided Frank through the great room, looking into Frank's eyes. His pupils were enormous. That damn drug. How much had he taken? Even as Frank held Mike's gaze, unblinking, his eyes kept darting. There was no telling what it was doing to poor Frank's brain. Smart people, and this guy obviously was smart, could be so stupid sometimes.

Mike brought Frank into Chase's bedroom and sat down with him on the bed. Frank grabbed Mike by the shoulders and moved to kiss him.

Mike held him back.

"Frank, Frank, no, it's not like that."

"It's not? Come on."

"No, Frank. We're friends, Frank. We're just gonna hang here for a minute."

"I don't have any friends like you, Mike."

"Well, you do now."

"Oh, God."

Frank fell back on the bed and sobbed.

#

"So that happened," said Carlos.

The entire room exhaled, then laughed.

"Very impressive young man, this Mike," said Ike.

"Yes," said Chase. "Very."

Ike turned toward the dinner table. He rubbed his hands together. "Well then, why don't let's all sit down and have something to eat? I'm famished."

"Splendid idea, Ike!" said Brooks.

With Billy and Barnie volunteering to distribute the last sprays of fresh mint, Shawn completed the first course plates and set them on the table. Chase stood at the bar and watched as his guests took their seats.

"Chase." Ike beckoned him to the table.

"Chase," said Billy, standing behind his chair. He tilted his head toward Chase's chair. "*Chico.*"

Chase took a sip of his champagne. He took another. Who was this guy, anyway? Where did he learn how to do that? What gave him the right?

"Chase," Ike repeated.

"Right," said Chase.

Chase wandered over to the head of the table. Billy watched as Chase pulled out his chair and sat down, before sitting down himself. Chase went for another sip of champagne. Billy caught his arm.

"Unh-uh," said Billy. "Maybe give it a minute."

Chase rolled his eyes, but obeyed. He scooted his chair in and fussed with the silverware.

"Well," said Sharon, settling in at Ike's right hand, "that Frank seems like a nice enough boy."

Ike burst out laughing. Brooks followed, then Kat. Carlos and Rachel smiled to each other, while Emily and Jake fidgeted. Atlas raised and lowered his shoulders.

"I prefer the other guy," said Barnie, unfolding her napkin and looking around the table. "Holy smokes!"

"No kidding!" said Rachel.

"Personally, I am fond of the boy," said Ike. "Look, he's young, he's, eh, eh, troubled, okay? He's made . . . mistakes. But he's brilliant, from what I understand . . ." Ike tipped his hand to Brooks, who nodded, "and he works very, very hard.

If he can straighten himself out . . . Don't forget, he brought in a lot of new work on my case. You people should be grateful."

"Yes," said Brooks, nodding again.

Carlos shook his head and swirled his bourbon.

"But Ike, speaking only for myself, I'm not at all comfortable with *how* he brought in the work. Raising an extremely dubious claim, and, by the way . . ." Carlos tipped his hand toward Chase, "going behind the originating partner's back to do it–"

"Well . . ." said Ike.

"No, I agree with Carlos," said Rachel. "Look, I'm not gonna lie, it's the kind of thing other lawyers do all the time, invent wild claims just to bleed the other side, because it's so hard to prove intent. But we, we like to tell ourselves, at least–and you–that we're not like other lawyers. And I believe it, truly. I would not be at this firm if I didn't."

"Brooks," said Ike, "come on, back me up here."

"Yes," said Brooks, "well, uh, yes, uh, rather–"

"Oh, dear," Sharon sighed. "I was the one who said no work talk, and look what I started. What a feckin' eejit."

Ike scooted his chair back. "I'm gonna go get that bottle of pinot."

Brooks stood. "Allow me, Ike."

"No, no, Brooks, I got it, I got it. You sit."

#

Mike sat in silence, watching Frank cry, waiting for him to stop, waiting for a knock on the door, someone, anyone, Shawn, to tell him to get back to work.

"No."

He was here for a reason.

He lay back next to Frank and stared up at the ceiling with him. He just listened, listened until the crying turned to whimpering, until the whimpering turned to silence.

"You know, Frank, when you think you've finally found a way to escape something, that's usually when you end up coming face-to-face with it."

Frank turned his head and looked at Mike.

"Do you know what I mean, Frank?"

Frank nodded.

"What are you trying to escape?"

"I don't know."

"Are you sure?"

"God, this is so embarrassing."

"Why?"

"I've always dreamed of meeting a guy like you, but now, when I meet him, well . . . you must think I'm such a pathetic loser."

"I think you're a kind, sensitive man who's maybe having a tough time."

"Oh, you're just making it worse. Please stop being so nice to me. Please just be a jerk to me, just like you would if you saw me out somewhere."

"Wow, man, who's being a jerk?"

"Why did you do that? Why did you bring me in here? Into this bedroom? Into *his* bedroom?"

"I don't know. I guess it was just instinct. I guess, maybe, I was feeling a little protective of him, and it looked like—"

"Protective of him?" Frank sat up. "You hardly—wait. Do you guys know each other? No, never mind, of course you do. Look at you, look at him. You guys all know each other. Did you two, are you two—"

"Frank, please, calm down. Please." Mike sat up and put a hand on Frank's chest. Frank's breathing was growing agitated again. "Just forget I said anything about Chase. This is just me and you, two friends chilling. Okay?"

Frank lay back down.

"Yeah, okay."

Mike lay back down.

Frank closed his eyes. No, it wasn't okay. It was unfair. It was cruel. Mike was cruel. There was this beautiful life, for beautiful men, and they all went to the same beautiful parties and were beautiful together, and Frank didn't know how to stop hoping that someday he would be like them, one of them. He didn't take the Ecstasy to escape; he took it to belong.

"You think I've got it so great, Frank? I'm thirty-two years old, I went to an Ivy League school, and I'm a freaking bartender. At least you have a real job."

"Ha!"

"And I can't seem to stay in a relationship."

"You? But you're so perfect."

"But I'm not, Frank. That's what I'm trying to tell you. You shouldn't measure me, or Chase, or yourself, by what you see on the outside. Especially yourself. Try to see what's really going on with people. Let people see the real you. You might be surprised."

Frank put a hand on Mike's chest. Mike took a hold of it. Frank turned, moved his hand to Mike's cheek.

"Don't, Frank."

"I love you, Mike."

Mike pushed him away and sat up. "No you don't, Frank. You've known me for, what, an hour?"

"I'm letting you see the real me."

"Oh, God. This isn't what I meant."

"I've never felt this way about anyone before."

"Have you ever taken Ecstasy before?"

"I know what I feel."

"I promise you, you don't. I've seen it too many times. A guy, a really sweet, beautiful, good guy, thinks he's in love with me, but he's just rolling on E."

"Do you ever fall in love with him?"

"Sure I do. All the fucking time."

"But not with me."

"Oh, Frank. You'll see. You'll wake up tomorrow and you'll see. Trust me."

"I do. I do trust you, Mike. But tomorrow I'll still think you're the most beautiful man I've ever seen."

"Well, that's objectively true."

Frank laughed. This was what it must be like, to be so confident you could even make fun of how beautiful you were. And this beautiful, confident man was his friend. And Frank would still love him even after the drug wore off.

\#

Chase tapped lightly at the bedroom door and opened it. He held Frank's jacket. Atlas stood behind Chase, putting his jacket on. Mike and Frank lay on their backs on Chase's bed, laughing.

"So . . . guys?" said Chase.

They stopped laughing and sat up.

"So, yeah, Atlas here is kinda ready to go, and so . . ."

"Really, Atlas?" said Frank.

"Yeah, Frank, really," said Atlas.

"Already? How long have we been in here?"

Chase checked his watch. "I don't know, a while."

"Long enough for your dinner to get cold," said Atlas.

Frank stood up and yawned. "Oh, that's okay, I'm not really hungry."

"That's not the point, Frank."

Mike stood up and stretched.

The four men walked out of the room and down the hall and stopped at the elevator. Chase opened the door, shook hands with Atlas and Frank.

Frank stopped. He turned. He gave Mike a hug and held him. Mike looked at Chase and patted Frank on the back. Frank released him and got on the elevator with Atlas and looked down at the floor. He raised a hand to his cheek as the door closed.

Chase turned to Mike.

"So, good talk?"

Mike laughed. "Sorry. Again."

"Again?"

Mike turned to head to his post.

Chase caught his arm.

Mike turned back and looked at him. "Yes, Chase?"

"Mike, I . . ."

"Chase? Everything okay?"

"Dude. Just thank you for that, before, with Frank. You saved my freakin' life, bro. Or at least my party."

"Oh, good. I'm just relieved you didn't think I was showing off or whatever."

"Are you kidding me right now? It was just instinct. You can't help it if everyone wants to . . . if everyone thinks you're . . . hey, man, could you fix me up a drink?"

"Right away, chief."

"Thanks. And hey, one more thing."

"Yes?"

"Look, I don't want to put you out, but I got a bit of an earful about it from Shawn, you know, and I mean, Ike, he's very impulsive, right, and inviting you to sit with us–"

"No, no, I get it. Absolutely. You don't need to say another word. Honestly, I'd rather be working than–"

"Exactly. Thanks for understanding, my man. You're just gonna have to find a way to let Ike down easy. For real, I think he wants to adopt you. Or marry you, I don't know."

"Mike and Ike, I love it!"

Chase laughed. Mike smiled. Their eyes met.

"So that drink," said Chase.

"Right." Mike turned away.

Chase watched him go.

Mike took his place behind the counter, broke up some ice, and started on Chase's drink. From the dinner table, Carlos stood up and called out for another bourbon. Mike nodded and set up another glass. He looked up to see Chase settling in at the table, next to his boy Billy. They were so tight, those two. Billy was always there, holding him up, keeping him steady. Mike could see it, feel it, as they sat together, Billy's hand just within Chase's reach, Billy's eyes on Chase even when they weren't.

Billy caught Mike watching and nodded to him. Mike nodded back.

Mike had seen the whole thing, that night. How playful Chase and Billy were together. How deflated Chase got when his boy disappeared. How quickly he picked himself up, found a rebound, realized the guy was just a rebound and sent him away. Mike had no delusions about taking Billy's place, but there might not be room in Chase's heart for anyone else.

He brought Chase and Carlos their drinks. He checked in with the rest of the table. Ike motioned him over. Mike leaned in, listened, nodded, and headed back to the bar. He opened the cabinet and took out another pinot.

With Frank and Atlas gone, Rachel moved over to sit next to Billy, and Jake moved over to stay next to Rachel. Rachel and Jake having moved, Carlos and Emily took their seats next to Chase.

Rachel poured the last of the old pinot into Billy's glass and leaned over to whisper. "So what's the story with Chase and the bartender?"

Billy touched Rachel's hand and looked over at Chase.

"I don't know as much as you guys about tennis, obvy," said Chase to Carlos and Emily. "All I can tell you is Rafa is hotter than Roger. Not. Even. Close."

Carlos sat back and laughed. He picked up his fresh bourbon.

Emily leaned in. "Well, if we're talking about who's hotter . . ."

Billy picked up his wine glass and brought it almost to his lips. He leaned over to Rachel. "They hooked up."

Rachel pumped a fist. "I knew it!"

Chase, Carlos, and Emily stopped to look over at Rachel; she stared down at her plate.

Billy touched Chase's arm. "Never mind, *hijo*."

Chase turned back to Emily.

"Nah, Taylor Fritz isn't really my type. Too pretty. But what about that Borna Coric? *Ay, dios mío!*"

"A couple month ago?" said Rachel to Billy.

"Okay . . ." said Billy.

"He came in one Monday morning, he was in a *very* good mood, but he wouldn't talk about it, of course. A couple hours later . . . he didn't think I could tell, but I could tell."

"Mike sent him a text."

"Ah."

"It wasn't as bad as he thinks. I tried to tell him, he doesn't really know what it meant, but he's so insecure sometimes."

"I mean, they think they're being so cool, but how hard are they trying not to look at each other?"

"Right? All we need is a little spark."

\#

Brooks and Kat were the next to leave. Early day tomorrow. Farmer's market. Followed by Rachel and Nick. Rachel's mom was great with little Ella, but they couldn't stand to leave her home without them past midnight.

Ike and Carlos wandered over to the bar; Mike, sommelier, conducted a tasting with the best pre-drought reds from Victor Donaldson's vineyard–white was barely even wine, Carlos said. Sharon and Emily couldn't keep up and so headed over to the couch for the silent finale of "My Favorite Wife." Chase helped Shawn with the cleanup; Billy and Barnie insisted on helping, too; Chase fought them, half-heartedly, then gave in.

Ike called across to the kitchen. "Chase, my boy, come have a drink with us. I notice you have remained far too sober this evening."

"Come on, Chase," said Carlos, who had not remained far too sober, "let your perfect hair down."

Chase looked over; Mike looked down at the counter and slid a glass back and forth. Chase looked at Billy.

"It's fate, Chase," said Billy

Chase rolled his eyes.

"What's fate?" said Barnie.

"So now you want me to drink?" said Chase.

"*Ándale.*"

"What's fate?" said Barnie.

"A man who does not partake of the very fine wine of his own collection, in his own home, among his own dear friends, is to me a very strange and disturbing state of affairs," said Ike. "Should I take this personally, Chase? What do you think, Mike?"

"Oh, it's not really my place to say."

"Oh, it's not really his place to say." Ike swung his arm around Mike's neck. "Do you hear this, Chase? Nonsense, young man, it is very much your place to say. You do yourself a great disservice, underestimating yourself in this way. The greatest disservice you can do. Chase! Why the dramatic hesitation? Am I missing something? Mike, am I missing something?"

Ike looked at Mike. He looked at Chase. He looked back at Mike. He held out his hands and pointed one at each of them. "No, no, wait. Wait, wait, wait, wait, wait." He snapped his fingers. "Yes, now I get it. Now I get it. Something has been going on this entire evening, a little *sotto voce* . . . yes, I knew it! I knew I was sensing some sort of a, a, a vibration?"

"Vibe," said Billy.

Ike pointed to Billy. "Vibe! Thank you, my wise young friend Billy. A *vibe* between you two. All evening, I have been sensing this."

"Ike . . ." said Mike.

"Ike . . ." said Chase.

"This is not the first time you two are meeting, is it? You two, you are hardly strangers. You have a, you have a history, don't you?"

"Ike . . ." said Mike.

"Ike . . ." said Chase.

"Ah, do not try to deny it, gentlemen. Look at the two of you. It is a beautiful thing. A beautiful thing."

"Look at the two of you, for fuck's sake," said Carlos.

"Chase, have I not told you, you are an excellent judge of character? You think I am kidding when I say this."

"No, Ike, I know you're not kidding, but–"

"Well, *this* young man . . ." Ike slapped Mike on the shoulder. "*This* is a man of character. I don't know what has gone on between you–well, I have an idea–but you listen to me now, Chase, listen to me. Do not let this man get away from you. I forbid it."

Chase looked at Mike. Mike looked at Chase.

"Oh, *that's* fate," said Barnie.

CHAPTER EIGHT

Mike stood in the doorway, his bowtie untied and hanging from his collar. Chase sat on the edge of the bed looking at his phone, going through his emails.

"So what's up?" said Mike.

Chase looked up. "What's up?" He went back to his emails.

"Chase."

"Yeah."

"Chase, look at me."

"Hang on one sec."

"Are we good?"

"I don't know, Mike. You tell me."

"Come on, man. Look at me."

Chase looked at him. "We're good, Mike. It's all good. Okay?"

Mike took a step into the room.

"What are you doing?" said Chase.

"Nothing."

Mike came forward, approached the edge of the bed. "Put the phone down, Chase. Please."

Chase put the phone down and looked up. "Sorry, man, I've got a big hearing on Monday, there's a lot I still have to–"

Mike leaned down and touched a finger to Chase's lips. Chase closed his eyes and fell back on the bed. Mike followed him down and kissed him.

"Mike," said Chase. "Mike, Mike, Mike, Mike, Mike." Chase pounded the bed with his fist. "Where did you go? Where did you go?"

Mike kissed the single tear running down Chase's cheek.

"Chase. I'm sorry, I'm sorry. I'm sorry. I should have believed in you. I should have trusted you. I had such a good feeling about you, but I, you, I got scared. You seemed like such a player, and you were rolling on Ecstasy, or Molly, whatever, and I thought–"

"You mean *we* were rolling on Ecstasy."

"No. Not me. I don't do that stuff."

"Honestly?"

"Don't you want to know what you're feeling is real? Don't you ever hook up with someone and you just think he's so amazing, but when the drug wears off you don't anymore?"

Chase wrapped his arms around Mike's back and squeezed him tight.

"Is that what you thought, that I . . . ?"

"No–I mean–yes–I thought–"

"Oh, Mike. It never wore off. It just turned into . . . I almost couldn't take it. All that time, when you didn't–I mean, I just knew, or at least I thought . . . Mike, I still think you're amazing. More amazing. More amazing-er. You can see that now, can't you?"

"I could see it the moment that elevator door opened."

Chase laughed. "You should have seen the look on Billy's face. He–shit! Billy!" He sat up. "Billy?" He jumped off the bed and hurried to the entryway, with Mike following, just in time to see the elevator door close. He went to the monitor and waited. He watched as Billy got off the elevator and waved to the doorman and left. "God, I hope he's not upset. We were kind of rude. I should text him."

Mike turned Chase toward him and wrapped his arms around him.

"I wouldn't worry too much about Billy."

"Nah. You're right."

Chase took Mike's hand and led him back to the bedroom. He stopped in the doorway and held Mike's head in both hands.

"Mike, I want to look into your eyes, and never look away. I want you to see me. I want you to know me."

"I feel like I've known you forever."

"You do?"

"I do."

"I want to lose myself in you. Abandon myself to you. I want to give you all of me. No more holding back."

"No more holding back."

Chase went to unbutton Mike's shirt. He took his time, stopping to feel Mike's skin and kiss his chest.

"You beautiful, beautiful man."

"Oh, Chase." Mike stroked Chase's hair, lifted his face by the chin.

Chase rose and met Mike's lips with his. He wiped a single tear from Mike's cheek.

"Look at us," said Chase. "A couple of delicate flowers."

"Sad sacks," said Mike.

"Drama queens."

"Emotional basket cases."

They smiled. They had known each other forever, but they hardly knew each other.

"There's so much I want to tell you," said Mike.

"What's the rush?"

"No rush."

Mike grabbed Chase, nearly lifting him off the ground, and rushed him to the bed, falling on top of him. He kissed him all over his face. "No rush. No rush. No rush." He kissed Chase's neck. "No rush, no rush, no rush."

Chase squirmed. He held Mike's head to his chest. Mike reached down and untucked Chase's shirt, lifting it partway up his torso. He kissed Chase's stomach, just below his chest. Chase squirmed again. Mike rested his head there, ran his hand up and down Chase's flank, closed his eyes and breathed in. Chase closed his eyes and stroked Mike's hair and breathed in. It was almost enough, just like this.

Mike looked up at Chase. Chase looked down at Mike.

They sprang up and finished taking off their shirts and tossed them to the floor. Chase grabbed Mike and brought him down again, positioned himself over him, slid his hands and arms under Mike's bare back and pulled them both up on the bed, until they were lying down, Chase on top of Mike, and Mike wrapped his hands around Chase's back and held him. They laughed.

Chase kissed Mike on the mouth, softly.

"What were you and Frank laughing about?"

Mike kissed him back, softly.

"Mr. Evans, you know what a man tells his bartender is confidential."

"Ah, yes, the bartender-patron privilege. But were you acting in your capacity as bartender at the time, Mr. Lacey?"

"I will tell you that that boy is a mess."

Chase kissed him again, and Mike kissed him back, not so softly this time.

"A fucking mess," said Chase. "I'd like to think I had something to do with that."

"Oh, no. I see what you're trying to do, Evans. I can neither confirm nor deny that you had something to do with it."

"You don't have to. I know I did."

"So there."

"So there."

Mike reached down and unzipped Chase's pants and pulled them down below his hips. He slipped his hands under Chase's briefs, stroked his ass.

"And there," said Mike.

Chase unzipped Mike's pants and pulled them down below his hips.

"And there," said Chase. "Oh! Going commando tonight. Very brave." Chase stroked Mike's bare ass.

"No, just low on clean underwear."

"Dude, shut up!"

"Totally serious."

"No you're not."

"No I'm not. Or am I?"

"Whatever. Let's . . ."

"Yeah."

They pulled their pants and one pair of briefs off and lay naked on the bed together.

"Mm, much better," said Chase.

Mike turned and lay on his stomach and Chase got on top of him and wrapped his arms around Mike's chest. "You feel so good." His hands traveled down and found Mike's hard cock. "Nice." He rested his own hard cock against Mike's ass and swayed his hips.

"Nice," said Mike. "Hey, boss?"

"Mm." Chase got harder. "Yeah, boy?"

Mike shook his head. "Nuh-uh."

"What?" said Chase.

"Not boy."

"Oh, okay. Uh, yeah, bitch?"

Mike laughed and twisted himself around to lie on his back, adjusting his hips into position under Chase. He looked up and smiled.

"Try again, boss."

"Wait. Wait. Uh, yeah, baby?"

"Mm." Mike got harder. "Getting warmer."

"Uh, yeah, Mike?"

"Ah." Mike got harder still. "Disco."

"Mike."

"Boss."

"Mike."

"Boss."

"Not 'boss.'"

"Not 'boss'?"

"'Mr. Evans.'"

"Mr. Evans? Oooh."

They both got harder and a little wet.

"Mr. Evans, Mr. Evans, how'd I do today, Mr. Evans?"

"You crushed it, Mike. Everyone loves you, Mike."

"Mr. Evans, Mr. Evans, may I fuck you, boss?"

"Oh, shit." Chase grabbed his cock. "I don't know, Mike. Do you think you've earned it?"

"I know I have."

"Oh, fuck. I like your attitude, boy, uh, Mike. But . . ."

Mike held Chase by the waist and grinded. They grinded together. Mike pushed up with his hips.

"But–oh fuck–but . . ." Chase arched his back. "Jesus. Not yet. Not sure you've shown the–oh fuck–the aptitude."

Mike pushed harder. He grabbed Chase's ass and spread his cheeks. "Whatever I have to do, Mr. Evans. I know I can do it, Mr. Evans."

Chase cried out. He lifted his hips and pulled himself toward Mike's face. He stroked his cock and held it over Mike's mouth. He dripped pre-cum.

"Oh fuck," said Mike. "Gimme that cock, Mr. Evans."

"Suck my cock, Mike. Suck my cock if you wanna fuck me."

"Oh fuck yeah!"

Chase grabbed a pillow and placed it under Mike's head. He took a hold of his cock and brought it to Mike's lips. Mike stuck out his tongue and licked the tip of Chase's cock.

"You want more?"

"Yes, Mr. Evans. I want that cock."

Chase slid forward a little more and gave Mike more of his cock. Mike took it and sucked, sucked Mr. Evans's hard cock, picked up his head off the pillow and got to sucking real good, such a nice cock, the nicest, so sweet, so smooth, Mr. Evans knew how to give it to him, tease him, enough but not enough. Mike's mouth was so wet and warm, he sucked so tight, he got his tongue in there spread real good, so warm and wet, he felt so good on Chase's cock, so pretty to look at, those big green eyes that perfect hair and that right on point beard he could come all over, make a mess of it, his pretty face could make Chase come. Chase did that thing he didn't think guys really did, he arched his back and threw his head back and ran his hands along his own chest, and Mike loved it, he loved watching Mr. Evans, stroking his own chest, so sexy, so confident, so beautiful; he followed Mr. Evans's hands with his own, took his hands and together they stroked Chase's hot fucking body. Mike grabbed Mr. Evans's perfect ass, holy fuck it was so perfect, just the right amount of round and tight and muscled, and he pushed that ass toward him so he could get more of that beautiful, perfect cock in his mouth.

"Oh, God," said Chase. "I need, I want . . . oh fuck."

Chase flipped over and gave Mike his cock that way, fucked his face, and he grabbed Mike's cock and sucked it. It was so hard and straight, he looked right down on it and Mike lifted his hips, gave him more, and Mike had Mr. Evans's cock in his mouth, his face was so close to that perfect ass, all he could think about was that ass, how much he wanted to fuck Mr. Evans. Chase slid forward and dove down and wrapped his arms around Mike's legs and found Mike's ass; Mike slid back and pushed his head up and found Mr. Evans's ass, and they licked around the edge and kissed and sucked around the edge and rammed their tongues in, rammed their tongues up each other's ass, his sweet, sweet ass, it was so fucking sweet, he could eat this ass forever, until his face was sopping wet.

He had to stop. He couldn't stop he had to stop. Mike took Mr. Evans by the waist and pushed him up, and Chase rolled himself off and onto his back. He sat up on his elbows and looked at Mike, his face so far away, he missed looking at that face, he missed kissing that mouth, he could really kiss that mouth, that sopping wet mouth and that sopping wet face. Chase turned himself around and got himself on top of Mike and kissed him, kissed all of his wet face, opened his mouth and kissed Mike's wet mouth, his tongue licked Mike's tongue. Mike closed his mouth on Mr. Evans's mouth and sucked his tongue, they sucked each other's tongues. Mike was so hard and wet and he was so hot for Mr. Evans, so, so hot. He was like no one he'd ever been with before.

"Mr. Evans, Mr. Evans, Mr. Evans."

Chase nodded and reached over to the nightstand and found the lube. "Oh, just a little more."

Chase sucked Mike's cock, his beautiful cock, swirled his tongue all the way around. He held it with both hands and sucked, stroked it and followed his hands with his mouth. It was so wet, it was dripping everywhere, getting Chase's face wet again.

"Mr. Evans."

"Mike."

Chase sat on top of Mike's cock and let it glide between his cheeks, feeling the size of it, Chase was getting so hard and leaking; he stroked his slick cock up and down, he spread his cheeks and spread his legs and lowered himself, his knees all the way down on the bed, his feet flexed behind him. He held onto Mike's upper body and rocked himself; Mike held onto Mr. Evans, by the hips, and rocked with him.

"I don't know," said Chase. "I don't know if I can."

"You can, Mr. Evans. I know you can."

"It'll be tight."

"I know. Just tell me what you need. Tell me, Mr. Evans."

"I need you to call me Chase."

"Of course."

Mike pushed harder; Chase rocked harder.

Mike grabbed the lube. He dripped it all over his cock and stroked. Chase took the lube and dripped it on his fingers and lubed himself.

"Chase."

"Mike."

"Let's fuck, Chase."

"Let's fuck. Let's do this."

"You're nervous."

"A little, yeah."

"It's okay. It's me. It's me and you."

"Me and you."

"I'm nervous too."

Chase grabbed Mike's cock.

"Doesn't feel like it to me. "

Mike pushed himself up against Chase's ass and grabbed onto Chase's shoulders and pulled himself up and kissed him. Chase closed his eyes and kissed him back, kissed him without stopping, and as they kissed and kissed Mike applied some pressure with his cock against Chase's ass. Chase's breath became more labored, but he stayed with the kiss, felt Mike's cock up against his ass, it was tight, he tried not to fight it, tried to relax, let go. Mike gently stroked Chase's ass, gently pressed his cock, let Chase take the lead, set the pace; Mike knew a little bit about getting fucked and he knew Chase knew a little bit less. He was being brave and he was being sweet, doing this because Mike wanted it, which only made him want it more, made him press a little harder and grip Chase's ass a little tighter. Chase gritted his teeth and grunted, but he didn't let up, he let Mike push, he grunted but he liked it, liked the way it felt, liked pleasing Mike, and he took a deep breath and exhaled and opened himself and pushed himself, let Mike push back; he let out a groan; Mike let out a groan; they groaned together, took turns groaning, pushing and letting go and pushing and letting go; and tops and bottoms and dominant and submissive was bullshit, it was bullshit, this was hot and this was great and it felt so fucking good, and it felt good because it was Mike and because it was Chase, they were fucking, Mike was fucking him, he was fucking Chase, they rocked and rocked and pushed and pushed and groaned and groaned and groaned.

"Fuck me, Mike. Fuck my ass. Give me your fucking cock, fuck my ass."

"You feel so good, your ass is so fucking tight, you're such a good fuck, Chase, I could fuck you forever, fuck you and fuck you."

"Fuck me and fuck me. Fuck me. Fuck my tight fucking ass."

"You're so fucking hot."

"You're so fucking hot."

Chase held one hand back behind him on the bed and raised and lowered his hips, raised and lowered his ass onto Mike's cock; Mike pushed up with his hips, raised and lowered his hips, thrust his cock deeper up Chase's ass, thrust and thrust; they pushed faster, faster, harder, deeper; with his other hand Chase jerked himself off, stroked his cock. Mike set his hands down on the bed and pushed himself up; he held onto Chase and held his cock in Chase's ass and got himself up and leaned forward and Chase leaned back; he eased Chase backward and Chase fell back onto the bed and straightened his legs on the bed under Mike; Mike straightened his legs out behind him until he was lying on top of Chase, still fucking him hard. Chase let go and let Mike all the way in and let out a gasp; breathed in deep and let out another gasp; Mike pounded him, pounded him, he looked but Chase closed his eyes and turned his head, not to look away but to feel it, really feel it; he wrapped his arms around Mike's back and held him, hung onto him, and Mike got his arms under Chase's back and held onto him; they kissed again and held each other and moved together, Mike's cock and Chase's ass, Mike's cock and Chase's ass, fucking so hard and fast.

Mike's groaning got louder, louder, his breathing heavier. "I'm gonna, I'm gonna . . ."

Mike raised his hips; Chase pulled Mike's hips back toward him.

"Don't pull out, don't pull out."

"Really?"

Chase nodded. "Come inside me, Mike, come inside me. Fucking breed me."

"Aw, fuck."

Mike let out one last, endless groan, one last, long thrust; he thrust his cock as deep as he could and he came, his whole body shuddered, and he came, thrust his cock and came, and Chase feeling him shudder and looking up and seeing this god of a man, all his beautiful muscles tight and rippling, Chase feeling him and seeing him let out one last, endless groan and came, came in hot, long bursts that reached up to his chest and warmed the places where their skin pressed together; Mike breathed deep and exhaled, breathed deep and exhaled, let go of his tight, rippling muscles and collapsed on top of Chase, kissing him, kissing him all over his face, his tongue deep in Chase's mouth, his hands gripping Chase's head and holding their mouths together; Chase closed his eyes, opened his eyes, looked into Mike's eyes. They held each other's stare like that while they kissed, still fucking, kissing and fucking.

Mike propped himself up on his hands and slowly eased back with his hips.

"No, no," said Chase, "let's stay like this for a minute."

Mike eased back down.

"Oh my God," said Chase, slapping Mike's ass. "What the fuck was that?"

"I think that's what they call 'the second time.'"

"Hmm." Chase stroked his chin. "Second time, second time. No, that's not ringing any bells."

"Ha ha," said Mike.

"Yeah, ha ha," said Chase.

"I mean, but you've had boyfriends before, right?"

"No. Nope. Unless you count–"

"Billy."

"Billy."

"Okay. I really need to . . ."

"Okay."

Mike eased back again and pulled out and collapsed on his back.

"Is that bad?" said Chase.

"No. No, no, no. To be honest, I've never had a real boyfriend either. Mostly just close friends I fucked around with sometimes."

"How very sophisticated of you. Didn't that get weird?"

"Only every time. The last one, Clifford, he kicked me out because it wasn't enough for him."

"Wait, you were living with him?"

"Yeah?"

Chase squinted. "His place."

"Yeah."

"But only as long as you were fucking him enough?"

Mike sat up. "It's not like that."

Chase sat up. "What's it like?"

Mike reached out and placed his hand on Chase's shoulder. "Chase."

Chase looked him right in the eye. "No, really, I want to know. What's it like?"

Mike took his hand away. "I'm feeling a lot of hostility from you right now."

"I'm feeling a lot of . . . I don't know what I'm feeling from you right now."

Mike slumped. "Oh, God. Okay. Look. Clifford was really good to me and he loved me in his way and sometimes it felt like that was what I needed. But I didn't want to give up my freedom, and I think he wanted to sort of, I don't know, control–"

"Keep you."

"I never really thought of it like that, but sure. Okay. Keep me. He wanted to keep me."

"And the other friends you sometimes fucked?"

Mike nodded.

"And me? Is that what you're looking for? Someone to keep you?"

"We aren't–"

"Some rich dude with a penthouse to keep you?"

"Chase! Wow, man. Hold up. Hold up."

"Yep. I'm such a fucking idiot. I should've known. When it feels like it's too good to be true . . ."

"You're not seriously . . . for real, Chase, you're being incredibly fucked up right now. I don't know, maybe my first instinct about you was the right one."

"Well, I'd rather be just some player than just some–"

"Don't."

"Why not?"

"Anyway, that's not what I meant. I meant you still have a lot to learn."

"Oh, I do, do I?"

"Yeah. You do."

"I guess you don't need to worry about that now though do you?"

"I guess not."

"Fine."

"Fine."

"I can't fucking believe I let you fuck me. Jesus."

Mike stood up.

Chase pounded the bed with his fist.

Mike looked at Chase. Chase looked away.

CHAPTER NINE

Mike got off the elevator, thanked the doorman, and left the building, stopping to wait for the town car. And to calm down. And to wipe the tears from his face.

He missed Clifford. He loved Clifford. He should have said he loved Clifford. He shouldn't have folded so fast when Chase said Clifford was keeping him. It just reduced everything, reduced him and Clifford, their life, to something it wasn't. Something cheap.

It wouldn't have made any difference. Chase was just looking for an excuse. An excuse to keep playing the player, stringing Billy along forever. That suited him better, that power.

They shouldn't have fucked again. They should have waited. When it's so new, guys blow everything up, they get sensitive and they misread things. Even hardened players like Chase.

Chase wasn't really that hardened. More like he had a shell and he retreated into it at the first sign of actually feeling something. But they fucked the night they met, and you can't put that genie back in the bottle.

It was fate. Fate brought them back together before they were ready.

He wasn't ready. For this new life, untethered, so much to get used to. Living with roommates again after so long. Paying rent. One of those things, so many things, that never cross your mind when you're living in a gilded bubble. He loved his friends from the party scene, and they would do whatever they could for him, but sleeping on their couch, borrowing drawers and closet space, it was hard to stay upbeat. From up close, after the dance, in the light of day, their lives were going nowhere. They were just killing time, getting older, doing the same old things. He refused to fall into the trap. For him, this had to be temporary.

What was taking the town car so long? What was he thinking? There was no town car. He checked his GPS. He swung his duffle bag over his shoulder and walked toward the subway. He passed homeless people on the sidewalk, in the fetal position in sleeping bags or hiding under black plastic trash bags. Even in gentrified downtown, just an elevator ride away from a glittering dinner party, with killer views and a wine cabinet personally stocked by a billionaire, the real world reasserted itself. How had they come to this? Where had they taken a wrong turn, or had they? How many wrong turns away was he? Did he even have a say? Was he just feeling sorry for himself?

At least he had made a start. He had his job at Radioactive. "Dude," the roommates said, "they don't care if you don't know shit about tending bar, if you look good without a shirt they'll train you." He was working his way up, to better, busier shifts. He was picking up side gigs, like tonight. He probably wouldn't hear from Shawn again, which was fine. He was done with tonight. Rear view mirror.

Radioactive was sprawling and always reinventing itself, indoor/outdoor, crowded, overpriced, with half a dozen bars under giant red glass chandeliers in twisting shapes like the head of Medusa. It was a bit of a tourist trap, but it wasn't a bad place to work. The thumping music, the flashing lights, the go-go boys: the party scene, but with training wheels and a curfew. The best trick they pulled was convincing the patrons that all the guys behind the bar were straight. That certainly wasn't Mike's experience. It was just part of the come-on. The less available you were, the better the tips.

Just up the hill from the subway station, he nearly tripped over a particularly pathetic man, who sat in the middle of the sidewalk, cross-legged, half-wrapped in a tattered, leaf-covered blanket, face sunburned and feet blackened, rocking and shivering in the mild weather. He looked up at Mike, eyes wide, hand out, silent. Mike stopped. He kept going. He stopped again, turned around, returned to the man. He reached into his pocket and found a ten and handed it to him, because why not?

"God bless you," the man said.

He reached the top of the stairs that led down to the subway, and stood there, looking down, missing those ten dollars. He shouldn't have done that. He didn't have cash to just throw around anymore. No mad money, no town car. Subways and buses, Über on a good night.

He took the long flight down to the turnstiles, tapped his card, took a short flight down to the platform, and stood there, waiting for the westbound train to take him home. A man in black sweatpants and a dark blue hoodie and tattered shoes lumbered up and down the staircase, shouting an incoherent, obscenity-laced lecture at himself. Another sat on the ground, holding a trash bag packed with his random belongings. Mike had his duffle bag and the pride of his Spartan lifestyle. There was no comparison.

The speakers announced the other train, the eastbound, which honked and flashed its lights and rushed into the station. The nearest car was standing-room only, filled with young people out on their Saturday night, just getting started.

The doors opened. Mike looked over and scanned the riders, as if a familiar face might be hidden among them. He looked away, down at the ground; he was behaving like a lonely man, and he wasn't lonely. Alone, but never lonely.

Ever since Feli, there had always been someone around, someone to go out with. Or to stay in with, but mostly out. Not that he couldn't fend for himself, of course; he just never had to. If he wanted to, he had his crowd; they were always there, waiting for him. But how would they see him now, without Feli orbiting him, or Jordan, or Clifford, or any of the others in between? It wouldn't be the same. Maybe it shouldn't be the same. Maybe that was the point, that after Clifford it was finally time to break the pattern. Yes! He was working on breaking old patterns. *That* was what he should have said to Chase!

The eastbound train's warning bells rang. Mike broke into a big smile and sprinted across to the doors just as they were closing; a kid in a brown knit cap pulled down the cord to open them; Mike hopped on. His big smile grew even bigger. The crowd smiled back, jostled around, and opened a space for him.

\#

They held After Hours at The Odyssey, an old, run down Art Deco movie palace from the Golden Age, standing tall at the eastern edge of a wide downtown boulevard, its glory days long behind but on the cusp of a revival, thanks to a new round of gentrification and the interest of a new generation of party promoters. When Mike reached the front of the long, slow-moving line, the shaved-headed, thickly built bouncer in a black muscle shirt and a headset patted him on the back and unhooked the rope. Just before the entrance, a man in a backwards baseball cap and a red tank top and a crucifix on a black lanyard stood at a card table covered with a black tablecloth. He smiled.

"Hey, handsome," said the man.

"Hey, yourself," said Mike.

"That'll be sixty, cash only."

Mike gaped at him. "Dollars?"

"Yes, sir. Cash only." The man indicated a portable ATM behind him.

One more thing he'd never had to think about. Mike apologized, turned around and went back outside. The bouncer patted him on the back again. He dropped his duffle bag and leaned against the building. No, it was better this way. If he really wanted to break the pattern, it should be a good, clean break.

It was getting cold out. He squatted down and unzipped the bag.

"Hey, stranger, need a light?"

Mike looked up. It was Poor Rob, in his retro Captain America t-shirt, looking as handsome and hopelessly single as ever, with his receding hairline and his blue-gray bedroom eyes.

"Rob!" Mike sprang up and hugged him. "Aren't you a sight for sore eyes!"

"The fuck you doing out here? Panhandling?"

Mike laughed. "So good to see a familiar face."

"Daddy inside already?"

"Clifford? No, he's back home. We're all done."

"Oh, shame. Good guy, Cliff."

Mike snapped his fingers. "Next!"

"Atta boy."

Rob stuffed his hands in his pockets and rocked on his toes. He sneaked a look over Mike's shoulder toward the club entrance. "Yeah, so anyway, I'm headed in. You coming, Mike?"

"Hmm, don't think so."

Rob squinted at him and frowned. "What?" He shuffled his feet, stared down at Mike's duffle bag. He scratched his head. He looked up again, with a new, hopeful look on his face. "My treat."

Mike brightened. "For real?"

Rob snorted. "Uh, yeah. Duh."

"I'll pay you back, I promise."

"Please. Whatever. Come on, dude." Rob took Mike's hand. They stepped up to the short, fast-moving VIP line.

At the coat check, Rob made a shield for Mike while Mike stuffed his dress shirt and slacks into the duffle bag and nearly tripped over himself pulling on his jeans.

"You're cracking me up, bro. Where's your fucking underwear?"

"Long story."

Rob picked a spot at the back of the dance floor, facing the stage and the blinding bright screen, the horde of men's bodies in silhouette before them. The two stood there, side by side, arms folded over their chests, swaying, sipping their water. Mike glanced at Rob but Rob was looking into the crowd, smiling, shaking his head, laughing. Mike sighed and looked into the crowd with him.

"What are you laughing about?" Mike asked.

"Me? Oh, dude, nothing." Rob laughed again. He reached into his pocket. "You need some Ecstasy, Mike, or are you already rolling?"

"Neither."

"Oh, you mean both. Got it." Rob looked around, took a plastic bag from his pocket and held it at his waist, for only Mike to see: inside were two pink tablets.

Mike sipped his water. "No, dude, I mean neither. That shit'll kill you."

Rob laughed harder, threw his head back. "Give me a fucking break, sweetheart. I've seen you out. I've seen your eyes."

"That's just how my eyes are. Look at them right now."

"Uh, because you're high right now?"

"Right," said Mike. "I'm just lying to you, for no reason."

"No, you're just fucking with me, for the fun of it."

"Whatever. Anyway, no thanks."

Rob put the bag back in his pocket and took a sip of water. "You're totally serious right now, aren't you?"

They both stared into the crowd again, folded their arms over their chests again.

Rob turned to Mike. "How do you—no, forget it."

"This DJ is so good, right?" said Mike. "God, I really want to get out there and dance. It's been so long!" He jumped up and down. "Let's get out there, Poor Rob."

"Actually, it kind of figures, in an extremely fucking annoying way. You're one of those guys."

"Which guys?"

"You know. You float around on a cloud, everything comes easy to you, everyone wants you. Your life is one endless high."

Mike laughed. "Wow."

"Nailed it, didn't I?"

Mike patted Rob on the shoulder. "You're just as clueless as—you're as clueless as fuck."

"Just as clueless as who?"

"No one. Nothing."

"I'm sorry, man. He must have broken your heart."

"Who?"

"Cliff. Who else?"

Mike closed his eyes. Nobody else. There was nobody else. He was free. Clean slate. Breaking the pattern.

Rob rubbed Mike's back. "Hey."

"Hey."

"Come on. What are we waiting for? Let's dance already."

"Ha!"

Mike smiled and took Rob's hand. Together they bounded into the thick of the dance floor. They found an open spot and Rob released his hand but Mike held on, took Rob's other hand, then let go of both hands and wrapped his arms around Rob instead. He spoke into Rob's ear. "Everyone's looking at you."

"Oh. My. God. They're looking at *you*, dumbass."

"At us. Dumbass."

"You should seriously drop Ecstasy with me. You have no idea what you're missing."

Mike shook his head.

Rob reached into his pocket and took out the plastic bag.

"Just split one with me. It's really good stuff. If you like it, we'll split another one."

"I don't know. It feels like you're working me."

"That's because I am. A little."

Rob kissed Mike's neck. Mike let him.

"Rob."

"You need it, Mike. It'll open your eyes. Your big, beautiful eyes."

"You have to understand, Rob. Whatever happens, this is strictly NSA. I'm still–"

"NSA, NSA. Yes, yes, NSA. I'm down."

"You're such an asshole."

"I know."

Rob handed Mike his water to hold and took out a tablet. He snapped it in two.

"Open wide."

Mike looked around.

"Dude," said Rob, "open your fucking mouth."

Mike rolled his eyes and opened his mouth. Rob put one half on Mike's tongue, one half on his own tongue. They washed them down.

Rob raised both fists in the air, threw his head back, and catcalled. "You won't regret it."

"Promise?"

Rob patted Mike's cheek. "Promise."

"How long does it take?"

"Stop it already! It's just me, Poor Rob. You don't need to keep up this act."

"It's not an act."

"Twenty minutes. Thirty tops. And this is some good shit. I've got the hookup, bro. You'll know."

"What should we do in the meantime?"

"Uh, dance?"

"Take off your shirt. Here, let me."

Mike grabbed the bottom of Rob's Captain America t-shirt and pulled it up. Rob raised his arms. Rob pulled it up the rest of the way and hung it from his back pocket.

"Yes!" said Rob. He posed for Mike, flexing his biceps and pumping his chest.

Mike felt him up and down. "Yes!" said Mike.

"Right?"

Another pair of hands stroked Rob's chest from behind. Mike lifted the hands off Rob's chest and pulled Rob away.

"Don't fight over me, boys. There's plenty of me to go around. If you know what I mean."

The hands returned, now accompanied by a handsome face, with dark eyes and dark hair, resting on Rob's shoulder. Mike took the face in his hands and kissed him. Rob turned his head and joined in, the three of them kissing each other in pairs and all together.

"Twenty minutes?" said Mike.

"This is just anticipation. You'll know."

"And what's this?"

Mike rubbed his hard-on against Rob's.

Rob wrapped his arms around Mike and closed his eyes and kissed him. Mike closed his eyes and kissed Rob back, holding him, feeling the handsome third man coming around behind him, kissing the back of Mike's neck, pressing his hard-on against Mike's ass. Another man took the handsome man's place behind Rob, reached his hands out to hold the shoulders of the man behind Mike. They swayed to the beat, everyone with his eyes closed, everyone with a head on someone's shoulder.

The strobe lights flashed all at once, lighting the club brighter than daylight, then stuttered to the beat, making everyone appear to dance in slow motion.

"Are we there yet?"

"You'll know!"

Rob turned around and made out with the man behind him. Mike turned around and made out with the man behind him. He held one hand behind his back and found Rob's hand, and they clasped them together. Something warm flooded Mike's veins and his lungs. With his other hand he held on tight to the man he was kissing, kissed him hard, so hard he inhaled the man's breath. The man was already in love with him.

He was back in South Beach, with Jordan and the friends, wandering off when they dropped their Ecstasy, wondering if they noticed, wondering if they were disappointed in him. When he joined the gods, Mike, the New Kid, they must have assumed he was a Party Boy just like them. When he didn't want a bump, of K or coke or Tina, they must have assumed his E was pure, he had the hookup, bro. They never asked, because it didn't matter. He was one of them.

He was still kissing the man who was in love with him. The man thought Mike was all that. The man couldn't believe his good fortune. The man was in heaven. If the man wasn't kissing him he'd be telling his friends about the hot guy he kissed for days. The man couldn't let go because then he might never get Mike back. Mike would move on to someone better.

Chase wasn't wrong, and Mike knew it. He knew what he was doing with Clifford and all the others, and when they caught on, and they always caught on, they kicked him to the curb. There weren't different kinds of love, one for him and one for them; there was only one kind of love, and he never trusted them with it. Love wasn't something you felt. Love was a decision you made. Yes, a decision you made.

He released the man who was in love with him–who *thought* he was in love with him–and he turned around, just as Rob turned around to face him.

"Rob!"

Rob smiled and nodded and opened his eyes wide. "You feel it!"

"I feel it!"

"What's it like?"

"Holy shit!"

"Right?"

They gave each other a big hug and rocked from side to side.

"Holy shit!" Mike repeated.

"Right?"

"Am I fucking crying right now or what?"

"You look so beautiful, Mike. Your tears are beautiful."

"Rob! Rob! I figured it out!"

Rob rested his arms over Mike's shoulders and held Mike's his face in his hands.

"You did, Mike? Tell me."

"Love isn't something you feel. Love is a decision you make."

Rob smiled his biggest smile. He threw his head back and laughed and laughed and laughed. He patted Mike on the head and mussed his hair. "Okay, Mikey, I believe you now."

"What?"

"This really is your first time on Ecstasy."

"I never lie."

"Maybe not, but you gotta get over yourself, dude. Stop thinking so much and just feel it!"

"I do feel it."

"Good! Feel it some more! Trust me, in forty-eight hours you're going to be laughing at your bullshit, if you even remember it."

"It's not bullshit."

"Forty-eight hours. For you, maybe longer."

"Maybe never."

"Wrong."

Mike closed his eyes. It was almost too much, just feeling it. The flashing strobe lights were so bright he could see them through his eyelids. He could see them in color, in yellow and amber and green and red and pink. The lights and the colors vibrated. He vibrated with them. He opened his eyes. He looked up. Multi-colored lasers from a dozen emitters dotting the walls shot across the sky and fanned out and pulsed and criss-crossed. He'd seen it before, a thousand times, but he'd never seen it before. It was magnificent, miraculous. The beat surged from the speakers through the floor and surged from the floor through his feet and from his feet through his body to his broad shoulders. He held his arms out wide and breathed deep and felt the tears streaming down and laughed.

He remembered everything, every night, every song, every man, the ones he met and the ones he saw from a distance, the looks on their faces, their beatific smiles, the secrets they kept, the mistakes they made, the connections they missed, the lives they could have lived, the men who hurt them, they men they wanted. They told him everything, because they saw something in him. He never knew what they saw, he still didn't know, but he knew.

Rob gave Mike his hand. There was something in it. The other half of the other pink tablet. Rob winked. Mike opened his mouth and stuck out his tongue. Rob took the half, opened his mouth, put it on his own tongue, and took Mike by the back of the neck and kissed him. He passed the tablet from his mouth to Mike's. Mike swallowed, went for his water, but Rob wouldn't let him go and kept kissing him. Mike closed his eyes and shrugged and let Rob have him.

Rob was a good kisser. There was something reassuring about the way he kissed, something familiar. As if he knew what Mike needed. As if they had done this before?

"Rob, have we . . . ?"

"Just go with it, Mike."

Rob, have we . . . ?

Just go with it, Mike.

It was a drug, not magic. They weren't having a conversation in their minds. Mike was just hearing the conversation in his mind.

No, Mike, we are having a conversation in our minds. It's a magic drug.

No, no.

Yes, just trust me.

Mike scanned Rob's eyes for clues, but they were opaque, flat, vacant. Rob was absent and present at the same time, bobbing his head, swaying his shoulders, keeping the beat with his feet, squeezing Mike and grinding, sliding his hands into Mike's back pockets. Mike took Rob's shoulders and gently pushed himself away.

"Hey," said Rob.

Mike looked up and spun around, slowly, catching his breath, straining to hear the music, to clear his head, to find some other eyes to look into. He was sad, desperate Frank, on the outside looking in. He was Billy, sweet, sad Billy, too good for his friend Chase. He was his own father, absent and present at the same time, forever disappointed. He was Clifford, or Jordan, or Spencer or Scott or Keith, absent and present at the same time, forever disappointed.

Through the amber fog he saw two good-looking men, one white and one Latino, pouring water on themselves and laughing, and he could tell that they were friends who once had been lovers, who found that friendship suited them better. He envied them. The Latin one floated off, consumed by the fog, and the other one looked lost, but only for a moment. The other one found someone else, someone he didn't know, and he led him on, it was clear he was leading him on, but the victim was all in.

Mike knew what was going to happen next, as if he had already seen it. It was a scene that replayed itself over and over, Saturday night after Saturday night; he had played the role himself, both roles, many times. The predator leaned over and spoke into the victim's ear; the victim pulled back, sad and angry; the predator held up a hand to run through the victim's hair, but the victim turned away and fled into the fog.

"Mike."

"Uh huh."

"You're stuck in your head. Get out of your head."

"What?"

Mike drifted away, through the fog, through the crowd, keeping an eye glued to the man, deliberate but not hurried. The man would be there, waiting, whenever he got there. The man looked over and saw him and half-smiled and looked away, but he was good. The man had game. The man was a player. That was fine. Mike knew how to play a player. The man was rolling on Ecstasy, which gave Mike an advantage, since Mike never–

Rob grabbed Mike by the wrist and stopped him. He came around to face him. "Mike. Are you okay?"

Mike looked over Rob's shoulder. "He's gone, Rob."

"Who's gone?" Rob turned to look where Mike was looking.

"No one."

"Clifford."

"No one."

Rob wiped away the tears from Mike's cheeks.

"Aw, Mike. I'm so sorry, really. I shouldn't have given you that other half."

"I'm fine. It doesn't matter. Let's get out of here. Your place?"

"Oh, I don't know. In your condition . . ."

"What condition?" Mike kissed Rob and stuck a hand down his pants, grabbed his hard cock. "We don't have to do anything, Rob, it's okay. Come on."

"You're not in your right mind."

"Like you give a fuck."

"Oh, Mike. You're so fucking hot. I want you so bad."

"Come on."

"Mirrors" played on the satellite radio. Justin's voice, the tension between joy and pain and desire, filled Mike's head as they kissed. The driver behind them sat on the horn, flashing his high-beams, finally pulling around and screeching through the intersection.

Rob opened the apartment door and Mike grabbed him, shut the door behind them, pushed Rob up against the door and kissed him. They kissed until they had to stop and take a breath.

"I don't know if I can make it to your bedroom," said Mike.

"Can you make it to the couch?"

Rob sat up, looming over him. "My God, let me just look at you. You are so fucking hot." He stroked his own cock. "I could come just looking at you. You're so beautiful, Mike. You're perfect. I can't . . ." Rob stroked Mike's arms. "Your skin is so smooth, it feels so good . . . look at your shoulders, they're so square, you look so strong, your fucking perfect chest." He grabbed Mike's cock. "Fuck, your beautiful fucking cock. You're fucking hotter than I remember."

"Than you remember?"

"So fucking hot, it's driving me nuts."

"I so wanna fuck you right now."

"Can I suck your cock first?"

Rob didn't wait for an answer; he lay down facing Mike and took his cock in his mouth. Mike lay back and looked down and just watched, stretched out his arms and locked his fingers behind his head and closed his eyes and just fed into Rob's rhythm. Rob took a deep breath and went down,

down, down, sucking hard, stroking Mike's stomach, his chest, sticking his fingers in Mike's mouth. Mike held Rob's hands and sucked on Rob's fingers while Rob sucked on his cock, until he couldn't get any harder, and then he got harder, and harder. Rob looked up, nodding, closed his eyes, nodding; Mike rocked his hips; Rob groaned, saying "Mm-hmm, mm-hmm." Mike rocked harder, really putting his back into it. Rob cried out, "Oh fuck, oh fuck."

"Holy fuck, Rob, you're a fucking master."

"Mm-hmm, mm-hmm."

"Take my fucking cock, baby. Take all of it."

"Mm-hmm, mm-hmm."

Rob took all of it, the whole fucking thing, and Mike couldn't do anything anymore, anything but breathe, so that was what he did, breathe, learn to breathe, breathe for the first time. Rob's mouth was so wet, so soft, he was a major cocksucker, a fucking master. Mike's cock was just getting sucked in and stroked as he hung on to Rob's head. He was fucking Rob in the face, in the mouth, in the throat, deep against the back of Rob's throat, the tip of his cock rubbing against him, and he was flying, soaring, his breath so deep and full, flying through the galaxy, hearing the wind and feeling the wind rushing by him and through him, flying among the stars; the black sky was thick with them, but they were real, not the movie kind, but the kind when you're out in the desert, only not in the desert looking up but up there among them, living up there among the stars; they formed a constellation in the shape of infinity and infinity meant death, and his body tensed and he came flying back, on rewind, as Rob climbed on top of him and kissed him.

"Where'd you go, Mike?"

"Where'd I go? Nowhere. I'm right here."

"You wanna fuck me now?"

"You don't wanna just keep–"

"I thought you wanted to fuck me."

Mike kissed him back. "Yeah. I do. Let's fuck. I just–that's a tough act to follow."

Rob laughed and patted Mike on the cheek.

"You ain't seen nothing yet, movie star."

Mike's cock was throbbing, visibly throbbing, leaking and dripping, pre-cum spreading everywhere, making everything slippery, making Rob slippery, and Rob stroked Mike's wet, throbbing cock and stuck a hand in his mouth and a hand in Mike's mouth. He did it again, licked all over his fingers and his palm, opened his other palm for Mike to lick.

"Do you like it, Mike, do you like the way you taste?"

Mike nodded.

"Do you know how fucking everything you are?"

Mike nodded.

"You're everything, Mike. You're the beginning, you're the end, you're everything."

Mike nodded.

"I mean it."

Mike nodded.

"But you won't remember. I know you won't."

"I will."

"No, you won't. But it's better that way. I can say anything to you now, and I don't have to worry about what you'll think of me two days from now."

"You never have to worry about that. I've got you, Rob. I've got you."

"Oh, fuck, you're gonna make me cry. How are you even possible?"

"Rob."

"Yeah?"

"Sit on my cock."

Rob looked him in the eye, looked through him almost, not vacant now but his mind was moving, searching for something, and he closed his eyes but he was still searching, which was a neat trick because he got Mike to close his eyes and search with him, with flashlights and miner's helmets, in a pitch black cave with no walls either of them could see, while Rob lubed himself with Mike's pre-cum and his own pre-cum and eased himself onto Mike's rock-hard, throbbing cock, groaning, crying almost, taking a break and starting again and easing Mike's cock farther into himself.

What are you looking for?

I won't know until I find it.

You and me both.

"Oh, yeah, Mike. You and me, Mike. You and me."

"Aw, fuck. That is fucking tight. Maybe even tighter than, tighter than fuck."

"Tighter than who?"

"So fucking tight, Rob."

"Tighter than who? You can tell me."

"Chase. Tighter than Chase. I don't think he ever bottomed before."

"Oh yeah? Before when?"

Mike thrust himself in deep.

"Oh my God!" Rob inhaled and shook all over. "Before when?"

"Aw fuck. Before tonight."

"Tonight?"

Mike laughed. "Can you believe it?"

"You're a fucking animal!"

"Fuck yeah I am! I'm gonna fuck you so hard."

"Harder than Chase?"

"I–I don't know."

"Come on. Harder than Chase?"

"That's different. He. I. We. I."

"You're in love with him."

"No no no."

"Maybe a little."

"I'm with you now."

"Maybe a little?"

"Stop talking about Chase!"

Mike let out a roar and leaned forward and slammed his cock up Rob's tight ass, as hard as he could. Rob pushed back, and it was like a ratchet, it made him tighter, made him cry out.

"Oh my God! holy motherfucking fuck, your fucking cock! Holy fuck!"

Rob's face contorted and grimaced, his body writhed and twisted.

"Take that cock, boy, take that fucking cock."

"Oh fuck, fuck me, Mike, fuck me so fucking hard. Oh fuck, oh fuck, oh fuck."

"Ride my cock, ride that motherfucker. Give me that tight fucking ass."

Mike sat up and took Rob in his arms, they were covered in sweat and rocking, and Mike thrust his hips, and Rob rode Mike's cock, putting all of himself into it, crying out in ecstasy and pain with each thrust.

"Oh my God, Mike, oh my God, Mike, I love you, Mike. I fucking love you."

Mike nodded.

"You can even remember if you want to I don't care."

Mike nodded.

"You're so, so everything, Mike, you're *everything*, I can't stand it, I fucking love you, oh fuck, fuck me, I want you to come inside me. Come on, I wanna feel your hot cum inside me, man, come on, come on, I love you, I love you so goddamn much, I want you to come, Mike. Mike, Mike, Mike."

"Get ready."

Mike held his cock all the way in and pressed his hips up against Rob's ass. He held on tight and turned both of them together and planted his feet on the floor. He got a good grip around Rob's lower back and sprung up from the couch, taking all of Rob's weight, and with Rob's weight thrusting down and Mike's hips thrusting up he went in deeper than he thought possible, and Rob hung onto Mike and moaned and groaned and cried, and Mike's powerful legs buckled a little, not under Rob's weight, but because he was out of breath and weak from the power of everything, of Rob's words which were real and not just words, he meant them and it was thrilling, and Mike regained his strength and carried Rob across the room until he had him against the wall, but he didn't let him down, he just fucked the living fuck out of him, right up against the wall, fucked him with everything he had, fucked him and fucked him and fucked him.

"Fuck me, Mike, fuck me, oh yeah, fuck me, fuck me."

Mike knew what was going to happen now, there was nothing he could do, it was out of his hands, and his entire body shuddered and clenched, and he was coming and coming and coming, his hot cum all the way up Rob's ass, and Rob was coming too, coming and coming and coming, his hot cum spurting up between them, and Mike could feel it rising from deep down inside him, from that place that connected him to everything, and it reached his lungs and his throat and his lips and he said it, he said it, he said it.

CHAPTER TEN

Chase left the car at the office and walked to the courthouse, wearing his best dark blue suit and powder blue tie, light brown leather briefcase in hand. It wasn't too far, not quite two miles, the weather was brisk, and the air would do him good.

All day Sunday, from sunrise to midnight, he had sat staring at his laptop, immunized to distraction, revising and revising and revising his outline, poring over everything, all the briefs, all the cases, everyone's notes and suggestions and caveats, looking for any holes in Syndicated's argument he might have missed, any holes in his own argument to defend against attack. He went back through every piece of intel on the judge, her political connections, her country club memberships, her past rulings, the times the Court of Appeal reversed her and why, other lawyers' reviews of her intelligence, her preparedness, her thoroughness, her temperament, the tone of her voice.

He had stood in front of the mirror and rehearsed his argument until he had it down to the last syllable. There was no way to predict how much of it he would get through, but he had to be prepared, and it kept him occupied. It was the best part of the job, the part he went to law school for. Judges told him he changed their minds; opposing counsel told him he left them tongue-tied. He had even invited Ike to sit in the gallery and watch–on his way out the door, drunk and still glowing from his matchmaking triumph, before everything went to shit, as usual.

Maybe Mike was right, his first instinct had been right. It was just the Ecstasy talking. Chase was just a player. Chase had a lot of growing up to do. No, that was too easy, it let Mike off the hook too easy. If Chase was so lacking in so many ways, what did that say about Mike, that he could have seen all that and still convinced himself that there was something meaningful between them? What did he need so badly that he was willing to overlook so much to have it?

Yeah, it was awesome, being young and rich. It came with a lot of perks. He was lucky. He never dared complain. But there were wolves out there, flatterers and users, and he had to learn how to spot them before they found his weak spot. Sometimes the packaging was so beautiful, but that's all it was, packaging. Scratch the surface and there was something selfish and mean underneath. Sometimes you really felt something, you knew it was real, you were sure it was real, but even then you better not let your guard down. You could let it down for an hour, a night, but when the sun came up you raised it again, steeled yourself against your fantasies, planted your flag in the real world, atop your castle, drawbridge up. That was the difference between Billy and all those other losers. Chase kept a chamber for Billy in the castle. Billy had his faults, God knows, but he was real. The drawbridge always came down for Billy. He was the same inside and out.

The Superior Court building occupied an entire downtown block, but it was the opposite of grand and imposing. A deteriorating, rain-stained, tile-clad slab in the International Style from the 1950s, it was more horizontal than vertical, more like an above-ground bunker than a hallowed edifice of justice. Chase walked past the lackluster Grand Avenue entrance, its fresco of Great Lawmakers Through the Ages scowling down at him, to a more congenial spot, the bright, manicured gardens that spanned the distance between the courthouse and the other municipal buildings. He strolled among the old-fashioned tiered fountains glistening in the sun, the purple jacarandas and orange birds of paradise, the drought-tolerant grasses in every shade of green and blue, and stopped to sit for a moment on a hot-pink metal bench and gather his thoughts one final time. He never would have been here in the first place, had it not been for Frank Sutcliffe, but he was here and he was ready and he was going to crush it, and Ike would remember who really had his back.

He got up and made his way along a shaded walkway, its square, stuccoed columns covered with moss, past an atrium of overgrown ferns, to the side entrance. A crowd of lawyers in dark suits and skirts and prospective jurors in street clothes formed a long line at the metal detector. He checked his watch. He walked past the line and approached a portly, graying sheriff's deputy in a green and khaki uniform at the front.

"Dude, ya gotta help me out. Custody hearing. That b–, uh, sorry, my ex is gonna take my kids away if I don't get in there on time."

The deputy stuck his thumbs in his waistband. "Back of the line, please, sir."

Chase checked his watch again. "Come on, man. Do me a solid. My kids. They're four and two. I'll never see them again." He turned and scanned the line, loosened his tie, rubbed the back of his neck, and rolled his shoulders. He turned again to the deputy and raised his voice. "My kids, man. Susie and Jimmy. They'll hate me forever. I gotta get in there." He turned to the crowd. "Can you believe this guy? My kids!" He turned back to the deputy. "Look, officer, I know you're just doing your job, but–"

"Let him in," said a tall African-American man in a dress shirt and jeans near the front.

"Let me in," said Chase. "I'm begging you." Chase pictured his childhood dog, Clarence, a black Lab, the day they put him down. Clarence wasn't ready to go. Chase never forgave his parents. Tears welled up in his eyes.

"Please, sir, please . . . My kids."

The guard shook his head and clucked his teeth.

"You can cut in front of me," said the African-American man. He turned to address the line. "Anyone got a problem with that?"

"No!" the line called out, with the exception of a few lawyers, who abstained, incredulous smirks on their faces.

"Oh, sir," said Chase, "thank you so much. Thank you, my good man." Chase wiped his tears and took his place in front of the man.

The man murmured under his breath. "Custody hearing, my ass."

Chase turned to him and winked. "I owe you one."

Safely through the metal detector, Chase fought his way through the crowd on the other side and hopped on an elevator. He got off on the fourth floor and walked the worn marble corridor. Several doors down, he found Carlos, sitting on the long wooden bench outside the courtroom, wearing a black suit, typing on his phone.

"We're up second," said Carlos. "You ready?"

Chase took a deep breath. "I think so. Been inside?"

Carlos nodded. "No tentative ruling. Hey, great party Saturday. Ike was *en fuego*."

"And you were shitfaced, my man. Any sign of him?"

Carlos checked his watch. "Nope. No message either. How'd it go with your bartender friend?"

"Hoo boy, look who's here. Dan fucking Rivetti, as I live and breathe."

Carlos turned around. "Dan fucking Rivetti. And his ornaments."

If Chase was among an elite class of lawyers, Daniel P. Rivetti was the über-elite. The kind who held press conferences, appeared as a guest panelist on CNN, had his own publicist. He represented politicians, studio heads, Mafiosi, and other criminals, anyone who could afford his fee. He wore three-thousand dollar suits stitched by his personal tailors in Milan and Hong Kong; shuttled among multiple residences on both coasts and in Paris and London and Barcelona; employed a full-time driver to take him from the beach house to the house in the hills to the office to the courthouse (when he didn't send his minions in his place), so he wouldn't lose a precious minute of billable time, which was rumored to have reached two-thousand an hour. And, as befitted a man of his station, he was widely acclaimed among his peers as a hyper-aggressive, ethically challenged, unrepentant asshole.

"If he's arguing this," said Carlos, "I have to think he's worried."

Rivetti strode down the corridor, accompanied by two young associates carrying his bags, one blonde, one brunette, in matching black skirt suits and white blouses. He was of average height, had a full head of salt-and-pepper hair, a square jaw, and a fresh European tan.

Carlos rose.

"Morning, gentlemen," said Rivetti. He shook their hands. "Any tentative? Ladies, can you go inside, check us in?"

The associates smiled, nodded, and noiselessly entered the courtroom.

"Motion emphatically denied, my good man," said Chase.

"If wishes were horses, Mr. Evans." Rivetti patted Chase on the shoulder. "Though I must congratulate you on your creativity. I assume the breach of contract claim was your idea, whiz kid?"

"Let's just say it was a team effort, Dan," said Carlos.

"Nice save, Bautista. I wouldn't want to be left holding the bag on this one either."

"No," said Chase, "you hire pretty young associates to hold *your* bags."

Carlos howled with laughter.

Rivetti glared at Chase. "Very clever, kid. They happen to be excellent lawyers."

The blonde associate opened the door a crack and popped her head out. "She's wrapping up the first matter, Dan. We're up next."

"Great!" said Rivetti. "I have a plane to catch. Gentlemen?" He opened the door the rest of the way and ushered Carlos and Chase before him. He gave Chase an exaggerated smile.

Chase smiled back. "Thanks, my man!"

The door opened onto a large box of a courtroom, with old, dark oak paneling reaching to the high ceilings, and a gallery of several rows of worn wooden benches filled to capacity with suits and skirts spanning a wide range of quality and style. The state seal hung dead center from the far wall. On either side of it, framing an enormous desk two steps up, flew two American flags. Behind the desk, looming over the assembled, sat the Honorable Marlene Kovacs, Judge of the Superior Court. She wore the standard black robe with a white collar and had graying, straight, shoulder-length hair and weathered skin. She looked down at the counsel's table over reading glasses.

"Clerk, call the next matter, please," said the judge, in a thin, low-pitched voice. She spoke with a surprisingly thick Slavic accent.

The clerk cleared her throat and read rapid-fire from the docket sheet. "The Syndicated Corporation versus Aronsoncorp, Superior Court case number B_____, motion of plaintiff and cross-defendant Syndicated to dismiss count one of the cross-complaint of Aronsoncorp for breach of contract."

"Counsel, please state your appearances," said the judge.

Rivetti rose from the gallery and passed through a pair of low, swinging doors, and stood at the counsel's table. The associates proceeded noiselessly behind him. "Daniel Rivetti, Megan Moriarty, and Caitlin White for plaintiff and cross-defendant The Syndicated Corporation, Your Honor."

Chase and Carlos followed them in.

"Chase Evans and Carlos Bautista for defendant and cross-complainant Aronsoncorp, Your Honor."

Carlos patted Chase on the back and whispered, "Nicely done, *whiz kid*. You've already got that asshole rattled."

Chase smiled. He scanned the gallery, nodded back to a few familiar faces. No sign of Ike.

"Be seated, counsel," said the judge. "Now. I must say this is a rather, well, *novel* breach of contract claim, Mr. Evans, this idea that merely by bringing a lawsuit one party can breach their contract with the other. The implication, it seems to me, is that every time someone sues for breach of contract, the defendant will counter-sue, essentially to punish the plaintiff for seeking their day in court. Am I wrong, Mr. Evans?"

Chase pushed back his chair and rose. He buttoned his jacket.

"Well, Your Honor, naturally I hesitate to say you are wrong. Uh, in so many words."

The judge smiled. "Please, young man. I'm not infallible."

Chase smiled back. "Well, Ma'am, far be it from me."

She nodded. "In any event . . ."

"In any event, allow me to, shall we say, *clarify* Aronsoncorp's position. We are not arguing that filing a lawsuit is a breach of contract. What we are saying is, Syndicated breached the contract by terminating it, openly and publicly. We have been operating under this license agreement for years, paying the license fees, accounting to Syndicated for our sales. Now suddenly they announce to all the world that this license is no longer valid. They happen to make this announcement by suing us, but it doesn't matter whether they sue, or issue a press release, or write a strongly worded letter. The damage is done."

The judge leaned forward and removed her glasses.

"Let me see if I understand, counsel. The termination and the lawsuit occur simultaneously but you consider them two different acts?"

"Exactly right, Your Honor, exactly right. They are two different acts. The termination occurs whether or not Syndicated never sues. Just a long-winded way of saying that you are *not* wrong, Your Honor. Your record is intact."

"Indeed." The judge chuckled. "I see, I see. Well, I remain skeptical, but–"

Rivetti rose, gripping a notepad. "If I may, Your Honor."

The judge leaned back, put her glasses back on, and flopped some papers onto her desk.

"By all means, Mr. Rivetti."

"Thank you, Judge. Now–"

The judge narrowed her eyes. "It's 'Your Honor.'"

"My apologies. Your Honor. My young, uh, shall we say, *enthusiastic* opposing counsel here is playing a cute little game of semantics with you, and I hope, I am quite confident you won't be taken in by it. There was only one act, the act of filing the complaint, which this fellow, which Mr., uh–"

"Evans," said the judge. "Mr. Evans. Please, Mr. Rivetti, a little collegiality and respect toward your fellow member of the Bar."

"Yes, Your Honor, of course. Mr. Evans. Surely we can *allege* that they breached the contract without breaching it ourselves. How else can we seek to recover our damages, if not with a lawsuit?"

"But there is only one license agreement, is there not?"

"Well, yes."

"And both sides now alleging a breach of this same agreement, correct?"

"I suppose technically yes, but, as I say–"

"So why doesn't, um . . ." The judge sifted through her papers. "Why doesn't Aronsoncorp have as much right as your client to its day in court? If you think their claim is meritless, well, you can have your discovery and we can revisit the issue of who breached what and how down the road. But at this stage we are not getting into the factual questions. Just the law, Mr. Rivetti, just the law."

"But that's not–they are inventing–with all due respect, Ma'am, the cross-complaint is a sham. It contains absolutely no credible, factual basis for this so-called breach of contract claim. It's a sham, plain and simple. A *sham*, Your Honor."

"If I may," said Chase, "what counsel seems to be saying, Your Honor, is that it's a sham."

A few lawyers in the gallery giggled.

"This is just priceless, really," said Rivetti. "Counsel is making light of the fact that he is engaging in a transparent attempt to silence and, and to intimidate my client. In all honesty, in all my years of practice, I have never seen such conduct. I find it a deeply, *deeply* offensive, attack on my client's First Amendment–"

"I'm sorry, Your Honor," said Chase, "but Mr. Rivetti raising his voice doesn't make his argument any less laughable. I assume he's referring to the anti-SLAPP statute, which he contorts mightily, I mean *mightily*, to fit within the allegations of our cross-complaint. I admire the effort, Your Honor, really, it's quite a pretty bit of lawyering."

Chase looked over at Rivetti and smiled.

"But it is, well, how do I put this gently? It's absurd, Your Honor. Silence The Syndicated Corporation? Deny them their First Amendment rights? Please. They're not a bunch of investigative reporters on a shoestring budget. They don't qualify for the protections of anti-SLAPP. They're a big Fortune 500 corporation selling consumer products, with a market capitalization in the billions. No one is going to go out of business litigating these claims."

"Correct, Mr. Evans," said the judge. "In fact, I would venture a guess that a couple of law firms are going to be doing quite well thanks to this case."

The giggling in the gallery rose to laughter.

"I'm sure you're not deeply, deeply offended by *that*, Mr. Rivetti."

The laughter spread.

Rivetti's face reddened.

The judge banged her gavel. "Silence!"

Rivetti forced a laugh. "Well put, Ma'am, very well put. On that very point, Your Honor, I feel I must not neglect to point out to the court that the conduct of counsel for Aronsoncorp in bringing this claim is highly, *highly* suspect, and positively reeks of bad faith. Mr. Evans and his firm stand to gain–"

"Your Honor," said Chase, "I can't allow–"

"Let me finish, Evans, Mr. Evans." said Rivetti.

"By all means, Mr. Rivetti." Chase turned to him. "Take as much time as you like." He looked at Carlos; Carlos winked.

"Thank you!" said Rivetti. "As I was saying, Mr. Evans and his firm are walking a very, very thin ethical line here, and it is quite clear under the Code of Professional Conduct–"

"Mr. Rivetti!" The judge banged her gavel again. Her face was now redder than Rivetti's.

The gallery fell silent.

The judge lowered her reading glasses. "I'm sure we're all quite familiar with your . . . *illustrious* career, Mr. Rivetti; however, I was not aware that the governor had named you my . . . replacement?"

"Ma'am?"

"Your opposing counsel's ethics is none of your concern, sir, and you know it. If there is some violation of the Code of Professional Conduct, if there is going to be an ethics referral to the State Bar, *etcetera*, that is the province of this court. You are well beyond your brief here, Mr. Rivetti, and, frankly, in light of your unfortunate remarks, I have to wonder who is the one walking the very thin ethical line, as you call it. I'm going to overlook your outburst, Mr. Rivetti, this time. However, your motion to dismiss is denied. Aronsoncorp's breach of contract claim stands."

Silently, hand at his side, Chase clenched a fist in triumph.

"But Your Honor," said Rivetti.

"Sit *down*, Mr. Rivetti."

Rivetti sat and tossed his notepad to the table.

"Now. As you know, gentleman–and ladies–where an issue has not been raised by the parties, the court has discretion to rule on its own motion. Normally I am quite reluctant to do this, but . . ." She glanced at Rivetti. "Well, in any event . . ." She sifted through her papers. "I am looking specifically at the fraud count, let me see, count 3, of plaintiff Syndicated's complaint, and I see only the most bare-bones allegations."

"Your Honor–"

She pointed at him. "Not another word, Mr. Rivetti, or I swear to God I will hold you in contempt. I don't know if you are accustomed to other judges indulging you or, or what, but in my courtroom you are not Mister Fancy Big Shot; in my courtroom you are just another lawyer, understood?"

The gallery murmured. The judge banged her gavel.

"Now, where was I? Oh yes, as I was saying, you have not made sufficient specific allegations for each element of a fraud claim. And of course a fraud claim in connection with breach of contract is strongly disfavored in this state. In the event I am going to dismiss that claim. I'm going to give you thirty days' leave to amend." She leaned forward and raised her index finger. "And I'm giving you *one* opportunity–one– to amend this fraud claim. And if it is still defective at that time I will dismiss it with prejudice. I invite counsel for Aronsoncorp to move to strike the prayer for punitive damages as well."

"Absolutely, your Honor," said Chase.

"Well, fuck," Rivetti muttered under his breath. He looked down and slid his pen around on the notepad. "Fuck fuck fuck."

"So!" The judge straightened her papers and looked up. "I believe we are done here. Defendant and cross-complainant Aronsoncorp to give notice." She banged her gavel. "Clerk, call the next matter, please."

\#

"That was phenomenal, Chase," said Carlos. "Fucking phenomenal." He fanned himself and broke into a falsetto. "Oh, young man, I'm not infallible, tee-hee."

They pulled out of the parking lot and started back to the office.

"Let's get Rachel on the phone."

Chase picked up Carlos's phone and dialed.

"Oh my God, you guys." Rachel's voice came through the car speakers. "How'd it go?"

"Asshole!" Carlos shouted.

"Excuse me?"

"No, not you, Rachel. Some asshole just cut me off. It went *unbelievably* well. Our boy is a freaking genius. The judge fucking *loved* him, and she *hated* Dan Rivetti, that arrogant prick. You should have seen his face."

"Rivetti argued this? Whoa. So how did she–"

"So can you conference Ike in?" said Chase.

"Ike? I thought he was in court with you."

"He didn't show up," said Carlos.

"Okay, yeah, let me . . . oh, crap, I don't know how to . . . Barnie!" Rachel called out. "Can you come here please?"

Barnie's melodramatic sighing echoed down the hallway all the way to the phone.

"I need to conference Ike in," said Rachel.

Barnie's heels tapped into Rachel's office. "Oh, easy-peasy, Rach', just press right here and–no, no, not–"

The line went dead.

"Jesus God," said Chase.

"Dial again," said Carlos.

"Yeah, yeah, hang on."

Rachel picked up before it rang. "Yeah, sorry, guys, I've got it now. Oh, crap, what is Ike's–"

"Chillax, hon'," said Barnie, "I got it. So, boys, you'll hear our fabulous hold music for a sec while I bring Ike in."

They waited. The line rang.

"Mr. Aronson's office?"

"Oh, hey, Janet, it's Chase."

Janet's voice rose two octaves. "Well, hello, Mr. Chase?"

"I've got Carlos and Rachel on the line. Can you get me Ike?"

"Oh, so sorry, Chase? Ike is in a meeting? I can connect you to Mr. Marshall instead?"

Carlos looked at Chase, raised an eyebrow. Chase shrugged.

"Okay, thanks, Janet? Go ahead and connect us?"

"Hold the line, please."

Chase slapped his forehead. "Jesus, she's got *me* doing it now."

The phone rang.

"Mr. Marshall's office."

"Janet?"

"Yes, Chase? I'm Mr. Marshall's assistant too?"

170

"But why did you–"

"It's a different line? If I want Mr. Marshall to–"

"Oh, never mind. Can you connect us?"

"Hold the line, please."

The phone rang.

"Brooks Marshall."

"Brooks!" said Chase.

"Well, hello, Chase. How did it go?"

"Mother fucker!" shouted Carlos.

"Excuse me?"

"Oh, no, not you, Brooks. Someone just cut me off."

Chase rolled his eyes. "Sorry, Brooks, some crazy drivers up in here. It went great, Brooks. Better than we could have expected."

"Oh. Is that so?"

"The judge denied the motion to dismiss."

"She did. Ah. That's, that's terrific."

"*And* she struck their fraud claim, on her own motion."

"Really? Well, now, that is very good, isn't it? Very, very good."

Chase looked at Carlos. Carlos shrugged.

"I think she doesn't like Dan Rivetti very much," said Chase.

"That is brilliant!" said Rachel. "Freaking brilliant! Chase, what did you do?"

"Just argued the law, Rachel, what else? So Brooks, this means–"

"Well, everyone," said Brooks, "I've got to go. Good job, all. I'm sure Ike will be pleased as punch. Thanks. Bye now."

He hung up.

"Okay," said Rachel, "is it just me, or was he just a little . . . underwhelmed just now? I mean, this is a huge win for us."

"If you ask me," said Chase, "there's something fishy going on. I think maybe we need to have another little word with Frank."

"Frank," said Rachel.
"Fucking Frank," said Carlos.

CHAPTER ELEVEN

Francis hopped on the elevator, sporting new wraparound sunglasses and dancing in place to a song about mirrors coming through his new noise-cancelling headphones. He nodded to the other passengers, just the right measure between civil and friendly, because they needed his approval but it was beyond his considerable powers to fill the void in their humble little lives. He caught a glimpse of quite an attractive lad in the elevator's polished steel doors, with a newly shaved head and neat three-day beard, and wouldn't you know, the lad was Francis his very same self. The form-fitting, casual pink dress shirt, no tie, and casual black dress slacks, cotton with just a little spandex, announced to all the world that this young man was someone to be reckoned with.

The elevator door opened and he bounced right off, spring in his step, did a graceful little turn so that the receptionist, what was her name, could take him all in and drop her jaw in wonder. To her great misfortune, she happened to be on the telephone, as a receptionist might be, ha ha, squinting through the bright late morning glare at her computer screen. That was a shame, for her. Next time. No, not next time. He would walk through the lobby and right past her for once, rather than slink away like a mouse through the nearest door and go straight to his office. In fact there was a kitchen for him to head towards. Did he need an excuse? No, come to think of it, he did not! What was her name what was her name goddammit what was her name? Marissa! That was close!

"Good morning, Marissa!"

Marissa nearly leapt out of her chair, so awestruck was she. She looked at Francis, even stared for half a second, though she did her best to hide the fact. She pointed to her ears. Such an odd little bird, Marissa.

Francis squinted at her and her strange ways.

She motioned to him to remove something from his head. Ah, the stylish new headphones.

"Oh!" Francis smiled and removed them. "Begging your pardon, Marissa."

"Oh, no worries. It happens more often than you might think, believe me. Anyway, who are you here to see, Mr. . . . ?"

"Marissa! 'Tis I, Francis!"

"Francis?"

"Oh, dear, of course. Frank Sutcliffe, as it were."

"Mr. Sutcliffe! Wow, I totally did *not* recognize you!"

"Thank you!"

"Good for you! I mean, it's good to change it up now and then, right?"

Not *quite* the reaction he was anticipating, but Marissa was busy and distracted, multi-tasking, and perhaps not as skilled as one might have hoped at meeting the moment.

"Uh . . . right. Right you are, Marissa."

"Isn't your office that way, Mr. Sutcliffe?"

"Oh, you know, Miss M, changing it up, as you say. *N'est-ce pas?*"

"*Que sera, sera!*"

"If you'll excuse me, I believe I'll head to the kitchen and fix myself a little cup of pick-me-up this morning."

Marissa nodded. "You bet, Mr. Sutcliffe."

"In point of fact, my dearest, it's not Sut–"

"Uh huh." She frowned. "Sorry, I gotta get back to this." She picked up the phone. It was all too much for her.

That pick-me-up was not such an odd notion, as it happened, so he glided toward the kitchen off the little hall behind Marissa. It wasn't fatigue, nor was it the residual effect of the mind-altering substance he and that Atlas fellow had ingested together, though the synapses were firing in an unfamiliar though quite pleasing fashion, as if one's brain had been rewired. All was quite calm and even-keel, and when he closed his eyes, he heard the planet turning slowly on its axis, humming very quietly in the background.

Some staff, a man and a woman, it was Reynaldo and, and, well, they worked in the Records Department, that much was known, they were sharing a hearty late-morning laugh, about something, something he was not privy to. Yet he smiled along with them, and he looked in their direction, and they said "hey," in their pleasant, simple way. He stuck a pod in the coffee machine and closed his eyes. The coffee machine hissed, drowning out the humming of the planet.

He took his coffee and headed back across the reception area–dear Marissa, still multi-tasking–and down to his office, second-to-last on the hall.

"Morning, Frank," said Justin. He, too, was absorbed in his tasks and barely moved his eyes from his monitor.

Francis stopped to wait for a moment at cute little Justin's desk. He was quite the young "hottie," that was the term, with his little gelled haircut and his little blue jeans with cuffs. Of no interest to Francis, of course, how awkward would that be! Though it must have been quite the predicament for poor Justin.

Lining Justin's desk were framed photos of Justin with his friends in sombreros, blended cocktails in their hands; in cap and gown with what must have been his parents; with another handsome young man kissing him on the cheek. On the counter above his desk were neat little stacks of documents.

Justin turned in his chair and looked up. He exhaled. "What's up, Frank?"

"Well?"

"Well what?"

"Well, what do you think, young Justin?"

"What do I think of what?"

"Oh, Justin."

"Oh, Frank?"

"Never mind. Say, can you come into my office? I need your assistance with a rather pressing matter."

Justin rose and rolled his shoulders and picked up his coffee. "I've only got a minute, okay? I have to get this filing out."

Francis stepped into his narrow but perfectly adequate office; the lights came on. He turned them off; the sun provided ample lighting. He placed his sunglasses and coffee and headphones down on the desk. He settled into his chair and motioned to Justin to take the single guest chair. Justin remained standing. Rather cheeky, this one. But no matter.

"So. I'm going to need you to take care of some things for me, Justin. A new nameplate, new business cards, we'll need to change my bio on the firm website, of course."

"Yeah, sure. What are we changing?"

"My name. Henceforth I'm to be known as Francis Powell the Third."

"Francis Powell the *what* now? What?"

"I believe you heard me."

"Frank, that is just weird, even for you."

Francis laughed.

"Why in the world?"

"Oh, it's quite simple, really. You see, I changed my name out of shame when I was a boy of fifteen, as my father, rest his soul, embezzled from his own law firm and in short order shot himself in the head."

"Oh my God!"

"But as I am no longer a prisoner of this shame I intend to change my name back to the original, as it were. Don't tell my mother, ha ha. About the name change, that is. She is well aware of the gunshot to the head, ha ha."

"Frank!"

"And I'll also need you to determine what sort of paperwork one needs file with the state. And Social Security, all that, *etcetera*, whatever you with your great skills can conjure. Work your magic and find it, on the internet, or the World Wide Web, or wherever else, and fill out the forms as best you can. I have full confidence in you."

"You're not kidding, are you?"

"Justin. Do I ever kid about anything?"

"Good point."

Justin stood quite still, staring in awe.

"Very well. Thanks ever so, Justin. Didn't you have a filing?"

"Frank–"

"Francis."

"Francis. What the–what did you do to your hair?"

"Ah, aren't you the subtle one. Choosing your moments. Can you close the door behind you? Much appreciated."

Francis turned to look up at his monitor, indulging Justin's stare a moment longer, until the boy shook his head and left, closing the door behind him. Like some lingering spirit, Justin's mesmerized countenance appeared again through the glass wall, finally disappearing as he returned to his desk.

Francis put the headphones back on, leaned back, and set his feet on the desk. He closed his eyes. He sat up and picked up his coffee and leaned back again. The coffee served no practical purpose; it had value in and of itself, its harmonious flavor and its subtly sweet aroma. He took a deep breath. He was in Philadelphia, flying over the old neighborhood, the wind coursing through him and around him. The woman in his ears sang of this wind, or was that in his mind.

A knock at the door startled him awake; he nearly lost his balance but rescued the coffee, not a drop spilled. He leaned back and peered through the glass. Carlos. He sat up and took the headphones off and offered a hearty wave.

Carlos opened the door and entered. He turned on the lights and took the guest chair.

Francis blinked, closed his eyes, blinked. "What fair tidings do you bring, my friend?"

"The judge denied the motion."

Francis smiled. "Never doubted it for a moment. So you see, my idea was–"

"And she struck their fraud claim."

"Well now, *that* was quite unexpected, was it not?"

"She gave them one chance to amend. We'll need you to draft something for a new motion. And, you know, we'll move to strike the punitive damages. Mostly just boilerplate stuff, probably."

"Yes, yes, certainly, Carlos. Certainly. I'll get to work on that post-haste."

"Yeah, so we briefed Brooks just now, on the way back, and he couldn't wait to get off the phone. It was a little odd. I know you know him a little. By any chance have you heard anything? Is something going on with him?"

Francis tilted his head back. "Brooks, Brooks. Let me see. Hmm." He looked at Carlos. "Oh, here's something. Were you aware that Brooks and I are, oh, how do I put this–that Brooks and I are fucking?"

Carlos glared at him. "Excuse me?"

"You know, fucking. It's a sex act. Between two men it generally refers to–"

"Yeah, thanks, Frank, I know what fucking is. I'm just . . . I can't tell if you're kidding, or what. You can understand my, uh, extreme skepticism."

"Well, Carlos, I don't contend he's actually of the gay persuasion or any such. I would say, it's more a matter of him using me for some purpose or other."

"Using you? For what?"

Francis shrugged. "Who is to say? Time was I wondered about it, but really I don't anymore. I'm having a rollicking good time, what do I care?"

"You weren't having much fun on Saturday night."

"Ah!" Francis wagged a finger. "That was Frank." He tapped his chest with his thumb and winced. "This is Francis."

"Francis?"

"Francis Powell the Third. You know. I'm sure you know."

Carlos sat forward. "I'm just, I'm just reeling here, Frank. I don't know what—"

"Francis."

"Francis." Carlos leaned in closer. "Look, *Francis*, I don't know what the hell you think you're up to, but whatever it is, you're not smart enough to pull it off, I promise you."

Francis laughed.

Carlos slapped the arms of the guest chair and stood up. "Well, congratulations, *Francis*. You really dodged a bullet today, *Francis*. Make sure to beg Chase for your fucking job when you have a chance. Nice buzz-cut, by the way." He turned and left.

Francis rose and watched Carlos storm out the door. He had never seen him so unnerved. Indeed, he had never seen him unnerved at all. And what an obvious, transparent liar. Well, well, well, wasn't Francis ever making some waves. This was the power of honesty, of authenticity, of showing all of them the real Francis, at long last. The real Francis was *the shit*, as they say. There was nothing he couldn't do now.

He walked quickly past Justin and down the hall, back through the reception area.

"Busy morning, Mr. Sutcliffe?" asked Marissa.

"It's not Sut–yes, quite busy, Marissa." He continued to the hall on the other side of the floor, down toward the corner office. He passed Barnie's desk.

Barnie called out, "Hi, Francis!"

Francis stopped in his tracks. "What did you call me?"

"It's your name, right?"

"But how did you–"

"Twenty-nine years, Frank, twenty-nine years. I mean Francis."

"Uh . . ."

"Chase is on the phone."

"That's quite all right." He resumed his walk down the hall.

Barnie called after him. "Francis . . ."

Chase stood behind his monitor, talking on his headset and pacing, a tall, defined silhouette against the window. Frank blinked. The sun's glare slowly faded; the silhouette slowly brightened; its depth and color came into focus. Chase wore a white dress shirt and tight dark blue slacks, very flattering, quite flattering, pale blue tie, such perfect hair, that masculine jaw-line, those full lips, looking agitated but not unhappy, never unhappy. Francis tapped on the door, smiled brightly, and walked in. Chase moved toward him quickly, pointed to the headset, waved him off, shooed him out, and shut the door in his face. The glass wall shimmered with the impact.

Francis stared at the door. It was most definitely closed, and Chase was most definitely on the other side of it. Quite a conundrum. He set his hands on his hips. He leaned to one side, looked through the glass wall, and squinted against the glare, but from here it was too much, the silhouette was but a blur, and Francis teetered back to center. He recalled a moving image, in black and white, provenance unknown, of a man in a dark suit and fedora leaning so far over he was almost horizontal as an elevator door closed in front of him. Doubtless the intent was comical, yet at this particular moment the image filled him with dread.

He laughed.

The slightest breeze whispered to him. He looked over his shoulder. Carlos and Rachel came rushing down the hallway.

Rachel stopped. Her jaw dropped. "Whoa, nice buzz-cut, Frank."

"Why, tha–"

"It's Francis, Rachel," said Carlos.

"No, I really like it, Frank. Francis?" Rachel's head turned from Carlos to Francis to Carlos again. "Wait, Francis?"

Carlos knocked on the door and opened it; he and Rachel entered and closed the door behind them.

Francis inched a little closer. Three voices, a fourth on the speakerphone, loud but indistinct. Such commotion over his newly acquired status was probably out of proportion, yet hardly difficult to fathom. Change, though inevitable, was difficult for some. It could shake the firm to its foundation.

A point of reflected light struck his peripheral vision. He looked over his shoulder. Barnie stood at the end of the hall, her flaming red hair visible from space, staring at him. He looked away. He looked at the door.

The call could last an eternity, so many i's to dot and t's to cross, and Francis had better things to do. He swiveled on one foot and ambled down to Barnie's desk, hands in pockets, this close to whistling a merry tune.

He smiled and clasped his hands together. "So I suppose you would have got word of our great triumph today."

"*Our* great triumph, ell-oh-ell," said Barnie. She banged her keyboard. A bundle of energy, this one. "I'm drafting the notice now." She shook her head. "Oh-em-gee this system is so slow! Takes two minutes to open a frickin' document!"

Francis leaned down and set his elbows on the counter. "They have *you* drafting the notice?"

"Who else, Francis?"

"No, I only mean to say, I'm quite impressed!"

Barnie stopped typing and turned to him. "Okay. What do you want, hon'?"

Francis tapped his chest and winced. "Me? Moi? Not a thing? Not thing one!" He leaned over the counter. One line on Barnie's phone was engaged, but the font was too small to discern the caller I.D. "No, Barnie, I was merely going to ask you–I'm going downstairs to get some coffee, doncha know, and it occurred to me that perhaps you . . ."

"Oh for heaven's sake, not you too!" Barnie rose in a snap and thrust out her palm and tapped her foot. "Just give me your damn money and I'll go get the damn coffee myself. What do you want?"

"No, no, I'm quite happy to–"

"Francis . . ."

"Just a regular latte?" He pulled out his wallet and riffled through it and withdrew a twenty dollar bill. "Keep the change?"

She harrumphed. "Okay, dear. Bee-are-bee." She stomped off down the hall, heels tapping with vigor.

As her clatter receded, Francis looked hither and yon, and tip-toed around the counter to her desk. He looked down at her phone just as the light went off and the caller I.D. disappeared.

"Oh, bother."

Behind him, Barnie's printer whirred awake. Francis turned around. He looked down the hallway again, then at the printer as the paper slid into the output tray. He peeled back the first page.

SECOND AMENDED AND RESTATED EMPLOYMENT AGREEMENT

This Second Amended and Restated Employment Agreement ("Agreement"), entered into as of the execution date entered below ("Execution Date"), by and between Isaac "Ike" Aronson, Chairman of the Board ("COB") and Chief Executive Officer ("CEO") (or "Employee"), on the one hand, and Aronsoncorp ("Employer"), on the other, shall—

The door to Chase's office opened.

"Curses!"

Francis let go the page and stepped quickly around to the other side of the counter and leaned his hip and one elbow against it and smiled. He switched to the other hip, other elbow, and smiled. Chase, Carlos, and Rachel walked out, Chase pulling his suit jacket on.

"Because Carlos would get us all killed," said Rachel with a morbid chuckle.

"Fucking west side," said Chase, jingling his keys.

They marched right past Francis, nary a glance in his direction.

"Where are you sly n'er-do-wells off to in such haste?"

"Lunch, Frank," said Chase.

"But it's not even eleven!"

"We're hungry!" Carlos shouted.

Rachel paused mid-stride, long enough to grab the pages off the printer. She turned to Francis.

"See you later, Frank."

"It's Francis!" said Carlos.

Francis stood there, unmoved, as the three quite intent figures rapidly receded in the distance. They would take him into their confidence as to this intriguing new turn of events in the near future, but for the moment he was at liberty. It was perhaps a bit peculiar, their utter lack of gratitude, but an explanation was sure to be forthcoming.

Rather than distract poor Marissa in Reception, Francis took the scenic route back to his desk this time, along the outer corridor with its many and varied views of the city, and the many hard-working attorneys, visible through their glass walls, all quite entranced by their computer monitors, as was so often the case when he passed. Such a diligent bunch! Kudos! He turned a corner, then another, then reached his office. He closed the door, picked up the phone and dialed.

"Mr. Marshall's office?"

"Oh, hello there! This is Francis–uh, rather, Frank Sutcliffe. It's Janet, is it not?"

"Yes, it is, Mr. Sutton? How may I help you?"

"It's not–no, never mind. Is Brooks around by chance?"

"Let me check? May I ask what this is in regards to?"

"Are you quite–uh, it's in regards to, uh–just please tell him it's Frank Sutcliffe, won't you?"

"Hold the line please, Mr. Sutton?"

The phone rang.

"Brooks Marshall."

"Oh, hello, Brooks, it's, uh, it's Frank. Chase Evans and his cronies just left here. I've a hunch they're headed your way. Any idea why all the commotion?"

"Commotion in regards to?"

"Brooks! Don't be a, a, don't be such a dick."

"Excuse me?"

"I said, don't be such a d–"

"Yes, I heard. It doesn't sound like you though, Frank."

"Francis."

"Francis?"

"It's my name, as if you didn't know. Francis Powell the Third."

"Francis Powell the–oh Christ. I don't have time for this, Frank. What do you want?"

"You, you *wanted* us to lose in court today, didn't you? You wanted to, to make a fool of Ike, didn't you?"

"What? I–"

"Why, Brooks? You promised I'd make partner, you promised you'd leave your wife, just to undermine your own boss? I'm probably going to lose my job now, thanks to you! Oh I'm such a fool!"

"Leave my wife? Frank, have you completely lost your mind?"

"Oh, ha ha!"

"No, Frank, seriously. Are you listening to yourself? Leave my wife for you? Francis Powell the Third? Are you psychotic or something? I'm a happily married man, *straight* man, and you're just some sorry little loser, and you'll never mean a thing to Chase Evans–"

"Don't do this, Brooks–"

"You had some kind of episode Saturday night, maybe–"

"Brooks! Stop! I told them about us."

"Told them *what* about us?"

"Oh, go fuck yourself, Brooks! Really, just go fuck yourself." Francis hung up.

CHAPTER TWELVE

Mike awoke to a darkened living room. It was sweet of the roommates to keep the shades down and let him sleep, even though it must have been close to noon. They would have gotten a real kick out of him, spaced out, collapsing on his couch before dinner and lying there, lifeless, nearly an entire day. He was no different from them, in the end, despite all his high and mighty bullshit. But that wasn't such a terrible thing. Just the reality. He owed Rob, for opening his eyes. Whatever else happened between them yesterday, and whatever might happen in the future, he owed him for that.

He sat up, planted his feet on the carpet, gathered his blanket around him and stood. His lower back seized up; he groaned and grabbed it with both hands, letting the blanket drop. That shit would kill him, one little assault on his youth at a time. Never again. He looked down: he wore brand new, too tight, bright red briefs he had never seen before. Slowly, carefully, he bent over and gathered the blanket again.

He staggered to the kitchen and found a carafe of old coffee on the gray-tiled counter. He poured it into a sink filled with dirty plates and mugs and bowls and rinsed it. He took another look at the carafe; he picked up the sponge and dish soap and gave it a quick, proper wash. He opened the cupboard next to the sink and took out a bag of grounds, and started a fresh pot in the coffee maker. He stared at it, drumming his fingers on the counter. He looked over at the pile of dirty dishes in the sink. It was an awful lot of dishes. He wasn't the last one to wake up, was he? He was the first. The coffee maker reached a boil after an eternity and began to drip.

He washed out a mug from the sink and stared at it, his eyelids drooping, then closing, his head nodding, then dropping, snapping him awake, reigniting his lower back. The carafe was still filling but he picked it up and poured every drop into the mug and replaced the carafe on the warming plate. He took a sip and burned his tongue. He cursed and put the cup down.

On the far end of the counter was a half-smoked joint in a glass ashtray bearing the mark of a local dive. It was supposed to help with Ecstasy withdrawal. That was what they said, anyway; he had no way of knowing and no interest in finding out. He picked up the mug again, blew on the coffee, took a cautious sip.

"Oh, shit!"

He was supposed to get breakfast with Rob this morning. This morning? Yesterday morning? He ran back to the couch and found his phone between the cushions. He opened it to a new text from Rob.

you were right breakfast too early what was I thinking lunch?

Mike replied, *ha ha did I say that. Sounds good 1:00 patio 24/7 diner?*

...

...

...

perfect don't forget your sketches

Sketches? Sketches? How did Rob know about the sketches? Mike sat on the couch and closed his eyes. He sat on a different couch, a black leather one, and Rob sat beside him, a hand on his knee.

Well, what would you really want to do, if you never had to worry about money?

Over in the hall closet near the door he kept an old weather-beaten leather portfolio with all of his sketches, going back to high school. He took it out and unzipped it and set it down on the coffee table in front of the couch. He went back to the kitchen and got his coffee, took another sip, set it down next to the sketches.

He set aside the ones he had never finished, which slimmed down the pile by a lot. Quite a lot. He went through the wrestler sketches and picked the best two, with real faces, good faces, faces showing the strain and effort and pain. One of Marius, asleep in bed, at their happiest moment. There was Feliciano, with his fabulous shock of hair and cocky grin. A portrait of Chase drawn from memory, of that first night, in the mist. He had to keep it. It was too good to let go.

He collapsed back on the couch. "Okay, that's enough."

He drank some more coffee. He took off his blanket and stood up. He found his duffle bag behind the couch and rummaged through it; everything was hopelessly wrinkled or sweat-stained, or both. He took his coffee with him to the bathroom. He turned on the shower and stared at the spray.

\#

"Asshole!" said Chase.

"Excuse me?" said Ike, through the speaker.

"Oh, sorry, not you, Ike. Someone just cut me off." Chase grumbled, "Fucking west side."

"So Ike I'm looking at this redline of your employment agreement," said Rachel, sitting crammed into the back seat, "and it looks like they deleted the entire section about termination for cause."

"What?!" Carlos shouted. "When the fuck did they do that?"

Chase looked over at Carlos and shook his head.

"Ix-nay, ix-nay," Rachel whispered.

"What do I know from termination for cause?" said Ike. "Brooks said there was some little change he had to make about the pension, some new regulation. No one said anything about termination."

"Ike!" said Carlos. "How the fuck could you–"

"Hey-hey-hey!" said Rachel.

Chase reached over and stuck his palm over Carlos's mouth.

"Ike," said Chase, "you have to understand, this means the Board can just flat out fire you for no reason."

"Me?! Fire me?! Why would they do that?"

"Which is why, and I hate to have to keep reminding you, Ike, but you really need to run these things by me before you sign them."

"Well, excuse me, bub, I hope you don't mind if I'm busy trying to grow this business and I don't have time for all your lawyer mumbo–"

"Yes, I get it, Ike, I get it. We all get it. So have Janet set up a videoconference? With the Board of Directors? Oh shit I'm doing it again. And let's figure out what we have to do now."

"You'll be here when?"

"With this traffic, probably sometime tomorrow."

"Terrific. We'll need some time to find those idiots." Ike hung up.

"Jesus God, Carlos!" said Chase. "I assume you're gonna be a little more chill when we get to his office?"

"He's gonna blame us when he gets shit-canned from his own fucking company."

"He won't get shit-canned, dude."

"Yeah, dude," said Rachel.

Carlos laughed. "Oh, shit, I almost forgot."

"What?" said Chase and Rachel.

"You won't fucking believe what Frank–oh, pardon me, *Francis*–told me."

\#

Opening right onto the busy main boulevard, the patio of the 24/7 Diner boasted the best views in Boys Town. From early breakfast to late dinner, gym rats worked the wide sidewalk like a runway, trying out their new outfits, pre- and post-workout; boys out shopping swung their new bags with prominent labels, maxing out their credit cards; boys still recovering from their last bender moseyed along, trying to stay vertical. After dinner, the same wide sidewalk teemed with another crop of boys, dressed up for another night out, another night of fresh possibilities. Or at least some drinks.

Rob sat at a table in the sun, out of the shadow of a green and white umbrella, smiling behind his sunglasses and pink baseball cap. He wore a black t-shirt that read "I'm With Stupid," with the arrow pointing down. He sat up and waved as Mike approached on the sidewalk, portfolio under his arm.

Mike waved back, jogged up to the patio, and traversed over to the table. He stooped over Rob and kissed him on the cheek; Rob took Mike's chin and kissed him back, on the lips. He held Mike there a moment, looking at him as if, in their time apart, the terms had changed, and "no strings attached" had always been just three little words.

"Dude," said Rob, "you need to find some clean clothes."

"I know, right?" Mike took the chair in the shade and set his portfolio on the round white table.

Rob leaned forward. "So how do you feel?"

"I definitely need some more coffee. And I'm kind of feeling like, I don't know, chocolate chip waffles or something? Is that weird?"

"Oh, that's the weed."

"What weed?"

"Duh, the joint I gave you before you left. You know, to come down easier."

Mike shivered with a little wave of panic. "There was a half-smoked joint in the kitchen . . ."

"Well, there ya go." Rob propped his sunglasses on his baseball cap and opened the portfolio and sifted through the sketches. "These are nice, Mike, really nice." He looked at Mike and nodded his approval. "Oh, wow. This one. Smoldering. It's Chase, right?" He held up the portrait, showed it to Mike, then scanned it again. "I feel like I've seen this guy out."

"Did I tell you about Chase?"

"Mmm, more or less."

"More or less? What do you mean, more or less?"

"No, I definitely know this guy. Chase, yeah. I think I might have even met him once or twice. Kind of a glad-hander?"

"A what?"

"You know, man about town, always introducing himself, striking up a conversation, remembering your name. You know. Charmer."

"Yeah . . ."

Another wave of panic crashed over Mike. A horn honked. He looked up; a waiter in a white tunic and long black bangs and mirrored blue sunglasses poured his coffee. The waiter stared at him, looking away just in time to stop pouring before the cup overflowed. He flipped his bangs out of his face.

"No, wait, I know you," said the waiter. "You work over at Radioactive, right? It's . . . Mike?"

Mike recovered himself and smiled. "That's right. I'm sorry, I don't–"

"Kolton. No worries, baby, you must meet a million guys over there. Can I just say? Love how you're rocking that beard, Mike."

"Thanks, Kolton." Mike picked up his coffee. "Still trying to work up to the good stations."

"I mean, you know wherever you're at, *that's* the good station, right?"

"I like it! I'll try to remember that one."

"Listen, boy, I'm not talkin' philosophy. I'm saying, you're, like, Mike, you're *that* guy. The boys go there for you."

Mike looked over at Rob, shrugged, and looked at Kolton. "Oh, that's really sweet. Totally not true, but really sweet."

Kolton exhaled from his lower lip, sending his bangs flying upward again. He handed them their menus. "I'll be back in a minute, boys."

Rob rolled his eyes at Kolton walking away, then at Mike.

"Everywhere you go, Mike. I can't even. No wonder your boy Chase chickened out on you."

"Chickened out? That's not what happened, Rob."

"Yeah, yeah. I know what you *think* happened, but I'm telling you, that's *not* what happened."

"What do I think happened?"

"You think he called you a whore."

Somehow Mike's panic subsided a little.

"And what do *you* think happened?"

Rob put his sunglasses back on and eased back in his chair. "I think . . . I think your boy Mr. Popular is so used to being the center of attention, he was afraid he'd be competing with you."

Mike stared into his coffee. "That's ridiculous."

"Me though? I don't care. You can have all the attention you like."

Mike looked up. He winked. "Thanks."

"You're welcome. Anyway."

"Anyway."

Rob put the sketches back and zipped up the portfolio.

"Anyway, going out of town tomorrow, be back in a few days. Mind if I hang on to this for a minute?"

#

Billy was totally used to it. If he wanted to talk to Chase, he was the one who called. He was the one who texted. Sometimes it even took a few tries, but Chase was the busier one, and that was just how it worked. Every once in a while, he just wanted to give up, wait, let Chase come to him, but he could never wait long enough, and he always caved. Chase probably didn't even realize. But this time, it should have been different. This time, Chase was going to call, tell him everything, because he couldn't help himself. Saturday night was a big step for him, basically the perfect guy, the guy fate brought to him, twice. A guy he was so into, he forgot his best boy even existed for a minute. It was a big fucking deal.

Billy was being stupid. There was no way Chase wasn't going to call this time. He just had to wait a little longer. Chase and Mike spent the night together. Chase had to get ready for his motion hearing. Chase had to appear at his motion hearing. Chase had to go back to the office, deliver the good news or the bad news to the client and the team, plan the next move. After that. After that he would call.

Billy stared at the phone like some loser crushing on some boy. He picked it up. He put it down.

"*Cabron.*"

He picked it up and dialed.

"Billy, hey," said Chase, "can I hit you back? Just pulling into Ike's office, got a meeting with him, and then maybe after?"

"Uh, okay. Hey, where's his office? Maybe we can meet up?"

"Oh, great idea. How about 24/7 Diner, like, around two, two-thirty? I've got Carlos and Rachel with me."

"Hollah!" said Rachel.

"Who's Billy?" said Carlos.

Chase and Rachel yelled, their words lost over the crackling connection.

"Kidding, you guys! I wasn't *that* wasted."
"Yes you were!" Chase and Rachel cried in unison.
\#

Francis sat back in his chair, stroking his lightly stubbled chin. Perhaps he had pushed Brooks a tad too far, caused him to say things he didn't mean. It made perfect sense, really, as Francis was quite a changed man, not what Brooks had grown accustomed to. Certainly it made a lot more sense than what Brooks had blurted out in the heat of the moment, that business about being psychotic or what have you. Fiddle-faddle to that.

When Atlas called him crazy, that was more euphemistic, as in, you're quite an intriguing person, which was accurate and flattering. To be perfectly fair, Atlas was stung with jealousy at the time, which was silly, since, though Francis did call out Mike's name, it was merely out of the confusion brought on by the drugs (oh, and perhaps Francis was a tad in love with the man, but who wasn't?). Indeed, was it not more likely that Atlas was the crazy one? The straps, the candle wax, *etcetera*, those were all Atlas's idea. Francis was merely playing along, a good sport. And it was Atlas who, out of pettiness and spite, abandoned him there, tied to the bed. Yes, Atlas returned, sheepish, wracked by guilt, but not until late the next morning. Not until Francis had had time to ponder the many poor choices that had delivered him to this most desperate moment in his already sorry existence.

Francis got out of his chair and stood up straight. His chest was throbbing. He looked down at his new pink shirt: nothing was amiss, at least nothing anyone could observe. He stepped through his doorway and checked the hallway. He stepped back inside, closed the door, turned, and leaned against it. He unbuttoned his shirt and gingerly removed it and placed it over the back of the guest chair. He looked down at his chest: the bandage was intact, sticking to his raw skin, light blood stains visible but dry to the touch. He peeled back a tiny corner but could go no farther. Better to tolerate the pain that already plagued him than to risk even greater pain.

He put his shirt back on, buttoned it, and sat back down at his desk. He swiveled around to face the window; in the reflection stood Justin, behind the glass wall, staring right at him.

#

"My ace legal team!" said Ike, a spring in his step, before Chase, Rachel, and Carlos had even stepped through the double-doors to his sprawling office. "Please, over here."

He guided them into the living room at one end, with overstuffed couches and wing chairs upholstered in gold- and white-striped silk, and a heavy mahogany coffee table, all sitting atop an ornate Persian rug in subdued hues of red and yellow and blue, which in turn sat atop a dark walnut floor. A big screen on the wall ran Bloomberg, its stock tickers flashing green and red.

Ike shepherded them to a couch and eased himself into a wing chair opposite them and crossed his legs.

"So, Chase."

"Yes, Ike."

"How's Mike?"

Rachel leaned forward. "Wait, did I miss something?"

"Did you ever!" said Ike.

"Ike," said Carlos, "we've got a somewhat urgent–"

"Hush, hush." Ike waved him off. "It can wait."

Rachel smiled at Chase. "Yes, Carlos, it can wait."

"Ike," said Chase, "I'm afraid Carlos is right. The fate of your–"

"I'm telling you, boy-chick, it can wait! So . . ." Ike set his chin in his hands.

Chase exhaled. "Mike is fine, Ike. Just fine."

Ike rubbed his hands together. "It makes me so happy to see you so happy, my boy. Sharon can't wait to have you two over."

"That's very kind of you, Ike. Really."

"Oh, nonsense! You're like a son to me, Chase. Two sons! Such fine young men, both of you. You know, we only have girls, Sharon and I."

Ike bowed his head slightly, looking for a moment as if he might actually shed a tear. It was possible, probable even, that the old softie had become more emotionally invested in Mike than Chase ever was. The poor man was going to die of a broken heart when Chase came clean to him. Obviously, now was not the time.

"Thanks, Ike. I don't know what to say."

Chase saw Mike, back turned and heading out the door, black duffel back over his shoulder. He looked out the window, down at the country club golf course; he shook his head to clear away the memory. Now was definitely not the time.

"Well then!" said Ike. He sat forward and picked up a remote and aimed it at the big screen. One by one, the screen split into four smaller screens, each with a different middle-aged man in a dark gray business suit sitting at a conference table, a space age, triangle-shaped voice station in front of him. "Good afternoon, gentlemen."

Each man chimed in with "Good afternoon, Ike."

Ike introduced the four Board members, in New York, San Francisco, Chicago, and Houston, to his three lawyers.

"Where is the General Counsel?" New York asked.

"Ah!" said Ike. He stepped back to his desk and pressed a button on the phone. "Janet, please show the gentleman in!"

"Right away, Ike."

Ike turned around and faced the screen again. "Now, as we discussed on the phone, we scored a big victory today, thanks to these three brilliant lawyers. As a result, our settlement posture against Syndicated is much improved! Wouldn't you agree, gentlemen?"

Each man nodded.

"Wouldn't you agree, gentlemen?"

Each man piped up, more or less at once, projecting his own version of "Absolutely!"

"So yes, we had to spend a little money, but it was an excellent investment and it is already paying dividends. Am I right, gentlemen?"

"Absolutely!"

Ike walked over to the double doors and opened them just as Brooks Marshall raised a hand to knock. He swung his arm around Brooks's neck and walked him into the living room. "Please, Brooks, have a seat." He indicated another wing chair.

Brooks smiled, nodded his hellos and took a seat. He looked up at the busy screen and squinted in confusion.

"It seems odd, then, doesn't it," said Ike, "that my General Counsel would try to convince you to get rid of me, no?"

Brooks's face turned ashen. The Board Members cleared their throats, or coughed, or fidgeted in their chairs.

"Mr. Evans has a theory," said Ike. "Chase?"

"I do? Uh, yes. I do." Chase sat up. "Yes, yes, I do. I have a theory."

Chase looked at Rachel. Rachel widened her eyes and shook her head. He looked at Carlos. Carlos widened his eyes and shrugged and shook his head. He looked at Ike. Ike smiled and nodded.

"Into the camera, please," said Ike.

"Uh, right," said Chase. Chase found the camera in the corner above the screen. He stood up. "Now." He was Chase Evans. He was always prepared, even when he wasn't. "We know that Mr. Marshall very much expected us to lose this motion today. Right, Mr. Marshall? Brooks?" Chase turned to glare at him. "Brooks?"

Brooks looked at Chase, then at Ike, glowering back at him, then at the screen. "I will say I was, uh, pleasantly surprised, yes."

"Pleasantly surprised," said Chase. "Uh huh. Or maybe disappointed? That you lost your big chance to make a fool of Ike, and get him fired?"

"And get me fired!" said Ike, his face reddening.

"That's ridiculous," said Brooks.

"Well why else would you have revised Ike's employment agreement?"

"His employment agreement? Now hold on, Chase." Brooks turned to Ike. "Ike, I would never—"

"Oh," said Chase, "but there's more. We also know that Mr. Marshall made some, uh, some *promises* to one of my associates, Mr. Sutcliffe, in exchange for which Mr. Sutcliffe persuaded Ike to bring the breach of contract claim in the first place. I will spare you the precise details of those promises, unless Mr. Marshall would like to share them himself?"

"Okay, that is insane, Chase. I have no idea what you're talking about."

"Promises, by the way, which he was in no position to keep. Unless . . ." Chase looked at Ike.

"Go on, Chase," said Ike.

"Unless he, Mr. Marshall, unless he had the support of someone . . ."

"All right, all right," said Brooks. "You can stop. I don't need to hear any more of this bullshit. It was Syndicated. Okay? Happy?"

"Syndicated?" said Chase. "Yes. Of course. Syndicated."

"Syndicated!" Ike took a step toward Brooks.

Brooks rose from his chair.

"Rat bastard!" said Ike. "Sonofabitch! Everything you have, it's because I gave it to you! And you go and stab me in the back! Syndicated?!" He took another step.

Carlos rose and put himself between the two men.

Brooks spoke over Carlos's shoulder, stepping backward. "You were going to run this company into the ground, Ike, with all your vendettas and petty personal intrigues. I had to do *something*."

"Like what?" said Ike. "Fire me from my own company, and, and take my place, I suppose? Because *you* know more than jack shit about running a business?"

"And sell the company to Syndicated, Ike, and make us both very, very rich men."

"WHAT?!" Ike made a move to step around Ricardo as Brooks backed himself against the double doors.

"Ike!" said Chase.

Ike stopped and looked over at Chase. Chase tilted his head toward the screen. Ike looked up. He pointed at Brooks.

"This? This is who you want leading my company? Gentlemen?"

"Certainly not."

"Absolutely not."

"I hardly think . . ."

"Never could imagine . . ."

"Under the circumstances," said San Francisco, "we may want to consider terminating our General Counsel."

"Unbelievable!" said Brooks. "What a bunch of—"

"Consider?!" said Ike. "I insist! I'm still CEO. It's still my company! Why don't we vote on it now? All in favor say 'aye'!"

"Aye!" said the four at once.

"Thank you, gentlemen!"

Ike switched the screen back to Bloomberg. He turned, sniffed, and tapped Carlos on the shoulder. Carlos stepped out of the way. Ike inched closer to Brooks. Brooks kept his eyes glued to Ike while behind him he slid a trembling hand along the double doors, up, down, sideways. Ike brought his face right up to Brooks's face. He smiled, grabbed the doorknob, and turned it. The door fell open. Brooks slipped out. Ike closed the door behind him.

Ike turned and smiled and wiped his hands.

"Good riddance to bad rubbish!"

"My God," said Rachel, "what a worm!"

"Well, my dear friends," said Ike. "You know what they say. You come at the king, you make sure and hit him!"

Carlos laughed. "You best not miss."

"What?"

"You come at the king, you best—"

"That's right, Ike," said Chase, as he placed a hand on Carlos's shoulder. "You make sure and hit him. You come at the king, you make sure and hit him."

"Exactly," said Ike.

"Exactly." Chase looked at Carlos and smiled.

\#

Billy walked from the office to the 24/7, wearing jeans and a t-shirt and Adidas; if you were one of the higher-ups, every day was casual day at the LGBT Center. If you were one of the higher-ups, you took your lunch whenever you wanted, for however long you wanted. Unless there was some big meeting, and there was hardly ever some big meeting. You could even grab a beer or whatever if you wanted, not that he wanted.

As he got closer, more boys crowded the wide sidewalk, pretty busy for a Monday. Once upon a time, all of two months ago, Billy would have been in a bit of a haze, nursing a chemical hangover from Saturday night, reliving the dancing and the cruising and the hookup, maybe even dragging the hookup along with him, if they clicked enough. But that was a different era. He wasn't going out alone, though there were plenty of Saturday nights when he came this close. You get used to doing things a certain way, you can't just snap your fingers and do it a different way. He should have at least tried, just to see if the vibe was the same without his boy Chase. To see if he still had game, which no doubt he still did.

He walked up the two steps to the landing, then two steps to the door, and headed inside. The tall, skinny, heavily tattooed host stood behind a white acrylic desk, stacking menus and straightening receipts, in front of a big blue neon sign that read "24/7" in cursive script. The music was louder inside, but harder to hear, because of the crowd noise bouncing off the walls and the warehouse-style ceiling.

"We're gonna be four," said Billy, "but I'm not sure when they're getting here. Anything on the patio?"

"Sorry, honey," said the host, "nothing at the moment. I can put you on the list?"

"I'm so sad! I was really looking forward to sitting in the sun. Such a gorgeous day!"

"Totally. Why don't you take a two-top out there until your posse gets here?" The host hooded his eyes and looked out the window. "Yeah, there's still one in the sun."

"Sweet. Thanks, baby."

The host handed him a menu.

Billy headed back outside; he spotted the empty two-top, among a row of two-tops one step above the rest of the patio, behind a railing. On the way over he saw a good-looking white guy sitting just outside the shadow of his umbrella taking in the rays, wearing a pink baseball cap and sunglasses and that tired old "I'm With Stupid" t-shirt, as if the arrow pointing down made it any less tired. The guy looked familiar, and Billy must have looked familiar too, because the guy looked right at him, and kept on looking as he walked by. Nothing to write home about; you could hide a lot behind a baseball cap and shades.

Billy took the chair facing into the sun. The guy turned his head, eyes peering just over his shades, and quickly turned away. Billy didn't flinch, just read his menu; he was so not thirsty right now. Too bad for you, white boy.

His phone vibrated.

Hey hijo sorry meeting running late. Drink later maybe?

The last-minute flake-out. Billy was used to that, too, and the odds on that drink were too low to bet on, but at least the boy was trying. A good sign.

It was a nice day, he had his table in the sun, plus he was hungry. He got up, glanced over at I'm With Stupid but got only the back of his head, and went back inside.

"Just gonna be me, turns out."

"Oh, okay," said the host, "go ahead and keep the two-top then. I'll send Kolton out in a sec."

"Thanks, baby."

Actually it was better this way. It would have been a little awkward totally not cruising I'm With Stupid for an hour and also hanging out kicking it all legalistic with Chase and Rachel and Carlos at the same time. Billy stepped back outside and totally didn't look over to where I'm With Stupid was sitting, but he did happen to notice that the chair was empty. He turned and caught a glimpse of I'm With Stupid heading down the steps to the sidewalk, carrying an old leather portfolio, jogging like he was late for an appointment or something. Billy spent approximately one second being minimally disappointed, then he headed to his table. He took maybe three steps. From out of the shadows, like something in a dream, Mike appeared in front of him, with a sweet, shy smile on his face.

"Oh my God, Mike!" Billy gave him a big hug. "That's so funny, I was supposed to meet Chase here, did you guys . . . boy, you look a mess! Late night Saturday, right?"

"Well . . ."

"*And* Sunday?"

"Uh . . ."

"That's cool, you don't have to tell me. But your friend, I'm With Stupid, is he single? Is he cute without the shades and baseball cap? Oh my God, that's so rude, never mind."

"Ha. Okay."

"But seriously, is he single?"

"You're meeting Chase here?"

"Yeah, we were, but he got busy with work. You know how that is already probably, right? I'm sure he had to get an early start Sunday morning? So yeah we might be getting a drink later. You should text him. Oh, sorry, you don't need me to–"

"Billy."

Mike got a gentle but firm grip on the sides of Billy's upper arms, and he looked at Billy in that way that he had of looking at you, and Billy felt his heart breaking a little.

"Billy, what did Chase tell you?"

"Exactly nothing, *hijo*. Not one word. So busy, right? Like, it's just me, his bestest bestie, but whatever, okay?"

"Billy."

Something was off. Mike's clothes were wrinkled and sweat-stained, like he hadn't change since Saturday. He smelled like cigarettes and maybe weed. He looked around, but not at anything, just out in space.

"Mike. What is it? What's wrong?"

Mike blinked and came back to earth. "It's fine. Everything is fine, Billy."

"Wait. Are you, I mean, are you *with* that guy?"

"What guy?"

"Mike. Come on."

"Oh, Rob? Oh, no, no! Well, I mean, well, no. He's, no, he's a friend. He's gonna help me out finding a real job."

"But why did he just . . . I mean, uh. Well, a real job, that's great."

"Yeah."

"So."

"So."

"Okay, so I'm gonna go sit down. I'm starving! So I'll see you soon, okay?"

"Sure, yeah."

Billy gave Mike another hug, held it for a second, dug his chin into Mike's shoulder. Mike held him too, rubbed his back a little, the way a good friend would do. They let each other go, and Billy watched as Mike walked down the stairs and out to the sidewalk, standing tall, chin up, turning heads, like always, even though he looked a little bit homeless.

Rob Massing

PART THREE

CHAPTER THIRTEEN

Mike gave the doorman his name, and the doorman gave him the keys.

He took the elevator up and let himself into the apartment. There was the black leather couch, right where they'd left it. He set down his duffle bag, took off his shoes and socks, and dropped himself onto the couch, which exhaled with his weight. At his feet was a plush, shiny gray rug; he sank his feet in and wiggled his toes. The rug spread out before him, reaching about halfway across the room, coming to a stop just below a big, black television, hanging from micro-thin cables, with the brand name in baby blue floating around on the screen. He picked up the remote sitting on the arm of the couch and chose a button at random; the television ascended noiselessly into the ceiling.

He laughed: got it on the first try.

The television's absence revealed a panoramic view of the twinkling west side through the wide window: long, bright boulevards, dotted with low-rise office buildings; low, unlit hills in the distance; beyond them, the black ocean, blending into the black sky.

He got up and went to the window and placed a hand on the cool glass. Somehow he had missed all of this the last time. He didn't deserve it. Rob was a good guy, but that was the problem. Rob had no idea what he was in for. *You can have all the attention you want.* He probably even thought he meant it. They all did, until they didn't.

Mike turned around. The place was spotless, gleaming, and it smelled like jasmine. A bouquet of sunflowers in a white vase sat on a table for two next to him. There was more leather furniture, glossy wooden side tables with polished white terra cotta lamps with light blue shades, their bulbs on low.

He found a hallway and a door. He opened it into a bedroom, made up for a guest, with a blond wood chest five-drawers high and a carpeted walk-in closet, empty except for the dozens of gleaming chrome hangers. On the bed, on top of a thick white comforter, were neatly stacked piles of jeans, slacks, polo shirts in several colors, and t-shirts, and a note.

Mike-

Feel free to borrow these. I think we are the same size or close enough. Back Friday or Saturday. My cousin Ken may be crashing here at some point. He's straight but cool ha ha.

Kisses,

Rob

As Mike went to set the note down, he saw, sticking out of the back pocket of a pair of jeans, a thin wad of cash.

He sat down at the edge of the bed and buried his head in his hands. This wasn't Rob's doing. Mike had arranged this, without even trying. Why was he so weak, so passive? Why did he always follow the path of least resistance? All he had to do was get up, go home, and take his clothes to the laundry room right there in the building. But the roommates. The dirty dishes. The old carpet. The stale smell. The stale smell of going nowhere.

He could offer to pay rent. He could buy some groceries and some wine and cook dinner when Rob got back. He wasn't totally useless. He didn't *really* know what Rob was hoping for anyway. He didn't really know what *he* was hoping for anyway.

He turned on the light in the bathroom. It gave a soft, amber-white glow; he stepped onto the gray slate floor, which warmed his feet. In the mirror stood a man he barely recognized: an old, homeless man with a drawn, tired face, circles under his eyes, a scraggly beard, and dirty, wrinkled clothes. He stripped down to his birthday suit: at least the body was mostly intact. There was one square, shallow sink in the center of the long granite counter, two neatly folded hand towels, and a stainless steel faucet with no handles. He placed a hand under the faucet and the water began to run. He dipped both hands in and splashed his face, ran some water through his hair, and combed it back with his fingers. He picked up a hand towel and dried off. He gave himself a light punch on the chin and smiled. He leaned in closer and tried the smile again.

Back in the bedroom, he put on a pair of jeans and a t-shirt. They fit well enough and felt soft and smooth and smelled fresh. He went out to the kitchen. He pressed a button on the wall, which turned on some tiny lights in the ceiling, then another button, which turned on three reproduction Art Deco pendants hanging over the island. A black granite island, surrounded by white, glass-fronted cabinets, above and below, and the works: six-burner stove, double-wide refrigerator, wine fridge, low profile microwave. He pressed a third button: mellow dance music came through speakers in the kitchen and the living room. It was like one of those reality shows where the first house they show you fulfills your wish list but is out of your price range.

He could make some dinner, just for practice. There was a nice grocery store nearby, within walking distance, too nice for an aging party-boy-slash-bartender renting a couch from three aging party boys-slash-wanna-be-actors, but the bare minimum for a man of independent means, occupation unknown, who took off to an undisclosed location and left him to mind the penthouse in his absence.

Some guys just left money lying around in their back pockets, without thinking; it meant that little to them. The jeans Mike put on were just the easiest to grab, from the top of the pile. He could just as easily take out the cash and toss it on the kitchen counter. He had cash of his own; if it wasn't enough for fancy groceries, he had a credit card, and he paid down most of it every month. He had plenty.

He took out the cash and tossed it on the kitchen counter. Easy. There was something else in the pocket. Probably a reward for his resolve, because that was how the world worked. Said no one, ever. He pulled it out: a plastic bag, with a little pink tablet.

CHAPTER FOURTEEN

Finally, some rain. Every year they lived on the edge of disaster; every year was the year that the drought was about to overwhelm everything, felling every tree and turning every lawn brown and leaving the least among them to die of thirst. Now they would say yes, it's something, but it's nowhere near enough. And if it ever got to be enough, they would warn of flooding: the cement-lined river, one of the great public engineering projects of the last century, was out of date and past capacity. And when the floods receded, they would worry about the next fire season, because all that rain meant thick new growth, kindling waiting for a single match.

The storm swept across the windows in waves, the clouds so thick you couldn't see the buildings across the street. In his chair, eyes closed, Chase listened. The sound it made tapping against the windows was not unlike the sound it made tapping on the roof of the house he grew up in. He used to sit in the living room for hours and watch the drops dancing on the swimming pool in the backyard. After the storm passed you could look down the Valley's biggest streets and see so clearly, all the way to the mountains so many miles away–sometimes, if it got cold enough, with snow on top.

When he made partner, they presented him with a three-foot bamboo stick, which made a terrific racket when you picked it up, as the pebbles inside rolled from end to end. They said it was a native American rainstick, for making it rain, a tribute to his uncanny power to bring in business. It still sat in the corner, to remind him, to remind everyone, of his value to the firm.

It was quite a day, the day he made partner, with champagne, and too many glowing toasts to count, and back-slapping, and stock tips, and real estate advice, and a marked increase in the volume of ass-kissing. And quite a night, too. Out on the dance floor he must have given off a new scent, the pheromones of monthly draws and origination points, because they fell over themselves to get a whiff. He had his pick that night, and ever since.

In the end it was pretty comical, if you looked at it right, Chase and Billy talking over the din of the weekday happy hour crowd, each trying to gently break the news to the other. Good on I'm With Stupid, well done, snagging Mike on the rebound in record time, or maybe quietly keeping him in his back pocket all along. It didn't matter either way. Poor Billy was truly crushed, rationalizing, maybe they were just friends, blah blah, because it was more than just the failure of a little affair that Billy had to accept; it was the failure of his whole worldview. All that bullshit about fate, his undying belief in romantic love, despite all evidence to the contrary. Knowing Billy, he would eventually forget how wrong he had been and start believing all over again. But then, you had to love that about Billy.

Rachel entered Chase's office, with her arms crossed and her shoulders hunched, rubbing her sleeves as if still feeling the cold from outside. Her black hair was matted down, her

211

off-white wool sweater damp around her neck. She gently closed the door behind her.

"So should we call him Frank, or Francis?"

"His name is Frank."

"But don't you think–"

"I'm not letting him dictate the terms of his own surrender."

"Chase!" Rachel pushed her hair back behind her shoulders. She returned to rubbing her arms and began to pace. "Do you have to be so–"

A loud surge of rain splashed against the window.

"So what, Rachel? So rational?"

"Heartless." She stopped pacing and set her hands on her hips. "You fucked it up with Mike, didn't you?"

Chase blinked at her. "Excuse me?"

"The way you shut Ike down when we were in his office. I know you, Chase. You found some excuse."

"Wow. Just wow, Rachel. You really need to back off."

"And why is that?"

"This may come as a shock to you, but some guys aren't what they seem."

"That's right, Chase. That's right. You might just have to settle for a real person. Not some fantasy with no faults whose world totally revolves around you."

"What? Is that really what you think of me?"

"Look, Chase. I adore you. I think you're great. Any man would be lucky to have you."

"Yeah, blah blah blah."

"But even you can't expect perfection."

"I know that."

"I don't think you do though. I think you set impossible standards that nobody can meet, because you don't want to get hurt. Because underneath all that . . . you know, all that *Chase*, there's a big heart, and it's vulnerable, and that scares the shit out of you. But it's also the best part of you."

Chase laughed. "A heart? Who, me?"

"Crazy, right?"

He got up and went to the window. Dense, dark clouds swirled by, no end in sight. "I thought he was different, Rachel, I really did. No. Fuck!" He pounded a fist into his palm. "We're not talking about this. I can't–"

"You *know* he's different. He's the real deal. You can feel it. You're feeling it right now. Aren't you?"

"I mean . . ."

"Aren't you?"

"Just because I feel it, doesn't mean it's–"

"Yes it does, Chase! Stop thinking so damn much! Just listen to your heart. What's the worst that could happen?"

"Ha ha, really? The worst that could happen? Well, once he sees past the money and the penthouse and the gym body, he might figure out that there's not that much to me."

Rachel gasped. "Chase! You don't seriously believe that! My God, Chase, you're so much more than the money and the–"

The door swung open. Francis stood in the doorway, striking a pose, sporting another new outfit, powder blue dress shirt and dark blue slacks with a subtle plaid pattern.

"Hello, all. How'd'ya like me?"

Chase did his best to look neither at Francis nor at Rachel, but still he choked on a little spasm of laughter. Out of the corner of his eye he caught Rachel having only slightly more success.

"Hello, *Francis*." Chase walked across to him and patted him on the shoulder. "Come on in. Let's get this over with."

"Get what over with?"

Chase guided Francis to a guest chair and stepped around behind his desk. Francis slid out his chair and sat down. Rachel gave the door a nudge to close it and took the other guest chair.

"New suit?" said Francis.

Chase unbuttoned the jacket and sat down. "Special occasion."

213

"Well, you look very handsome."

"Jesus, Francis, don't–oh, never mind. So! On the plus side, there's, well, you're good at research, you put in the hours, you work hard. On the minus side, after nine years with the firm your writing is still mediocre, you've never brought in a single dollar in business. You exposed the firm to a huge risk and nearly destroyed my relationship with my biggest client. Does that–oh, also, lately you've been creeping out the staff. Does that sound about right?"

"Ah," said Francis. "I see what you're getting at."

"You do. That's great. So look. I've spoken with the rest of the Executive Committee, and we're happy to give you a glowing recommendation, but–"

"Chase, please," said Francis. "Can I just say something?"

Chase looked at Rachel. Rachel looked back, poker-faced.

"Go ahead, Frank. Francis."

"Well, that's just it, Chase, right there! Everything you say is true, but the problem isn't me. It's Frank. *Frank* is the one who's been such a disappointment to the firm, and to you personally, and I'm truly, truly sorry about that. But I'm not Frank, Chase, I'm not. I'm Francis. *Francis.* I'm really . . . if you really knew Francis, *really* knew him, you would see. I think you'd like him. He's, he's . . . he's like you Chase. Yes! He's so much like you. He's charming, and winning, and, and really *quite* attractive–if I do say so myself, ha ha–and, and, and he could be just as good as you at all the other stuff, the, the, the business stuff. I know what I have to do now, I understand, and I know I can do it. You'll see. Just give me a chance, just a little more time, and you'll see."

Rachel opened her mouth to speak but no words came out.

"Uh . . ." Chase took a breath. He squeezed his eyes shut. He opened them and looked at Rachel and shook his head.

"Oh, God, Frank. I'm really . . . I feel bad, I do. I feel like I'm somewhat responsible for this."

"Fear not!" Francis clasped his hands together and laughed. "*I'm* responsible! *I* did this!"

"Okay, now you've lost me," said Chase.

"That old newspaper clipping?"

"Newspaper clipping?"

"Oh, Chase, don't be coy now. You know." Frank winked and aimed his index finger at his temple. "About my father?"

"Aha!" said Rachel, pumping her fist. "I told you it wasn't me!" She turned to Francis. "Wait, what?"

"*I'm* the one who set this all in motion! I gave you that clipping. You used that to needle Frank. Frank freaked out, and . . . voila! Francis!"

"But . . ." said Rachel.

"Francis," said Chase. He stood up. "Frank. I'm sorry about this. Really. But the kind of help you need, I don't think . . ." He picked up the phone. "I think we're done here."

215

CHAPTER FIFTEEN

All the boys and the occasional girl who worked at Radioactive, the bartenders, the barbacks, the cocktail waiters, even the go-go boys, when they wore anything more than a g-string, everyone except the guy outside the bathroom who dealt you a paper towel, to dry yours hands, for which you rewarded him with a dollar, or a fiver if you'd had enough to drink or to vape, for which he rewarded you with a mint, or a bite-sized Snickers, or the indulgence to let you try out your Spanish on him—everyone wore a custom-fitted muscle shirt or tank top, black with a rainbow-colored logo, with the understanding that it was to be removed at each boy's individual discretion, though in a timely fashion, at some stage of the evening's proceedings, so as not to disappoint the straight tourists, who had traveled so far to visit The World's Best Gay Bar three years running, per BuzzFeed.

The tips increased when the shirts came off, an undeniable fact of nature, but there was still an art to maximizing those tips, an art which Mike had only begun to develop. It had something to do with the time of night, the pace and beat and volume of the music, the proximity of the go-go boys, and the size of the crowd, though the last cause had its own set of causes, including, at least to some degree, some unquantifiable something projected into the atmosphere by Mike himself. He dared not call it "sex appeal," and not just because he retained some of the humility his parents had drilled into him, but because it was a tired cliché that denied him any active role in the process, something you either had or you didn't.

"Charm" was a little better, but still too passive. There was a word, there must be a word, for the way he brought them in and made them want to stay, to stay and make a friend out of him, at the very least. "Seduction" wasn't right either, because it implied some insincerity on his part, something transactional and mercenary, and even though somewhere in the back of his mind the idea of a payoff lingered, that idea only got there because he had seen the results, not because he made it his objective. Through some mysterious process he preferred not to understand, for fear of ruining it through self-awareness, *not* making it the objective improved his chances of making it happen.

Except when it rained. The rain, because it was so rare, upended the calculus. Just as the suddenly slick roads rendered so many drivers reckless in their helplessness, the unthinkable prospect of anything less than a full house sent both staff and management into a panic. The veteran, which was not to say old, bartenders left hurried voice mails about the flu or a family emergency, or simply failed to show. Mike though, calm and level-headed and sensing an opportunity, like the understudy who knew the blocking and every line backwards and forwards, and already having earned the respect of his superiors for his consistently low pour cost and high pour speed, suggested himself for the biggest, busiest bar, under the biggest red chandelier, and they handed him the upgrade without the slightest hesitation.

They turned up the music early, and it echoed across the half-empty interior space in front of him, bouncing off the yellow stucco walls and dissipating out to the wet and slippery and abandoned red terra cotta tile patio behind him, and he danced as he shook the drinks, and he stopped to look up and listen, and maybe jut out his butt a little, as he poured them. Ayiesha, officially in charge of the station but all about the flow, leaned back against the counter and observed, arms folded over her chest, t-shirt tied above her midriff, happy to cede the limelight to the hot new virtuoso, since there wasn't yet much of an audience to witness it anyway.

"Hey," she said, barely moving a muscle. "Hey!"

"Ya."

"Where'd you learn to shake your booty like that?"

"Girl I been places."

"Mm-hmm."

"You know it."

The not-crowd huddled in the middle of the interior space, not-dancing, in isolated sets of fours and threes and twos, with the ones hovering within cruising distance of the new sensation Mike, who kept his shirt on but gave them back just enough to keep them thirsty. In the absence of prospects or courage they kept their eyes glued to the videos on the suspended TVs or on the giant screen in the back, on the wall behind an even emptier station. In what passed for a VIP section, a narrow roped-off space with half a dozen leather chairs and two leather ottomans and a brick fireplace, a pair of office-mates wearing ties and no jackets warmed themselves and looked over their shoulders expectantly, each other's company a distant second to the near certainty of someone #fabulousaf joining them any minute now.

A young go-go boy, bored of the sparse and stingy gawkers, abandoned his post on a black box and jumped up on the bar, his calves level with Mike's eyes, but at a respectful distance. He was thin and sinewy, his body not yet overbuilt from too much devotion to the gym and supplements, with dark, curly hair frosted blond, delicate features, and a perpetual snarl that, though juvenile in its execution, managed a certain unintended charm. He undulated and he twirled; his hand gestures said *come on, come over, com'ere*; the eyes in his nodding head said *I want you, you want me, let's do this*; he made all of himself available to anyone who looked, a growing contingent. One step and one bend and one kick at a time, and without disguising his intentions, he made his way over to where Mike worked; an indefinite number of beats after that he stood over him, looking down; he locked his eyes on Mike's and wouldn't let go. The boy was young, very young, early twenties at most, but in those fresh eyes Mike saw wisdom, and secrets, and something to learn.

The boy crouched down, hands on knees, and whispered to him, something unintelligible. Mike leaned in and cupped his ear. The boy came in closer but said nothing; instead, he gave Mike an open-mouthed kiss, raising a minor stir among the onlookers. Mike had a tab to close, or something, but it could wait; he held the kiss and touched the boy's cheek and allowed a hand to creep up the boy's tight, smooth stomach. He pulled himself away and laughed; was the kiss for him or was it for the audience?

The boy licked his lips and stood back up. He turned and faced outward, giving Mike a nice clear view from behind, and shooting back a look over his shoulder that suggested to the patrons trickling in that dancer and bartender were a package deal. He bent his knees and lowered himself until his naked backside nearly touched the counter; he steadied himself with one hand behind him while thrusting his hips up, slowly and repeatedly, an invitation to step up and fondle a leg or grab a knee or, more to the point, tuck a bill or two or five into his crotch. He was good, this boy. He was easy to believe. You wanted to believe.

Mike heard his name and turned his head; an unseen man called out a drink order and repeated his name; Mike searched for him and spotted him and smiled and nodded and put his head down and got to work. He heard his name again, and again; he spotted them and promised they were next and spun past Ayiesha, down to the well and up to the top shelf; the two crossed arms as they reached for adjacent bottles, premium vodka and extra premium vodka, made quick eye contact and smiled and turned around and scooped at the ice. As he placed the glasses on the counter he looked over to where the boy was thrusting, but he was gone, replaced by patrons leaning over and waving, their eyes wide at the sight of the hunky bartender spinning and dancing and reaching with his big arms. Mike peered over, past their stares, and found the boy back in place on his black box, surrounded and smiling his dirty smile and stroking his earnings. The boy caught him looking and stuck out his tongue and winked. Was it the same boy? Had he really been dancing on Mike's counter?

Mike wiped the sweat from his forehead with a cocktail napkin. The sweat from his chest and under his arms made his tight t-shirt even tighter, restricting his movement. He paused, took a step back, planted his feet and wiggled as he lifted the shirt up and over his head. The crowd cheered. He looked over; the boy's back was turned. He tossed the shirt to his barback, who tucked it under a shelf. He looked over again; the boy faced him and looked back, mouth slightly agape.

Mike tried new moves to sell his routine, shrugging and grinding and twisting and sliding as he took orders and mixed and poured and swiped credit cards and handed out receipts and smiled and said "what'll it be chief" and "you got it brother" and "thanks my man." A man took a drink and said "leave it open" and stepped away; the boy–it was the same boy–stepped up to take his place. Mike blinked, but he was still there.

"I want something," the boy said. "Can I have something?" He propped his elbows on the counter.

"Can you . . . uh . . ." Mike looked over at Ayiesha. She held up her thumb and forefinger, a small gap between them.

"Sure, what's your drink?"

"Uhhhhhhhhhm. Vokka?"

"Vodka?"

"Yeah. Vokka."

Mike watched the boy in his peripheral vision as he poured. The boy bounced his head around, eyes closed. Mike handed him his drink.

"Is that it?" the boy asked.

"You're working."

"So are you."

"I'm not drinking."

"I'm not talking about drinking, dude."

"What are you talking about?"

"Come on. Don't make me say. I want to do what you're doing."

"I'm not doing anything."

"But your eyes."

"That's just how they look. Sorry."

"Liar." The boy flipped him a middle finger, turned around, and leaned back against the bar. An older fan grabbed the boy's waist and swayed with him and spoke into his ear; the boy squinted and smiled and spoke into the fan's ear and gently pushed him away.

A change in tempo and a soaring voice stopped Mike mid-pour. He cocked his head: Justin again, the same remix that had played on Rob's car radio; Mike closed his eyes and breathed it in. Was he doomed to think of Rob every time he heard it?

He felt something. He opened his eyes. The boy stood staring at him, as if to answer his question. The boy was like singing a new song when an old one was stuck in your head.

The boy leaned in. "What are you doing after work?"

"Going home."

"Can I go home with you?"

"No."

"Why?"

"I have a rule against bringing boys home. It's not my place."

"Rules are made to be broken."

Mike shook his head and laughed.

#

The storm outside rattled the windows and lit up the sky. Mike hovered over the boy and looked down at him. The boy looked up and stroked Mike's chest.

"You're so jacked, Mike. Will you train with me?"

"No."

"Why?"

Mike leaned down and kissed him.

"Because you're perfect. I don't want you to get too jacked."

"Ugh! You old dudes are always saying shit like that."

"Old dudes?"

"Ha ha ha ha! That's right, Daddy!"

Mike grunted and yanked the boy's arms, sliding him down and making the black leather couch squeak, until his crotch met the boy's face. The boy squinted and slid his finger under the elastic of Mike's black briefs.

"Hmmm."

He nibbled at the fabric, opening his mouth and following the contours of Mike's stiffening cock.

"That's big, Daddy."

Mike threw his head back and groaned. He was nobody's Daddy. But this was his boy. His boy and his alone, tonight. The boy wanted him, wanted his indulgence, wanted to look up to him. That could work, tonight. He looked down into the boy's sad, waiting, pretty eyes, his need so well disguised by a veneer of world-weariness that you had to fear just how deep that need went. But none of that was Mike's problem. Not this boy, not this time. Not tonight.

"You want this big cock, baby?"

"Mm-hmm."

"You want it bad."

"Mm-hmm."

Mike slid his thumbs under the elastic and pulled the briefs down partway, revealing the tip, then a little more. The boy flashed his eyes wide open and lunged for it with his mouth. It slipped away and slapped his face. He sucked in a breath and let out a laugh and lunged again, swallowing a good mouthful. Mike pulled the briefs all the way down; the boy took the rest in his hands. Mike thrust his hips, stuffing more into the boy's mouth, pulling back and thrusting again and again; the boy sucked and slurped, getting it good and wet. Good and wet and way too close. The boy had skillz.

"I want you to come in my face, Daddy. I want you to shoot your load in my mouth. I want to swallow your hot cum. Fuck my mouth, fuck my mouth."

"Oh, fuck." The words, the way he said them, almost begging. Mike pulled out and grabbed his cock and gripped it tight. "Oh, fuck, not yet."

The boy laughed. "You totally want to. I know you do."

Mike took the boy's face in his hands. He bent down and stuck his tongue deep in the boy's mouth.

"I totally want to. I want to shoot all over you, boy."

"Come on, Daddy! Shoot all over me."

The boy pushed Mike's face away and slid down and took Mike's cock into his mouth. He closed his lips around it and sucked. Mike gasped and pulled away with his hips; the boy grabbed Mike's ass with both hands and fought him, flexing his arms tight as he pulled Mike's hips and Mike's cock in, back to his open mouth. He raised his head, forcing himself onto the cock, and wrapped his lips tight. There was nowhere left for Mike to move; pulling his hips back would only make it easier for the boy to suck, and suck, and suck.

"Suck it, suck it–oh fuck oh fuck!" Mike called out. "I'm gonna–oh fuck!" He erupted into the boy's mouth, and the boy held Mike's cock tight with his lips and sucked it in. "Oh fuck oh fuck!" There was more, much more; the boy opened his mouth wide and caught Mike's cum, as much as he could, what didn't shoot up into his face and his hair or down onto his neck and his chest. He closed his mouth and kept sucking, every last drop, and Mike writhed and grunted and shuddered, arching his back and opening his eyes to see another lightning flash, closing them to hear the thunder, opening them to look down at the boy's pretty, cum-covered face.

"Stop, stop!"

But the boy kept sucking, sucking Mike's spent but throbbing cock, smiling up at him, slurping up the cum left on the shaft. Mike grabbed the boy's shoulders and pushed him away. The boy licked his lips and smiled.

"Hope I didn't tire you out too much, Daddy."

"I'm just getting started with you, boy."

Mike got up from the couch, leaned over, and picked the boy up. "Man, you're light as a twig." He carried the boy in his arms, to the bedroom, and tossed him onto the bed. The boy rolled over and pressed his face into the pillow and lifted his ass in the air.

"Oh, fuck," said Mike, "look at your pretty ass."

Mike got behind the boy, on his knees, stared in awe and wonder, and spanked him. He grabbed the boy's cheeks and spread them.

"Eat my ass, Daddy, come on."

"You drive me nuts."

Mike bent down and licked the boy's cheeks, his tight, smooth, hairless cheeks, and circled his way closer. The boy let out a moan, his ache palpable. Mike came in closer still, pressing his tongue down harder, licking and sucking. The boy reached down to jerk himself off. His moans came faster.

"So sweet," said Mike. "Such a sweet little ass."

The boy tasted of briny sweat and musky pre-cum, the pre-cum trickling in tiny drops down the boy's cock as he stroked himself, down to his hairless balls and down along the flesh below his balls. Mike nuzzled it and sucked at it, teasing and poking the tight, tense hole as the boy shivered and cried. Such an angel, this little boy, yet hardly an angel. So much life lived, yet so little. So direct, yet so tentative, wanting so badly and trying so hard not to want at all. How did he end up there, on that black box, one step removed from turning tricks, or maybe not even; maybe this was the obvious thing Mike in his delirium was missing. The boy's pained little whines merged into one long, sustained, soaring groan, of anguish and desperation and delight, and he buried his face in the pillow and groaned and moaned and cried. He mumbled a string of something resembling words.

"What?"

The boy lifted his head. "I said, fuck me. Fuck my ass."

"I'm sorry, you'll have to speak up. Us old dudes are a little hard of hearing."

"Oh, please, Daddy, please, please fuck me!"

"You want me to fuck you, boy?"

"Yeah, Daddy, I want it bad!"

"How bad?"

"So, so bad! Please please please? Give me your cock. Fuck my ass!"

Mike grabbed him at the hips and pulled the boy to him; the front of Mike's thighs pressed up against the back of the boy's, his hard cock pressed up against the boy's tight ass. He stretched his arms down along the boy's back and held him by the neck. He turned the boy's face to him and kissed him, filling his mouth with the boy's sweet, cum-soaked tongue. The boy took his mouth away and turned his head; Mike grabbed it and turned it back to him and got his tongue into the boy's mouth. The boy took Mike's tongue and sucked it, and they kissed as Mike worked his cock into the crack between the boy's cheeks.

"Fuck me, Daddy. Fuck my ass."

Mike held his cock and pushed the tip in, flesh into flesh.

The boy took rapid short breaths and gritted his teeth and cried.

"It's so fucking big, Daddy."

"You're so fucking tight. You want more?"

"Oh, yeah, please please, give me more. Ow, fuck! Ow!"

Mike pushed a little bit in and pulled a little bit out, and each time the boy let out a cry, and as Mike pushed in deeper, into the boy's soft, tight flesh, the boy raised his body up, taking more and more. The boy pushed up until his arms were straight and his upper body hovered over the bed; Mike held himself up by one arm and let more of his weight fall on the boy's back. He took the other arm away; his full weight forced his cock all the way in.

"Oh fuck oh fuck," they said.

He stroked the boy's chest with both hands, stroked his stomach, grabbed the boy's cock; they stroked the boy's cock together as they fucked, the stroking matching the rhythm of the fucking, the boy's cock getting slicker as his pre-cum flowed.

The boy's arms bent and collapsed and he fell forward with a grunt; Mike fell and grunted with him, forcing his cock in farther, startling the boy, who let out a shout of almost grateful, almost amused pain. Mike raised himself and raised the boy by the hips; the boy rested his head on the pillow and turned it to one side to breathe. Mike held the boy's waist and fucked him hard and deep, as hard and deep as he could; the boy stroked himself and looked back at him.

"Fuck me, Mike, oh Mike, oh fuck, fuck me!"

"Oh yeah!"

Not Daddy, just Mike, he pulled out and jerked himself off and threw his head back and shuddered and shot his load all over the boy's back, so much cum he had to laugh; the boy jerked himself off and shot his ample load on the sheets, coming and shivering and coming, his shoulders flexing and relaxing and flexing; he turned himself over and got his mouth on Mike's cock, sucking up the last of Mike's load as it dripped out, and Mike laughed and held the boy's head and pulled it away. The boy smiled up at him.

Mike collapsed onto his back and pulled the boy on top of him and kissed him. He stroked the boy's hair with one hand and stroked his ass with the other.

"You're such a good fuck, Mike."

"You know it, baby."

"We should fuck on the reg yo."

Mike laughed. "On the reg yo."

"You got a rule against that too?"

"Nah. I just–"

"The old dude who gave you the keys. Figures. When I get me a setup like this no way am I his little bitch. I bet he's not even hot."

Mike pushed the boy off him. "Fuck you, you little bitch. I'm not his bitch. We're not–"

"Ha ha ha, just kidding, dumb fuck!"

Mike climbed on top of him. "You're fucking hilarious."

"Fuck me, not this tired song again."

"Huh?"

"Justin Timberlake. That old queen is so played out."

From the living room the opening bars wafted through the apartment.

"Shit! Rob!" Mike leapt up and ran to the bathroom, grabbed a towel, and wrapped it around his waist. "Stay right here."

"Yes, Daddy."

He hurried out of the bedroom and shut the door behind him.

A very tall, broad-shouldered man with thick, black hair and black-rimmed glasses, wearing a college sweatshirt and flattering white jeans, danced around the kitchen opening cabinets. As he reached for the refrigerator door he saw Mike and stopped. His eyes widened as he looked Mike up and down.

"Hey!" said the man. "You must be . . ."

"Hey! Mike. And you must be . . ."

"Ken. Oh, sorry, hope I didn't, didn't, uh . . ."

Mike laughed. "Nah, you're good."

Ken closed the refrigerator door and came forward, offering his hand.

"Uh," said Mike, "I'm kinda . . ." He wiped his hands on his towel.

"Huh? Oh! Oh, no worries." Ken laughed. "Anyway, nice to meet you. Looks like Rob's been trading up, hasn't he?"

"Excuse me?"

"I mean this apartment. Trading up, like, because–"

"Ah, okay. Yeah, the place is tricked out."

Ken nodded. "Tricked out. Yeah."

"Yeah."

"So . . ."

"So . . ."

"Look, man, you don't have to worry about, um . . ." Ken pointed toward the bedroom. "I won't tell Rob about, I mean, whatever, you know, whatever you–"

Mike stepped forward. "I'm not worried, *man*. You can tell Rob whatever you want."

Ken backed off. "Right, right, sorry! Didn't mean to be a dick or whatever. I'm going through some shit right now . . ."

"I mean, the boy came onto me. What choice did I have?"

"Ha! The boy? Like, how old?"

"Mm, I wanna say, I dunno, twenty-two?"

Ken smiled. "Nice!"

Mike hopped up and sat on the kitchen island. "What kind of shit?"

"Huh?"

"You're going through some shit?"

"Oh! Right." Ken opened the refrigerator. "You know, the usual blah blah blah." He grabbed a bottle of beer.

"Hey," said Mike, "would you . . ."

"Oh, sure!" Ken grabbed another bottle. He looked around. "Uh . . ."

Mike slid open a drawer next to him and picked out the bottle opener. Ken took it and opened their beers and handed one to Mike.

"I want to move in together, but she wants me to put a ring on it first. It's *kind* of becoming a thing? She's dropping hints about a deadline."

"How long you together?"

"Two years."

"Ooh, tricky."

"Yeah. And what about you guys?"

"Us guys?"

"You and Rob? I mean, you're moved in already."

"It's not like that. Why, did he say something?"

"No, not much. He's all about lowering expectations."

"That's good, because I'm not staying."

"Ah. The boy?"

"Oh, God no."

"Okay, okay. The boy is more of a symptom."

"Yup."

"Got it."

"How much of that did you hear, anyway?"

Ken winked. "How much of what?"

CHAPTER SIXTEEN

Frank pounded on the red front door. He waited. He paced. He pounded again. He stepped back and looked up, holding up a hand and squinting against the pouring rain. He stepped back a few feet more, slipping and nearly falling backward on the short front steps. All the windows were dark, their white curtains drawn. He turned and walked back down the brick path and turned again at the end of the path to face the house. He shivered; his hair and his work clothes were soaked through. His leather briefcase was soggy and heavy and dripping.

"Brooks! Brooks! Don't be such a fucking coward! Brooks!"

He stood and waited and clenched his fists until his hands ached.

"Brooooooooooooooooooooks!!"

On the second floor, in the corner room, a light switched on. A hand drew back the curtain, just a sliver.

"Coward," Frank muttered.

The curtain fell back; the light switched off.

Coward. You're such a coward. You're such a fucking coward. Get a grip. You really believe you can't live without this guy, don't you? What's wrong with you? What's wrong with you? Why this guy, of all the men in the world? Why do you choose the one you know, *you* know *will never feel the same way? He'll never love you, Frank. Never ever ever ever!*

This house was a lot like the one he grew up in. The same simple, imposing white façade, the even rows of windows with green faux shutters, the modest little front door. The wide, lush front lawn, the semi-circle driveway. Everything but the two shiny black Mercedes parked out in the open for all to see. His parents were never like that.

The porch light switched on. The front door opened. Brooks stood in the doorway, wearing gray sweatpants and a white t-shirt.

"For Christ's sake, Frank! You're soaking wet!"

"Why don't you answer your phone? Why don't you call me back?"

"Go home, Frank!"

"I lost my job!"

"You'll find another one. Now go home, dry off, get some rest. You're not in your right mind."

"That's right, Brooks! I'm not! That's why I'm going to stand out here and yell at you. I don't care. I'm gonna stand here and yell at you until you promise to help me."

"I can't help you, Frank!"

"Bullshit!"

Brooks's wife Kat appeared beside him in the doorway, dressed in a pink nightgown, folding her arms and gripping herself against the cold. She leaned over and spoke into Brooks's ear. He took a step away from her, shaking his head. She moved toward him and took both his hands in hers and spoke again. He pulled his hands away and held them up in surrender. She turned and looked at Frank.

"Please, Frank," she called out. "Please come inside. You'll catch your death out there."

"Come inside? Really?"

"Yes, dear. Really. Right, Brooks?"

"That's right. Please . . . come inside, Frank."

Frank looked at Brooks, and from Brooks to Kat; at a distance, through the downpour, their expressions gave little away. He stood there, his socks like sponges sloshing in his shoes, his slacks chafing at his skin, the power of decision lost to him. He could have stood in place forever, until he drowned, or died of exposure. It made no difference: whatever it was he ever thought he wanted, that was the thing he couldn't have. It was axiomatic. It was law.

He looked up. The rain slowed to a drizzle. The full moon appeared, its light dimmed by the thinning clouds. Brooks and Kat stood there in the doorway, motionless. Frank took a step toward them. Kat exhaled and smiled. He took another step. She held out a hand. He looked at Brooks. Brooks remained as he was, his face a blank stare.

"Fine," said Frank.

He walked up the path, up the steps, and stepped inside, looking only at Kat. She took his hand. She took his dripping briefcase and set it down on the marble floor. She closed the front door behind him.

"Don't just stand there like an idiot, Brooks. Find this young man something to change into."

She smiled at Frank. "Would you like some tea, dear?"

"Some tea? Oh, Mother."

Frank stared down at the floor and sobbed.

CHAPTER SEVENTEEN

The old Chase was back, and about time. People change, sometimes for the better, sometimes for the worse, but it doesn't have to be permanent, especially if it's not a good fit. Frank Sutcliffe: gone. What's-his-name: gone. They just slowed his roll, so peace out, and he was back on top, back on the market, and up to no good, right where he was meant to be. If anything was different about him, different from before, the boy deserved an award, Best Performance by a Homo, he was that good. But that was highly to extremely unlikely; there was no way he could front with Billy, who knew him best, who could hear not just the words the boy said but all the things he didn't say. Which could be a lot of things.

After the big storm, the weather warmed up, just in time for the weekend, and Billy and Chase drove around town in style, top down, tunes jamming, bass thumping. Billy hit the volume button but Chase, being Chase, made him turn it back down.

"Check us out, dude," he said, "Boys be looking already. No need to be douche-y about it."

It was a fair point. Attention was never in short supply, for either of them, even if it wasn't always easy to tell who was winning. Not that they were competing. They had their own demographics, and they almost never fell hard for the same boy. One of the keys to a lasting friendship in this town.

Billy eased back in his bucket seat as they crept along the boulevard, following the foot traffic, checking out the boys hanging outside the entrances to the bars. It was early and they were mostly clustered in happy little after-dinner sets. A guy who somewhat resembled I'm With Stupid strutted by, without his baseball cap, looking to be headed toward Radioactive all by his lonesome. His back was to them so it was a tough I.D., but they inched past him, and Billy turned his head, casual as could be, like he was making just a general survey, and sure enough. The shirt was plain black, no graphics, no words, and the jeans were tight but not too tight, and to be totally fair the dude was hot. Not in an obvious way, but like he didn't need anyone looking at him to know he was all that, he just knew. It was almost too much, seeing him there, alone, being all sure of himself, but there was no harm in just looking. Who knew what his deal was with Mike, and who even cared, and anyway Billy wasn't even a little bit thirsty.

"Whatcha lookin' at?" said Chase.

"Me? Nuthin'."

"Uh huh." Chase looked over his shoulder. "Black t-shirt?" He nodded his approval. "Ni-i-i-ice. I think he's checking you out."

"It's I'm With Stupid."

"Who?" Chase glanced at Billy. "Oh."

For a second, but just a second, temporary Chase, the one who got sidetracked by the bullshit, rose to the surface. But the real Chase fought back and won by knockout.

"I mean," said Billy, "I would totally hit that."

"Totally," said Chase, eyes back on the road.

"I think he's headed to Radioactive."

"Then let's go, Billy boy!"

"You for real?"

"Sure. Why the fuck not?"

"Other than Radioactive is tired?"

Chase laughed and patted Billy's knee. "Not when you're there, Billy boy." He turned up the music.

#

They sauntered into the Radioactive patio like the two badass motherfuckers they were, smiling and saying hey and moving right along, but slow and easy, and with Chase at Billy's side everything was the way it was supposed to be, the way it used to be, before Chase's little detour. No need to stop at the bar, or the other bar, or the other bar, or the other bar, not yet, if at all. It was so not professional to get messy, especially if there were going to be other substances later, which there were. They stopped to look up at the first go-go boy, a big beefy one with a shaved head and a lot of ink, and Chase went right up to him and of course the boy bent down and gave Chase a little kiss and whispered in his ear, and Chase whispered back and felt him up a little and slid a five into his trunks. He felt bad, he said to Billy, because the first boy you see when you walk in never gets much attention. They moved on, sometimes holding hands, sometimes Billy in the lead, sometimes Chase.

Everyone must have been desperate to get their drink on after the rain delay: the place was packed for so early, with bottlenecks around the narrow dance floor. If I'm With Stupid was there, which was not a sure thing, he could be anywhere. He could be a few feet away and they might not spot him. Chase told Billy not to worry, Billy could let Chase do all the scouting, so Billy could stay chill and not look all wide-eyed and needy, not that he was either of those things. Chase put his arm around Billy and told him to let all the boys wonder about them, I'm With Stupid included. Yes, the old Chase was definitely back.

They hit serious traffic near the big bar in the middle, so they took an outside lane, by the little red rope where the bougie boys of Boys Town sat on cushions around the fireplace acting all bougie. Like anyone was impressed. Man, the place was tired. And so hetero lately, like straight people didn't have enough places of their own or something. And the music, Greatest Dance Hits of the Nineties, so not edgy. No wonder they hardly ever came here anymore. What were they doing wasting their time, chasing after one random somewhat hot guy, some stranger he had seen once from a distance? Billy was so not the type to turn into basically a stalker. He was better than this; he knew how it worked, and it didn't work like this. What was this about? What was wrong with him?

"Chase, *chico*, I love you, but this place is tired."

"I love you too, babe." Chase pointed. "Is that him?"

"Where?"

"Eleven o'clock, elbows on the bar."

"Uhhhhh."

"Sweet! Come on, let's go!" Chase grabbed Billy's hand.

Even the way I'm With Stupid propped himself on his elbows, shoulders hunched, swinging a little bit from side to side, was sexy. He wasn't quite as chill as maybe he thought, like just a little, tiny bit of him was dying to know if anyone was checking him out, which only made him more adorable. He wasn't alone anymore, unless he was talking to himself, out loud, but he didn't have a pyscho vibe at all, but there wasn't anyone on either side of him either. Talking to the bartender was such a loser move, so if that was it then Billy was right in the first place, this was a mistake. Except a certain kind of dude could pull that off, depending on the bartender, if the bartender was really talking to him and not just being a good bartender who knew how to be nice to everyone.

Chase pulled a little bit too hard and Billy stumbled forward, and he righted himself and looked toward I'm With Stupid and there was the bartender and it was Mike, shirt off, that ridiculous body, that body even a straight dude could appreciate, leaning over the bar smiling and chatting with I'm With Stupid while he poured. Of course. It made perfect sense, in the most miserable kind of way. But who hangs out with his bartender boyfriend at the bar? It didn't matter. It was a disaster in the making and there was nothing to do but get away, get out of there, as fast as possible.

Billy yanked back on Chase's arm, dragging him back the other way, into heavy traffic, where there was at least a chance the crowd would be dense enough to block the view.

"Dude, seriously," said Billy. "I'm so over this place."

"Oh, no you don't, playa, this is so on. He's hot! He's into you!"

"You don't need to do this, Chase."

Chase stopped. "Well, how do you like that?" He folded his arms over his chest and stared.

"Chase—"

"That new bartender is very popular, isn't he?"

Chase smiled a little, the real Chase, like he was impressed or even proud, and there was no point saying anything to him, he was going to think what he was going to think, feel what he was going to feel. Billy reached out to pat him on the back, but the time wasn't right for that either, Chase had to have this little moment to himself. But not for long, because I'm With Stupid looked over, and his eyes landed on Chase, and something in Chase went still. Billy almost couldn't breathe. I'm With Stupid blinked and shifted and looked straight at Billy, or straight through him, who could say, nodding, smiling too much, like he was just enjoying the whole damn thing. With his eyes holding onto Billy like that, he leaned over and said something to Mike, and Mike said something to him, and Mike looked up at him and followed his eyes and turned his head and saw Billy and stopped. He saw Chase and stopped. Everything stopped.

Mike looked away and smiled and leaned over and took another drink order, and another, and another.

"Let's get out of here," said Billy.

"You high? We're on a mission, *hijo*."

"Come on, Chase. I'm not fucking around."

Chase turned to Billy and took his face in both hands.

"Billy. My sweet, sweet Billy. Can you please just trust me on this? You're my best friend in the entire world. I know you better than you know yourself. I only want what's best for you."

Billy just looked at Chase, at his beautiful eyes, his perfect handsome face, that face that hadn't changed since the day they met, except maybe to get a little more handsome, if that was possible, his lips a little fuller, his cheekbones a little stronger. He would never be the Chase he was, when they were Billy and Chase, for that split second way back when. They would never be Billy and Chase again, Billy's Chase and Chase's Billy. But love is love is love; they would always have love, no matter what else happened. No matter what fate held in store.

Billy took Chase's hands from his face and placed them on his shoulders.

"*Hijo*, what's best for me is what's best for you. If you're telling me we're going over there and I'm talking to I'm With Stupid, then that's what we're doing."

Chase kissed Billy on the mouth. "That's what I'm telling you, Billy." He grabbed Billy's cheek with his fingers and squeezed. "Oh my God, this face! Let's go, gorgeous."

"Okay." Billy smiled. "Let's go, buddy."

Billy took a deep breath and took Chase's hand and set out through the crowd, and everyone smiled at him as he passed by, like they knew something. No thinking, no guessing; every step was laid out in front of him, so clear and natural he could have done it with his eyes closed. Or in his sleep, because it was like a dream. Before he finished exhaling, he found himself standing right in front of I'm With Stupid, who leaned against the bar, sipping from a glass of champagne, smiling a real smile. There was no mistaking it–you could see the light go on in his eyes when Billy looked right at him.

"Hey," said Billy.

"Hey," said I'm With Stupid.

"I'm Billy."

"I'm Rob."

"Hey, Rob. Rob? We've been calling you I'm With Stupid, you know, because of the t-shirt? I mean, we do that sometimes, give people names, just because, you know, sometimes you don't know their names but there's something you can remember them by, like a placeholder? And I saw you the other day and you were wearing that shirt, but I guess it makes sense now since you're wearing just a plain black t-shirt that you should have an actual name, ha ha."

"I'm sorry," said Rob, "could you repeat that?"

Chase doubled over with laughter, and he gave Rob a high-five over Billy's head. He put his arm around Billy.

"That's my Billy."

"You must be Chase," said Rob.

Chase nodded. "You look familiar."

"Yeah, I think I've seen you guys out."

"Captain America shirt," said Chase.

"Yep, that's me. Honestly, it'd be a better name than I'm With Stupid."

"Rob works," said Billy.

Rob put down his champagne and stood face-to-face with Billy.

"Can I ask you something, Rob?" said Billy.

"Anything, babe."

"Are you single?"

Rob looked over at Mike. Mike's head was down. Rob looked back at Billy. He held Billy by the waist.

"Yep."

Billy smiled. "Sweet."

Chase unhooked his arm from Billy's shoulders and turned around. Everywhere he looked, the crowd's eyes were trained in the same direction, even as they talked and laughed and drank with each other: on Mike, busy, graceful, impossible Mike. He was in his element; he was a star. Mike picked up his head and smiled, as if to acknowledge their admiration, or just because he was enjoying himself.

This was the guy Chase thought he knew, before that miserable night. It didn't matter if there was some truth in the things Chase had said to him, in the names he hadn't quite called him. H   is words must have stung. It was obvious the moment they came out of his mouth. But he didn't realize just how cruel he had been, how unforgivably cruel, until now.

He looked back over at Rob, single Rob, wooing Billy, Billy holding his own, the two taking turns speaking into each other's ear, Billy's hand already on Rob's shoulder. Well done, Billy. What was best for Billy was best for Chase. Ha ha.

"Something to drink, Chase? On the house."

"Huh? Oh, hey, Mike, sorry, I'm so rude. Good to see you."

"Yeah."

"I mean it. Really good to see you."

Mike leaned forward and wiped the counter with a rag and stopped and looked up.

"You, too, Chase."

Chase offered his hand. Mike took it, smiled, and leaned all the way over the bar and gave Chase a solid pat on the back.

"Maybe something really weak?" said Chase. "Not too many calories?"

"Going out later?"

Chase tilted his head toward Billy. "Depends on stuff."

Mike smiled. "Got it."

"I'm actually considering hitting it sober."

"Whaaaaaaaat?"

"That's right," said Chase, "you heard correctly."

"Funny, I was actually considering dropping some E."

"Whaaaaaaaat? Listen to you."

"I know, right? My friend Rob over there talked me into trying it. I didn't hate it."

"But what about wanting to know if it's real, all that?"

"Yeah," said Mike, "what a load of blah blah blah. Guess I can be a little full of myself."

"Maybe a little." Chase waved a hand over the crowd. "But I can see why."

Mike blushed. "Nah. Anyway." He set Chase's drink on the bar.

"Thanks."

"No problem."

"Hey, Mike."

"Yeah?"

Chase looked him in the eye. "Oh, just . . . I mean . . . you look great."

Rob offered Billy some of his champagne, and Billy took a sip, but only just. They were celebrating because Rob hooked Mike up with a so-called serious job interview. Billy didn't ask him why being the hottest bartender at the most famous nightclub in town or possibly in the world wasn't a serious job; they just met, they had a little vibe going possibly, and this wasn't the time to get in his face. He didn't say anything about it to Chase, but then he didn't say anything at all about Mike to Chase. It was too raw, he didn't see the point risking any drama. Chase was just as pleasant as could be though, chatting with Mike for a minute, and taking a lap around the club, running into approximately one million friends, of course, because Chase had friends everywhere.

Rob never quite answered when Billy hinted about After Hours downtown–busy day tomorrow, not sure he was feeling it, heard the DJ was meh, all the usual excuses. But Rob's eyes, trying to look when Billy wasn't, his tight body that couldn't keep still, the little hunch in his shoulders, they all told the same story, even if he didn't know it himself. Billy went along, he was behind on a project at work, but Chase was so excited, didn't want to let his boy down, hadn't been out in a while, really ought to. Billy could have said anything, Rob wasn't going to commit. Which was fine. Let the guy have his fifteen minutes of player.

#

Billy and Chase ran upstairs to the VIP section first thing when they got to After Hours. There was a ton of free goodies laid out on the tables, cookies and candy bars and bananas and gum, but that was for much later, when they were so hungry they had no choice. They sat on a couch for a minute, but they looked at each other and nodded and got up and went to stand at the railing right near the sound guy and the lights guy, and they looked down at the dance floor and the stage and the screen. You really didn't get how tricked out the light show was when you were on the dance floor, which was why it was always a good idea to get the VIP ticket. It was a seriously 3-D experience, with the lasers floating below you and sometimes jumping up to eye level and sometimes dancing in waves. From down on the dance floor they streaked over your head, and they just looked like a bunch of straight lines in pretty colors, which was great in its own way when your mind was in the right place to appreciate it, so to speak.

Even upstairs on the balcony, Chase had to yell into Billy's ear over the music, and he went on whining about how broke he was, which was just so sad, boo freaking hoo. He offered his neighbor Victor Donaldson way too much for his apartment, the contractor kept raising her estimate for the remodel, the city was trying to kill him with the permits to break down the wall and reinforce the floor and the ceiling, and he had to leave some posts where the wall used to be, and let's not forget the fees and taxes for the reassessment, and on and on and on, and he shouldn't have let his heart outbid his head, all over some stupid three-sixty view. Billy had to give him a reality check. For one thing, he was lucky to have all that money to spend in the first place, and for another thing, he was going to be so proud of that view, and the parties were going to be so lit, it wasn't even funny.

"White people problems," Billy said.

"Oh, ha ha."

Chase said sit tight, and he slapped the railing and went off to get a bottled water at the bar for seven bucks, and Billy hung on to the railing and leaned over a little bit. There was a loud hissing sound, and a big puff of smoke filled the place in an instant, and the boys on the dance floor let out a roar, and more boys were streaming in and filling the place up in a hurry. Billy fidgeted. He looked behind him to the bar. Chase was chatting up someone new, a short, stocky gym rat with red hair and freckles, good-looking but not really Chase's type. Chase was smiling with him and gesturing and talking real close, hand on his shoulder, like he had some incredible secret to share. The ginger leaned back and laughed and clapped, and gave Chase a high-five.

"Whatever," said Billy.

Down below, a guy in a black t-shirt and a slightly balding head shuffled onto the dance floor and danced in circles. The t-shirt fit him well but a light swept by him and lit him up long enough to show writing on it, so not Rob. The guy found some boys to dance with and blended into the crowd. Another guy with a black baseball cap and no shirt was about Rob's height, and he looked good without his shirt on, very, very good, especially around the shoulders, but he jumped up and down and looked up at the lasers and he wore glasses and had a very close-trimmed beard, so unless Rob grew it in the last two hours it was his younger brother at best. Hot younger brother. Not hotter necessarily, but hot. And also younger.

Some guys hanging out at the railing huddled together and turned and headed over to the stairs. Some guys chilling on the couches got up and followed them down. Billy looked down at the dance floor. Everyone was facing the stage and cheering, and guys were raising their hands in the air, and up on the stage five go-go boys were grabbing their crotches and sticking out their tongues and flexing their chests and shaking their booties and even dancing a little, like real dancers, not just hot boys who got away with it, with synchronized steps and jumps and kicks and twirls, all right on the beat. Maybe they were flown in from Vegas, like the DJ. The images on the video screen got very bright, almost blinding, and the crowd cheered some more. There were super beautiful, super muscly, almost naked guys on a white beach, and the promotor's logo, and the DJ's name in big red letters, more almost naked guys, guys rolling in the sand and making out and tugging on each other's tiny swim trunks. Enough to make a boy thirsty, if he didn't check himself.

Billy felt a chill and tensed up and gasped; it was Chase, pressing a freezing bottled water against his neck. Hilarious. Billy turned around; Chase poked at his stomach with the bottle, but Billy backed away so he just missed.

"Give it here, boy," said Billy.

Billy grasped for the bottle. Chase pulled it away and spun around. Billy pounced on him and got him in a chokehold and rode him piggyback. Chase whined and rolled his shoulders back, but Billy hung on, laughing. He slid off and hunched over and held his knees like he was out of breath. Chase handed him the water.

"Thanks, loser," said Billy.

Billy took off down the stairs; Chase ran after him.

"You're the loser, loser," said Chase.

At the bottom of the stairs they looked around. Billy pointed.

Chase nodded. "Let's do it."

Except for the very edge of the dance floor, practically at the entrance, the place was wall-to-wall shirtless men, sweaty men, sexy and meh, hairy and smooth, tall and short, muscly and skinny and even overweight, young and less young, rolling on Ecstasy and wannabe rolling, dancing and swaying and standing still, looking up and looking at Daddy and looking for Daddy and looking nowhere special, content in themselves. But with some good dance floor karma, which Billy was rocking up to his eyelids ATM, he found a way to get in and fill the gaps, with just enough room to spare for Chase coming in behind him. They reached their spot, right in the middle, and Billy took a deep breath and exhaled, and took another deep breath and exhaled, and he looked up at the lasers, just a bunch of straight lines in pretty colors, and it was good.

"You feeling it yet?" said Chase.

"Feeling what?"

"Hello? The music?"

"Ah, the music, yeah. Think so."

"Yeah, me too."

"Much better than Radioactive."

"That's a low bar."

"Right?"

Chase looked at Billy and smiled, like he was remembering an inside joke; he didn't move much, just swaying and turning a little. He closed his eyes and dropped his arms to his sides. A lot of boys were checking him out, and checking Billy out, and Billy smiled when they looked but closed his eyes too, but he opened them and looked around again, but he closed them and kept them closed, but he opened them and didn't look anywhere, except maybe at the screen and the lasers, and he took a lot of deep breaths and pushed down the butterflies, but that was dumb so he breathed in the butterflies and they were good, so good. The music was just the right mix of melody and beat and basically just noise, it was so, so good, but everything was just slightly, slightly not perfect, but that was fine, imperfection was perfect too. Probably.

"Stop it," said Chase.

"Huh?" said Billy.

"He'll show, I promise."

"I don't even know what you're even talking about."

"I see you looking around, sad puppy. You're not as chill as you think."

"I am so chill."

"Okay."

Rob was one lucky dude, but Chase wasn't about to say anything to Billy. The less said, the better, as their history had taught them. The boy was crushing so hard though, he was at risk of saying too much himself. Chase was going to have to just stand down, a silent supporter, let him make his own mistakes, and hope for the best. As for Chase, maybe he was looking, maybe he wasn't. There was such a thing as just dancing, having a good time with your best boy, not setting an agenda. Ha ha, no there wasn't.

It wouldn't be such a terrible thing if Rob would just show up already; no need to play games, with anyone but especially not Billy. No, Billy could take care of himself. Stand down. Rob was probably right there in the crowd, panicking because he hadn't found Billy. Or scanning the crowd from the balcony. Chase looked up, but it was just lasers and fog. And anyway it wasn't his problem. Except it kind of was. Rob had a friend, didn't he? The friend was here too, wasn't he? Most likely. Unless he'd had a change of heart. Or they both had. That would be better. For Chase, but not for Billy. Probably.

What was he going to say? He needed a plan. Mike couldn't have been as unbothered as he acted tonight at Radioactive. Chase meant more to him than that. He must have meant more to him than that. Mike was just focused on his work, reserving his feelings for another place and time. Was this the other place and time? Mike said he might be rolling on Ecstasy. So yes.

Did Chase need Ecstasy too? He shuddered. "Fuck fuck fuck." Was he wrong about Mike? He had hurt him, yes, but was he wrong?

"Stop it," said Billy.

"Stop what?"

"He's gonna show, sad puppy, I promise you. "

"Who is?"

Everybody had a past. Everybody made mistakes. And what were Mike's mistakes anyway? Saying yes? To men who offered him everything? Giving them something like love in return? Maybe it was just real love in exchange for real love, and all that other stuff was beside the point. The truth was, Chase didn't know. The truth was, Chase couldn't know. And it didn't matter. It had nothing to do with him.

He wasn't those other guys. He was Chase Evans. Rachel was right. It was crazy, to fear that there was nothing more to him than his money and his gym body. Where the fuck did that come from, anyway? He was Chase Evans. Chase fucking Evans. He deserved to have everything he wanted. Maybe what he wanted was Mike. Time would tell.

A tall, lanky, fair-haired man with a beard smiled at Chase through the dense crowd. He turned around to hold onto his friends, or whoever they were. He disappeared and reappeared and disappeared; Chase looked and looked away and looked again. The man turned again and moved in Chase's direction, still smiling; he dragged another man with him, his near twin with dark hair. He gave Chase a long, thoughtful look; Chase gave him a long, thoughtful look back. He came closer; the lights brightened. There was some gray in the beard, and more in the hair. He was at least a decade older–impressive, but not quite right. Chase patted the man on the shoulder and looked away. The man and his dark-haired, younger companion passed by, single file, hand in hand.

Billy yelled into Chase's ear. "Chase! Why didn't you talk to them? I totally would've hit the dark one."

Chase laughed. "Sorry, bro. Maybe they'll come back."

"And the blond one is totally your type."

"Light brown. And gray. Water."

Billy handed Chase their bottle.

A pair of firm hands landed on Chase's shoulders. Chase froze. He turned his head a quarter turn, not enough to see much; the hands were big, the man must have been tall, taller than Chase. The man pulled himself close and wrapped his arms around Chase's chest, and they swayed together. The man's beard rubbed against Chase's neck.

"Mmm, you feel so good, Chase."

Chase smiled and turned around.

"Man, there are so many tall . . ." His face fell. The man was meth addict thin, his eye sockets were too deep, and his skin was badly pockmarked.

"I'm sorry," said Chase, "I don't . . ."

"You don't?"

Chase shook his head and shrugged.

"That's okay." The man stroked Chase's abs. "You still feel real good. You look even better."

"Ha, thanks."

"You looking, Chase?"

"Uh, sorry, I gotta go find my friend, uh . . ."

"Clark."

"Clark. Nice to meet you. I mean, nice to see you. Again."

"Whatever."

Clark backed away and turned around and found another boy to hold, and the crowd filled in behind him.

Chase turned toward Billy and rolled his eyes.

"Who the fuck was that?" said Billy.

"Duh. Clark."

"Oh, yeah. Clark."

"Exactly."

Billy laughed.

Another firm hand landed on Chase's shoulder. He turned his head. "Oh, for fuck's–oh, hey you!"

"What's up, fellas?"

Rob wore his big, know-it-all smile, and his blue-gray bedroom eyes twinkled and gleamed. He slid in between Chase and Billy and put his other hand on Billy's shoulder. Billy broke into a big smile, too, and he gave Rob a hug, and tousled Rob's hair, and pulled Rob's tight black shirt off and reached around tucked it into Rob's back pocket.

Billy stood back, arms crossed, and nodded. "I'm so not disappointed."

"Sorry I'm late."

"You're right on time, *papi*."

"Oh, speak Spanish to me, baby."

Billy wrapped his arms around Rob's waist. Rob wrapped his arms around Billy's waist. Rob stroked Billy's temple and kissed his cheek.

Chase closed his eyes and swayed to the music. He moved behind Rob and held him by the shoulders. Billy peeked around to see him, to get a nod or a smile or a thumbs-up or something, but Chase kept his eyes closed, and when he opened them, it was like he wasn't really there, like he was far away. So Billy looked at Rob. Rob he could see, clear into his thoughts. Mostly they were thoughts about sex, which was great because by some amazing coincidence mostly Billy's thoughts were about sex, too. Rob looked at him and they both smiled. Billy turned himself and pressed his back against Rob and took Rob's arms and wrapped them around his chest. Rob kissed Billy's neck, held him under the chin and kissed his cheek; Billy turned his head; Rob kissed him on the mouth. Billy opened his mouth and Rob opened his mouth and they tasted each other and inhaled each other and closed their eyes and forgot about everything else. While everyone around them moved, they were still,

still with each other and inside each other and lost with each other, lost together.

Billy came back long enough to find a void where Chase used to be; he stopped and looked around and around, but Chase was nowhere to be seen.

Rob grabbed Billy and brought him close again. "You're with me now."

"Yes. *Siempre junto a ti.*"

"Ah, Tito Puente."

"*Lo conoces?*"

"*Por supuesto.*"

"*Ay, papi.*"

Billy's face receded from view, and Chase was left alone, adrift. There was no way to find him again, at least not Billy as he had always been. They rode on new, different currents, their destinies no longer linked but their futures bright. Chase let go and let the crowd hold him up, lift him up, move him where it might. A sea of men, beautiful, strong men, united for a thrilling moment in their freedom, their optimism, their suspension of judgment.

THE END

Made in the USA
San Bernardino, CA
03 August 2019